The Ghost
of Ellen Dower

Conche Area, Newfoundland

The Ghost
of Ellen Dower

by Earl B. Pilgrim

Flanker Press Ltd.
St. John's, Newfoundland
2002

National Library of Canada Cataloguing in Publication Data

Pilgrim, Earl B. (Earl Baxter), 1939-
   The ghost of Ellen Dower / Earl B. Pilgrim.

ISBN 1-894463-22-6

   1. Dower, Ellen--Fiction. I. Title.

PS8581.I338G48 2002   C813'.54   C2002-903673-9
PR9199.3.P493G48 2002

PRINTED IN CANADA BY ROBINSON-BLACKMORE

Editor: Jerry Cranford

Cover Photo: Sara Rostotski

www.earlpilgrim.com

— FLANKER PRESS LTD. —

P O Box 2522, Stn C,
St. John's, Newfoundland, Canada, A1C 6K1

Toll Free: 1-866-739-4420   Telephone: (709) 739-4477
Facsimile: (709) 739-4420   E-mail: info@flankerpress.com
www.flankerpress.com

SPECIAL THANKS

Austin Gardner, Paul Bromley, Jim Whalen, Uncle Bernie Dower, Anthony Carroll, Vale Carroll, Bill Carroll, Anthony Power, John and Susan Bromley, Eugene and Ronald Byrne, Rex Cooper, Wallace Maynard, Alvin Sutton, Mark Lawlor, Father Brophy, Carl Pilgrim, Pearce and Anita Cull, Gary Newell, Austin Canning, Ivan Canning, Clifford Coombs, Ceasar and Barbara Pilgrim, Lindy and Kent Brophy, Tom and Gracie Maynard, Nadine Ellsworth, Baine and Nancy Pilgrim, Junior Canning, George and Iris Fillier, Gid and Alma Tucker, Norman and Marsha Pilgrim, Kala and Kristin Pilgrim, Christopher Ellsworth.

Thanks to Vera McDonald, Margo Cranford, and Jerry Locke for reading the manuscript.

Without the help of Paddy O'Neill, this book would not and could not have been written. Thanks, Paddy.

I would like to thank Beatrice, my wife, for her support in putting this book together. Without her help, none of my books would ever have been written.

Thanks to Shannon Ryan, author of *The Ice Hunters: A History of Newfoundland Sealing to 1914*.

To Cathy Noel, thanks for being the photographer's model for Ellen Dower.

Special thanks to Garry Cranford of Flanker Press.

Dedicated to Patrick "Paddy" O'Neill,
Historian of Conche

Prologue

By the coast of the Great Northern Peninsula, or, more specifically, to the north of Conche about fifteen miles, lies a small offshore point of land called Fishot Island. History says this island was among the first in Newfoundland to be inhabited by European settlers. During the years when pirates roamed the oceans, when ships of such dubious repute needed a place to hide, the mouth of Belvy Bay with its many hideaway coves became a haven to such men of the deep. And for this reason they sometimes called in at Fishot Island, to sound around or see if they could learn of military vessels lying in wait. Paddy O'Neill, who is touted as the historian of Conche, wrote one such tale in his paper *The Log of Conche* that held particular interest to me.

Many stories have been told about Maurice Power these past hundred years, old Maurice Power from Conche. One says he was a pirate who changed his name a couple of times. It goes that one stormy night a pirate ship bound for Belvy Bay came into Fishot Harbour seeking shelter.

Little is known of what went on aboard the ship and among the crew, except that a man by the name of Maurice de la Pour jumped overboard and swam ashore to escape the future his shipmates had planned for him.

At daylight the brawling cutthroats came ashore and searched the rickety houses on Fishot Island, but no sign of Maurice de la Pour could be found. In a rage, the tyrannical captain ordered all the dwellings burned. The crew managed to convince him after some time that their missing crewmate was not in town, and annoyed at the cries of the women and children, the captain gave up the search and left.

It wasn't long before Maurice de la Pour crawled out from under a rock and appeared in town. He was soon recognized as the escaped man the pirates were seeking. He asked the people in his French accent if they had any work for him ashore, but they were still shaken after their ordeal with the pirates. They just wanted to be rid of this man who had brought trouble and most likely would again.

Not welcome on Fishot Island, Maurice de la Pour headed south—avoiding the Conche area out of fear of meeting up with his former crewmates—and went on to the small town of Englee. There he secured a job with some French fish merchants as a keeper of their fishing rooms. He stayed there for just two years, before he was transferred to the Northeast Crouse area. Here the old Frenchman changed his name to Maurice Pour, fuelling speculation he was disguising his identity.

A year later he moved again, this time to a place called Silver Cove, within the boundary of Conche

Harbour. By now the old Frenchman's name had evolved into Maurice Power. He was the father of one Maurice Power, Jr., whose name struck fear into the hearts of people back in the 1800s.

* * *

WHILE TALKING TO PADDY O'NEILL, my source of information for this book, Maurice Power's lineage came into question. "I heard all about Maurice Power, Jr.'s background from my grandfather, Thomas Casey," Paddy said. "He was a well-grown man before Maurice Power, Jr. died."

When I visited Mr. O'Neill for the first time, he met me with a wide grin and said, "I know what you're here for, Earl. I heard that you're writing about my relative, Aunt Ellen Dower."

I greeted this grand old gentleman and shook hands with him. "Yes, I am," I said, "if I can get the story of what really happened."

He took out a pipe and said, "Well, you've come to the right place. I'm the only person alive now who can tell the true story of what went on between Aunt Ellen and Uncle Edward Dower."

I could see that his eighty-eight years had not lessened his memory any, and I could tell he was ready to talk. "First," I said, "I want to tell you what I plan to call it."

Paddy lit his pipe. "Yes," he replied, tapping his fingers on the table and giving me a look that said he was expecting a surprise.

"I am going to call it," I hesitated, "The Ghost of Ellen Dower."

He fell silent for a moment. "Earl," he said, "you have to make sure people know it's the *true* story of the ghost of Ellen Dower. A lot of people have already written about this, but they didn't know what they were talking about. I'll tell you the whole story now, if you have the nerve to write it."

I lifted my notebook and turned to a fresh page.

"Start talking," I said.

Part I

1

Edward Dower's hands were cramped and shivering so much he could barely hold the quill. The land grant lay flat on the table in front of him, awaiting his signature, and his wife Ellen sat next to him, waiting to take the document after it was signed. She had read it out loud to him once again, just to make doubly sure that all was in order. After all, Edward considered this land grant the key to his family's future.

He set his quill down and shifted around to face the Giant stove, holding his hands over it for a minute, rubbing them together to get the blood moving. "I think I'll have pains in my hands for the next month," he said. "'Twas cold enough out there to skin you." Edward spoke with a strong lilt that hearkened back to the Waterford area of Ireland.

* * *

EDWARD, OR UNCLE NED, as everyone called him, had been out all day hauling seal nets with the rest of the men from Conche. It was Christmas Eve, but the work demanded immediate attention. It started when a group of men out on Cape Fox had spotted a large herd of harp seals "by the thousands" heading south, right into their seal nets. The sealers returned to the village as quickly as possible to report the good news to John and Edward Dower, who owned most of the nets.

The Dower brothers owned a large business premises at Conche that expanded yearly. John and Edward employed a sizable number of the population, and they had a reputation for being fair employers. Their positive outlook kept their men productive, and fair monetary success was enjoyed by all. With success came reams of bookkeeping and other paperwork that could not be neglected, and Ellen made sure that accurate records were kept.

"The nets are becoming swamped with seals," their lead man had reported, and all hands were called to work. Within the hour they were bending the oars, heading out of Conche Harbour and pulling for Cape Fox. Snow and ice covered everything on land this time of the year, but the ocean was free of it, or so it seemed at first glance. It wasn't frozen over, but closer inspection yielded water thick with ice particles, a bay full of slush.

The swilers who had come overland to scan the ocean with spyglasses spotted the boats when they went around the outside. They followed them to the first net floating on the water and found it to be full of seals. Some had drowned submerged in the nets, and those that hadn't were quickly put out of their misery. The catch was made up of young bedlamers (seals that are but a year old) and old harps.

From there, the men had spread out to check the remaining nets and found them to be much the same, blocked with seals. Boatload after boatload were then untangled from the nets and taken into Conche, and still there were seals everywhere. The ocean was full of them.

Before the sun set, the people of Conche had landed a thousand seals. John and Edward's crew had taken over six hundred near their own wharf alone. That evening Conche was five thousand dollars richer, with the Dower firm harvesting three, the greatest share.

* * *

EDWARD WARMED HIS HANDS enough to hold the quill steady and scratched his signature across the bottom of the land grant. Ellen looked at her husband with concern. It was Christmas Eve, and paperwork was the last thing on her mind. "I don't understand you, Edward. The next thing you know, you're going to be crippled up. You should know that the cold water this time of year gets right into the bone."

Edward laughed. He was a tall, well-built man, with blazing red hair from his Waterford heritage. He could work sixteen hours a day and still be ready if called upon, day or night. He picked up the freshly signed document and waved it over the Giant to dry the ink. He looked at the attached letter and began to read aloud.

"'To Mr. Edward Dower, Conche, Newfoundland. Sir: Enclosed you will find a land grant for your property located at Conche in the Dominion of Newfoundland. It is to be pointed out to you that this grant will only become valid after we receive the enclosed document signed by you, Edward Dower. Return as quickly as possible, preferably by May 1872. Thank you.'

"All right, Ellen, my dear. We'll have to send this out with the mailman by the last week of March. It should arrive in St. John's on time."

Ellen said, "Better still, give me an envelope."

Edward opened a drawer and took out a brown envelope. He slid the document inside. "I think we should put this in the till until the time comes to post it in March," he said, looking up.

His wife nodded in agreement, though he could see her attention was focused elsewhere. Their nine children were waiting for them downstairs, and she was as excited as they were about tonight's coming festivities.

Christmas Eve in Conche was always a roaring time, even back in the 1800s. Although times were tough, the people there made sure they could afford a good Christmas. And so it was on this December 24 of 1871 that a square dance was scheduled to start at 9:00 P.M., and Edward and Ellen's two oldest daughters were getting ready to step it out. Someone called from downstairs for her mother to come and help get the house in order.

"Mother! Come down and help us. Don't you know that this is Christmas Eve? We're going to the dance!"

"All right, girls. I'll be down right away."

Ellen Dower was a very reliable and shrewd business person when at her best, but all she could concentrate on were tonight's celebrations. Edward gave the final touches to the envelope and was about to hand it to her just as the girls called again.

"Mother, come on down!"

"All right, I'm coming!" Ellen said, and jumped to her feet.

Edward stood up and placed the envelope in his wife's hands. "Here, my dear. Put it in a safe place until March."

"I think I'll put it in the cash box, Edward."

"Mother! Hey Mother, you better come down right away, because I think the cake is burning!"

"Goodness!" Ellen squawked. She dropped the envelope on the table and dashed downstairs.

Edward laughed. He conceded this was no time for his wife to be tormented with paperwork. It was Christmas Eve, the family was well, and on top of that, their firm had made over three thousand dollars today. It was a time for rejoicing and giving thanks and being with friends and family. It was time to enjoy the holiday season.

"I'll put it in the cash box myself," he said in a far-away voice.

The cash box was tucked away in his sea-chest, which was stored under the window in the upstairs loft room. It was always locked, and only he possessed the key. This solid oak chest contained Edward and Ellen Dower's most valuable possessions at a time when there were no banks with safety deposit boxes in any outport towns, and families had to provide their own. Edward's vault happened to be this large oak chest, which he took with him whenever he went to sea, whether it be to the Labrador for summer fishing, to St. John's, or overseas. While ashore, all his valuables he kept within, but before leaving for sea he would transfer them to another well-secured trunk.

Edward retrieved the key from the closet and went back upstairs. Unlocking the chest, he lifted the lid on its well-oiled hinges and took out the cash box, which was heavy with documents and money. In those days the merchants were sometimes paid in gold coins, and this cash box contained a lot of them. Merchants some-times received fifty per cent of their valued cargo in hard cash when they sold their fish and seal products. Often these gold coins came from direct sales to European markets.

Edward never used a St. John's bank. Instead, he paid his working people in goods and material, as was the custom of the day. Whenever Edward and John went to the market with a load of product, they returned with a load of groceries, goods, and fishing gear to be traded against fish received. The people accepted it without question, as this was the custom in Newfoundland at the time; in fact, people considered themselves lucky to get just bread and butter.

In this large sea-chest were several tills. Edward kept the larger denominations of bills in one, and as he opened the chest, it was there he decided he would put the land grant. It occurred to him that the keys to all the tills and the cash box were in a drawer in his downstairs bedroom. He fingered the envelope, thinking of Christmas Eve and reminding himself that he'd just had one of the most successful days of his life. He'd look for the keys later. It was time to join his family for Christmas. Looking from the envelope to the stairs leading down to the mirthful cries of his children, he determined he would at least hide the document. Edward was not normally a suspicious man, but so much was riding on the land grant making it to St. John's on time.

A thick cardboard lining made its way around the inside of the chest. It was there for two reasons. One was to ventilate against dampness, while the other was to protect the oak from wear and tear. Along the back of the chest, the cardboard lining was becoming unglued, and many times things of little or no value, such as newspaper clippings and old Christmas cards, were tucked inside it rather than thrown out. It is a well-known saying in Newfoundland: "I wonder what they've got stuffed away in the linings of their trunk?" This was said if someone was thought to have a lot of money in his house.

Edward reached into the chest and pulled the lining away from the wood to let the envelope slip down inside. When he released it, the lining went back in place very snugly, looking as if it had not been disturbed at all. "I'll take it out again after Christmas and lock it in the cash box," he assured himself.

Just then, one of his daughters called from down-stairs, this time more impatiently.

"All right," he replied, "just a moment."

After he placed the heavy cash box back into the chest and closed the lid, Edward locked it and put the land grant out of his mind once and for all. He brushed himself off as he stood, made his way to the woodbox, and lifted a junk of wood. The Giant's lid squealed as he slid it open. He deposited the kindling into its smoldering belly and closed the lid.

"I'm coming down," he called.

A voice drifted back up to him. "No, Father, don't come down yet. We're going to bring up a gift for you and Mother to open." This was a Christmas Eve tradition in the Dower home.

Edward sat at the table, and in a minute he heard the sound of feet coming up the stairs. His four daughters came in, with Ellen close behind. They were carrying two Christmas gifts wrapped in beautiful, brightly coloured paper. The girls were bubbling with excitement, and it was obvious Ellen was trying hard to contain herself as well. They placed the two gifts on the table. TO EDWARD, FROM ELLEN, MERRY CHRISTMAS was written across one, and on the other, TO MY DARLING WIFE ELLEN WITH LOVE, MERRY CHRISTMAS, EDWARD. Edward knew what Ellen's gift was, of course, but he had no idea what his family could have gotten him.

"All right," he said in a voice now filled with anticipation.

"We'll open Father's first," the oldest girl, Kizzie, said as she handed him a parcel.

Edward took the gift and leaned back in his chair. His present was soft, so it had to be a garment of some sort.

"I think I know what it is," he said, laughing.

"No, I bet you don't," Nora, his youngest daughter, said. "It's not a suit of clothes. Take a guess."

Edward held it close to his ear and gave it a shake. "No, I'm not going to guess. I'm going to open it."

His huge fingers fumbled with the string until he got a firm grip. He broke it and stripped the paper away, revealing a handsome tan-coloured overcoat. His eyes lit up and a wide smile spread across his face. He was very pleased, and Ellen and the girls came over to hug him.

It was time now for Ellen to open hers. "Sit down, Mother," Kizzie said in mock authority. Edward got up from his chair as his beloved wife sat and faced them all.

"Now, Mother, we want you to guess what it is."

Ellen lifted her gift and rolled it over. "No, I'm not going to guess either, because I want it to be a complete surprise."

"Has Father told you what it is?" Nora asked.

"Well, no, I haven't told her," Edward said quickly, and he hadn't. But he knew that his wife was going to like the gift he'd gotten for her.

"Open it, Mother!"

"I want something to cut the string with," she said.

"Just a minute," said Edward. He reached into his pocket and took out his knife. He opened it carefully and passed it to her, handle first. "Here you go," he said.

Ellen gripped the knife and snapped the string binding her gift, then peeled the paper away. To say she was surprised would be an understatement. She stood up, holding a new lambskin coat. She hugged it and looked like a woman in love as she stared at her husband.

"My, oh my," she breathed. "You don't mean it, Edward." She gasped. "It's beautiful. It's gorgeous!"

Edward was grinning from ear to ear. He didn't know what to say. The girls were eyeing their mother's new coat with open mouths. They had never seen anything like it.

"Father, where in the world did you get that coat?"

Edward laughed. "You know where I got it," he said. "From St. Nick, of course."

Each of the girls took turns feeling the material and trying it on while Ellen threw her arms around Edward and kissed him. Tears were running down her face.

"Don't cry, Ellen. 'Tis Christmas."

"They're tears of joy, Edward. Thank you."

When the excitement was over and everyone had taken a good look at each other's gifts, Ellen suggested they go back downstairs. One of the girls cried out, "We have to get ready for the dance!" With that, they all jumped to their feet and made their way to the stairs.

Kizzie said, "I'll be right there. First I have to clean up this mess."

"All right," said Ellen in a distant voice as she hugged her new coat. She watched wistfully as Kizzie swept the paper from the table and rolled it into a ball. She walked to the stove and slid the cover open, dumping the trash unceremoniously into the now roaring fire. Ellen and Kizzie were the last to leave, smiling with pleasure as they turned and descended the stairs to join their family in celebration.

2

Edward Dower was a man of many talents. The old-timers of Conche tell stories even today that he was a well-known ocean-going captain who took large vessels to many parts of the world, including Europe, Africa and the Caribbean. He was an excellent fisherman who used every technique that worked, everything from small boats to schooners. He was also a good businessman, proving himself even into the 1900s. But above all, any old-timer will tell you that he was a wonderful family man.

Edward was popular at the celebrations of the day, a man who could take the floor and step dance to any tune played on the accordion or fiddle. He was said to be a ladies' man, that women flocked to him wherever he went. Though he was not a womanizer, his blazing red hair and freckled face acted as a magnet for women looking for companionship.

John and Edward Dower were brothers, and John was the older of the two. However, John was content to leave the management of all business affairs in the capable hands of his younger brother. Edward was fearless on the ocean and could navigate it with great skill. The same old-timers used to say that Edward had his chart and log in his head, at a time when navigation on northern waters hadn't yet been put to paper. Mariners who traversed the seas, including those around northern Newfoundland, had to rely on their wits.

Before the dawn of the engine, seagoers rowed with oars or were driven by the wind to their destinations. Edward was well versed in weather signs, particularly the tides and the effects they had on ice movements. His success at the seal fishery was due in large part to this. He was the brother who most often commandeered the *Elsie*, while John and Ellen stayed in Conche and took care of the shore workings of the business.

The Dowers were successful and down-to-earth yet carried themselves well. They had received only the most basic education in the areas of reading, writing, and arithmetic, but associated with the most prominent people of the day. The two brothers grew up in a home where they learned to work hard and to love their neighbour as themselves. This was the credo of James Herbert Dower, their father. By following this, John and Edward were told, they stood a chance of getting almost anything to work.

Apart from his red hair, Edward resembled his older brother in many ways: he was tall, well built, resilient to the outdoor elements, and possessed catlike reflexes. The two brothers had also inherited the great quality of generosity from their parents. Their father's words left a lasting impression, because they were good to their neighbours and to strangers in need, no matter where from or how desperate the soul. John and Edward Dower never turned away any who came to their door, and the people along the French Shore respected them for it.

John was the happiest man in Conche when Edward married Ellen Casey from St. John's. Some said that John was also in love with her himself, but this was not so. His love for her was as a brother loves his sister. The newlyweds built a large, two-storey house in the middle of a grassy field, with the intention of raising a large family. They would need the space; in fifteen years they had nine children, five sons and four daughters.

Two years after Edward and Ellen married, John met a woman named Rose and fell madly in love with her. They married and moved in with his brother, ate from the same table, and pooled their money in the same till tucked away in Edward's old sea-chest. Whatever was under their roof was shared by the two families. It was said that their children looked alike, acted and talked alike, and the people of Conche had a hard time distinguishing which child was whose. These two families were blessed with the greatest harmony and peace anyone could experience.

As time passed and their families expanded, privacy became ever more important to the maturing children. Therefore, John and Edward and their wives sat together one night and decided they would build another house. The new house would go to John. "I think you're going to have the most children anyway," Edward had said with a laugh. It turned out to be true; John had twelve to Edward's nine.

The new house was built, but as the people of Conche will tell you, it was only a place for them to sleep. Most of them continued to live and eat at Edward's place with no questions asked.

* * *

DURING THE 1870s, life was tough in and around the colony of Newfoundland. The fish merchants ruled either directly or indirectly. They could destroy a village by strangling the flow of credit, leaving the fisherfolk no choice but to leave and settle elsewhere. But the livelihood of those living in Conche with the Dower Brothers firm was never in jeopardy.

When the Dowers prospered, the people shared in their fortune. When the people fell on hard times, John and Edward suffered also. Each fall the Dowers rolled a hundred barrels of flour into their private storeroom, and although they would eat only half of the winter supply, by the time spring came it was all gone, given away to needy families in the community. They kept large vegetable gardens, and cattle: goats, sheep, and sometimes cows. Although they were well off, they worked the land like everyone else.

John and Edward were men who went at the seals with great vigour, and they saw much success in the cod-fishery as well. Over the years, the town of Conche, teeming as it was with the coveted codfish, produced dozens of reputable fishermen. The town played host to schooners and crews in search of cod as well, and there were years when fishermen at Conche landed more than the catch of all of White Bay combined.

The Dower brothers were leaders of their time. John and Edward were daring businessmen, always in search of ways to improve their financial standing, and it seemed every new venture flourished. After participating in the sealing industry for years as landsmen, that is, working the seal nets and sending men and dogs out on foot, they determined that there was far more potential out there on the water.

Weighing the costs, and spending many a late night in conversation with their closest friends and advisors, they decided to investigate the possibility of acquiring a vessel. Not just any vessel, though. This one had to be large enough and strong enough to withstand the force of the Arctic ice and the pull of the mighty Labrador current. Without seeking an outside financier, they worked out a budget based on the pooled resources in Edward's till.

So, during the spring of 1871, Edward and John travelled to Halifax, Nova Scotia to look for a suitable vessel, one they could take to the cod-fishery in summer and which could endure the seal hunt in winter. They located a company that had just such a vessel for sale, and after giving her a thorough inspection, they purchased the *Elsie*. It had been built in Lunenburg, Nova Scotia from solid oak, a versatile ship intended for polar expeditions. When the Arctic ice pressed in on both her sides, her round hull wouldn't fracture but instead be pushed upward. The Dowers fell in love with her at first sight, despite their high estimation of repair costs.

While John and Edward stayed in Halifax, they each bought a gift to take back to their wives. Before leaving Conche, Ellen had given Edward specific instructions.

"Now, Edward, my dear," she said in a businesslike manner, "here's what I want you to buy me for Christmas."

Edward took one look at Ellen, with her hands on her hips, and laughed. He had it figured out. "Ellen, I'm not bringing back any more furniture or dishes. We've got too much of that stuff now."

"No," she said, "that's not what I want."

"What do you want, Ellen?"

"I want you to bring me back one of those lambskin coats. You know the type, with the wool inside, like the one Mrs. Findlay was wearing at the meeting that day in St. John's."

Edward remembered. Ellen hadn't stopped talking about it ever since she'd seen it. "All right, Ellen. If there's a coat like that on this side of the Atlantic, I'll find it."

In Halifax, Edward and John pounded the streets for well over an hour, their search for a lambskin coat turning up nothing. They were about to turn around and return to the hotel when Edward caught sight of something out of the corner of his eye. There, proudly displayed in a shop window up the street, was a coat made of pure lamb's skin. It was a thing of beauty that seemed to light up the shop all by itself. The luxurious material spilled to a three-quarters length, and a smart little hood completed the ensemble. Edward knew at once that Ellen would love it.

He said to John, "I would say there's not another coat like that in Newfoundland. Just wait 'til Mrs. Findlay sees this!" They laughed.

"You're right, Ned, I have to agree. Ellen deserves the best that you can get her."

"It's expensive," Edward said, not taking his eyes off the coat in the window, "but it's worth it."

* * *

THE ELSIE WAS A GALLANT VESSEL, a massive barquentine with a strong reinforced frame comprised of eighteen inches of solid oak. She had a large forecastle, where the cook and the majority of the crew would be staying. Below deck and toward the stern of the vessel was a low-built house about twelve feet square, extending to a point three feet above deck and with windows peeking out on both sides. This was the captain's quarters, built this way so that the windows would allow some light into the cabin. In this room were two extra bunks for added crew members, but under normal circumstances only the captain and his first mate would make use of it.

The vessel's sole means of propulsion was the wind that blew on the ocean. She was a magnificent sight to behold from both aboard and on shore, and Edward's chest swelled with pride as he set sail on this, a ship he could call his own. After leaving Halifax, the *Elsie*'s first port of call was St. John's, Newfoundland, where Edward was to pick up freight bound for Conche. After word of his arrival circulated, he met some business associates, and of course they decided to have a night on the town.

In one of the inns, Edward was introduced to a man by the name of Walter Joy, whose hometown was Harbour Main, a small community located in Conception Bay. Walter was a handsome man, a ship's carpenter and boat builder by trade. When he learned that they had just purchased the *Elsie*, he told Edward that he was interested in a job.

This was more than Edward could have hoped for, to run into someone with such a skill so soon after acquiring a ship. Edward hired him at once, and Walter packed his bags and joined the crew. Theirs was a friendship that began with no fanfare whatsoever, but one which lasted a lifetime.

* * *

AND SO IT WAS, as the *Elsie* sailed into Conche for the first time with all her flags flying, the people stood cheering and clapping their hands, with cries of "Our sealing vessel has finally arrived!" filling the air. Soon she was fitted out for her first trial, the Labrador fishery, and she did quite well, taking back over five hundred quintals of heavily salted cod. She was well on her way toward paying for herself.

The seal fishery was very important to the economy of Newfoundland as well as Labrador. In fact, seals were the second most valuable resource, the first of course being cod. There were vessels of all description taking part in both fisheries every winter and spring, the largest of them coming out of St. John's. The more opportunistic of the foreign seamen harvested the shores of Newfoundland and Labrador as well, but the lion's share of the industry was procured by Newfoundlanders.

A large part of the sealing was done by swilers operating onshore with seal nets and small boats. But times were changing. Schooners were being reinforced by the score and sent to the whelping areas of the icefields. This is a place in the pack ice where mature seals congregate to give birth to their pups, which are known as whitecoats. When the harp seal first gives birth, the coat of its young is stark white. Before long, the pup grows very fat by feeding on its mother's milk, which has the highest protein of any known substance. It was the oil rendered from this fat that fetched such a handsome price on the market and brought Newfoundlanders out by the thousands.

3

Christmas morning dawned cold and clear. Just about every home in Conche had its fire going, with columns of smoke drifting lazily into the air and criss-crossing in silky patterns. What little snow there was on the ground was marked by the passage of dog teams and children's riding sleighs. The young ones had forgotten about the snow for the time being, of course, anxious to see what presents had mysteriously appeared for them overnight.

This late December was like Christmas twice over for the Dower family. The shoreline was littered with dead harp seals still wearing their pelts, those the men had killed the day before. They had bled them as soon as they killed them, but the hides and fat would have to be removed and sorted today or tomorrow, before the ship that collected them arrived in Conche the first week of January.

Although this was Christmas Day, Edward and John summoned some men to the house to discuss the possibility of harvesting more seals.

"We've got two weeks before the collector comes," said John, turning to address each man at his table. "Between now and then we should be able to get another thousand seals ready."

"Or more," Edward said with a sly grin.

"You can't get too greedy, Uncle Ned," laughed one of the swilers.

"That's not greed, my man, that's bread and butter."

"Yes," John said in a matter-of-fact way, "and we need lots of it." His words brooked no argument, for everyone at the table remembered well the previous year. The catch had been scarce for everyone in town, and the Dowers had been called upon to feed most of their neighbours.

It was decided that on Boxing Day half of Edward's men would go out and haul the nets, while John supervised those who would stay in and secure the seals they had caught yesterday by preserving them in snow and ice. Anyone who wanted to work at them today had permission to do so, but John made it clear to everyone that today was Christmas Day and the work could wait until tomorrow. For now they could celebrate the season and this most successful year.

* * *

AFTER THE CHRISTMAS and New Year's celebrations passed and life returned to normal, the regular workings of the town of Conche recommenced. Firewood was cut for the coming winter, logs were split with overhead pit saws, and nets and other fishing gear were repaired or replaced as the situation demanded. Some men went to work constructing a new boat.

However, this winter was anything but normal for the Dower family, for they had bigger and better business ventures in mind. The *Elsie* had proven herself in the summer of the previous year, so their new man, Walter Joy, was readying her for the "front." This was the name people had for the icefields where ships went to hunt whitecoats during the winter and early spring. He set to work on the vessel immediately, making adjustments to the forecastle and installing more bunk beds in the sleeping quarters. Walter was experienced in the preparation of sealing vessels such as the *Elsie*, and Edward considered himself lucky to have met the man.

While in St. John's the previous year, they had secured a good price for whitecoats, and to their delight they learned that there was an unlimited market for them. They knew what they had to do. This winter they would head for the whelping grounds. The question was how many pelts the *Elsie* could stow below deck. Some said five thousand, while others said as many as ten. John and Edward would be satisfied if she could carry just five thousand.

It was a simple matter to acquire a crew for the *Elsie*. Thirty-four men were needed besides the captain and the cook to give them a full crew of thirty-six. Edward enlisted two of his own sons, Frank and Peter, and two of John's wanted to go as well. Walter Joy would be going, of course, to act as Edward's second-in-command. The others consisted of twenty-nine hand-picked sealers. Edward looked at his list of men, noting that they were strong, daring, energetic, and ready to tackle anything. They eagerly lent their hands to getting the *Elsie* in top shape and ready for the front.

Their aim was to have the *Elsie* ready by the first of March. Firewood and coal was put on board and stored below in the rear of the vessel, and the lockers were filled with enough food for three months. Barrels of fresh water for cooking and cleaning were hoisted on board and lowered through the hatch, along with the tools needed to kill seals: knives, two dozen sharpening steels, and a large manual grindstone.

The women had been busy preparing warm clothes for the sealers: extra socks, mitts, special rain clothes made waterproof by giving them an extra soaking in linseed oil. The linseed was as much an insulator from the cold as from the rain. Walter was put in charge of this project as well.

The men had no choice but to cut a channel through the ice in the days before the *Elsie* was to set sail. Between her anchoring point and the open water was a solid slab of winter ice through which they had to use pit saws to cut a path about a mile long. It was naturally decided by the two brothers that Edward would go to the seal hunt in the *Elsie* and John would stay home and run things. When the crew returned, space would be needed to store their load of pelts, so the older brother would have to begin expanding their warehouse immediately.

* * *

ON THE MORNING OF MARCH 1, 1872, Edward Dower, Walter Joy, and thirty-four of the finest sons Conche could produce were ready to go. Edward made a mental checklist and determined that everything they needed was on board. A crowd had gathered early in the morning to witness this important event. It had been arranged by the people earlier in the winter for Father Gore, the community's priest, to attend and give his blessing to the voyage and the vessel on the day of the *Elsie*'s departure.

At ten o'clock the people stood shivering in the chilly morning air as the ship lay in full splendour with all of her bunting flying. The throng observed John and Edward walking out to the vessel with a sleigh in tow. This last-minute loading included Edward's personal belongings, all packed up in his large oak chest.

Edward always said that his sea-chest had all the luck in the world attached to it and vowed that he would never go on any voyage without it. Indeed, in the years to come, this old chest would travel almost as many miles on the ocean as Edward himself. It accompanied him as far north as the Labrador and to the east far across the Atlantic.

But for now this chest with all of its hidden secrets was about to make a voyage to the greatest hunt in the world. It required two strong men to lift, and before long the hearty Conche crew had it up and over the rail. They carried it down below to Edward's quarters, where they stored it neatly at the foot of the captain's bunk.

Father Gore was pulled out onto the ice by a team of dogs manned by two drivers. He was dressed in his winter robes, and a large crucifix dangled around his neck. The people crossed themselves as he came to the side of the *Elsie*. The crew and captain had boarded the vessel and now stood near the rail, watching the priest as he began his farewell service.

First he read from his prayer book, then said a prayer for the men on board. He concluded with a short speech. "I am glad that you men are going to the seal hunt. What makes it all the more comforting is the fact that you are going out to earn bread and butter and not to do something for pleasure. Because this is what is ruining humanity today—pleasure," he said, pausing for effect.

His eyes swept over the assembled townspeople. Turning to regard the *Elsie*'s crew again, he continued, "I can assure you one thing, and that is the people will be praying for you every hour of every day. They will be praying for two things. One is for your safety. Two is that you will get a bumper load of seals." His face brightened into a beatific smile. "May God bless the *Elsie* and everyone on board," he concluded.

With that, he produced a bottle of holy water and sprinkled the side of the barque.

"Amen," the crew responded to the priest and the people onshore. Edward waved at Ellen, his wife, as she stood there on the wharf in her new coat. Family and friends cried and cheered all around her as she calmly waved back at her beloved husband.

Edward gave the order for the sails to be hoisted, and it was then that the women and children among the onlookers really broke down, crying as they watched their fathers, brothers and sons begin their perilous journey to the icefields and the unknown. The vessel bobbed and swayed like a drunk as it weaved down the narrow icy corridor. Soon it reached the open water, and the men waved their last goodbyes before turning out to sea to face whatever awaited them there.

* * *

THE GREATEST DISASTERS EVER to have happened in the history of Newfoundland, especially where loss of life is concerned, occurred in the sealing industry. Large sealing ships have been known to disappear along with their crews, leaving not a trace of anyone or anything. Vanishing, as it were, into thin air. And so it was, that whenever a sealing vessel left for the ice, be it a wooden hull or otherwise, the people in those small fishing villages worried and fretted daily. They were always on the lookout for signs of disaster or any indication that a vessel was in trouble. Every day in Conche saw people out on the cliffs near Cape Fox, always watching, their spyglasses at the ready.

There were no long-distance communications of any kind in 1872. Just sight and sound had to suffice, and even then, as the old saying goes, you believe only half of what you see and nothing of what you hear. The best optical instrument available at the time was the spyglass, and even they were of poor quality. Therefore, when a vessel left port to go on a voyage like the seal hunt, no news was expected from her until she came into view of the lookout on shore. On a clear day, a spy-glass could let you see forty miles or a little more, so lookouts kept a constant watch for vessels stuck in heavy ice.

Now, it is a documented fact that over the years people have had dreams and visions of things happening far away. Ninety-nine per cent of the time these prophecies turned out to be nothing more than bouts of fantasy brought on by worry and anxiety. Throughout history, fact and fiction have often mingled to the point where one cannot easily be distinguished from the other. But the fact remains. Ninety-nine per cent of alleged supernatural visions have proven to be nothing more than delusions.

But sometimes they came true.

4

After seeing the *Elsie* off, the townsfolk left the harbour ice and went back to their homes. The men resumed their usual tasks of mending nets, building boats, repairing sheds and cutting firewood, while the women took up their work inside the homes.

Besides the regular demands of the firm, John Dower was responsible for overseeing the expansion to its warehouse and wharf. Their grocery shop needed to be enlarged, too, but the most pressing issue was ensuring that the Dower storehouse was large enough to house a sizable catch. In the event that the *Elsie* struck the whitecoats, John would have to make room for five thousand or more of the precious pelts.

The foundation had already been laid late the previous fall, and there were more than enough materials to build an impressive structure, so he hired the best construction crew he could muster at short notice. The industrious men were happy to be part of John's team. There were many excited conversations among them as they rumoured and speculated about when the *Elsie* would hit the main patch and how many she would bring back. The women worked just as hard as the men at their own work, and they were scheduled to handle the shop for John while he was busy with the new warehouse.

It took a couple of days after the *Elsie* left port for John to get everything organized for the building project. First of all, he had to engage a group of men to clear the foundation and floor of snow. When that was done, the crew uncovered the perimeter of the structure. Next they carried the lumber and the framing into the old shed. The large iron stove blazed while they stacked the snow-covered materials near to dry.

"Listen, men," John said to his crew at the end of their first day on the job. "If the weather stays good, we should have this building closed in very quickly, in no more than a few days, I would say."

John's confidence in his workers' abilities was well placed. Within a week of Edward's departure, they were able to felt the roof and administer the finishing touches. He stepped back upon the project's completion and admired their handiwork. The man nearest him slapped him on the back and said, "John, you're pretty confident that they're going to get the seals."

"If Ned comes across them and they're prime to take," John said, "he'll go at it morning, noon, and night, that's for sure. Frank and Peter and the boys won't get much sleep." The men laughed. Whatever the case, they were now fully prepared to store as many pelts as Edward could get his hands on.

* * *

DURING THE FIRST WEEK of March, a small sailing skiff breezed into Conche and tied up at the edge of the ice. It was unusual for boats to be moving around the coast at this time of year, so a few men went out to see if those aboard were in trouble. They discovered the vessel had come from Canada Harbour, where the residents had gotten low on food and sent the boat in search of provisions.

In charge of this small boat was a well-known fisherman named Paddy Dempsey. He had been born and reared in Ireland, but came to Newfoundland on a fishing banker and landed at St. John's. Paddy ended up at Canada Harbour, where he married and raised a large family.

Paddy Dempsey helped his only passenger out onto the ice with the aid of the Conche men. A close friend of his in Englee by the name of Morgan Strong had asked him if he would pick up his daughter Emiline and bring her to Conche. She was seeing Frank Dower, son of Edward and Ellen. And now as she stepped onto the solid ice floe, Emiline Strong thanked Paddy for taking her to Conche, and together they walked arm in arm across the frozen bay, with thoughts of a warm meal quickening their stride.

Emiline knew that Ellen Dower was holding her breath, waiting for the two lovebirds to make up their minds and get married. She had kept house for the Dowers for two years, during which time she and Frank had gotten to know each other. Of course, she was welcomed with open arms by Aunt Ellen and the rest of the Dower clan, who treated her like one of their own. She was disappointed to learn, however, that Frank had left for the seal hunt on board the *Elsie* and might not be back for months.

"With Frank gone to the seal hunt, I guess I'll go on back home with Uncle Paddy this evening," she said after eating with Ellen and her family.

"And no you won't," Ellen declared. "You're staying here 'til the *Elsie* gets back, supposing she's gone 'til Christmas." That settled the matter, and Emiline stayed.

* * *

THAT NIGHT, the Conche ladies held their monthly meeting of the Women's Aid group, of which Ellen was president. At eight o'clock the women started crowding into the local hall. Everyone was present, eager to get together and talk about the men who were away at the ice. Ellen, Emiline, and the Dower girls were a few minutes late, but the minute they arrived, the meeting started. During the time she had worked as the Dowers' housekeeper, Emiline had been in every home at one time or another and was known to all the women at the function. Tonight she was their guest, and she smiled at all the familiar faces.

Whenever Ellen attended one of these meetings or other public events, she always looked her best. She instinctively knew how to dress well, and with her hair in the latest style of the day, she looked much younger than her forty-two years. When they entered the hall, everyone turned to admire Ellen's lambskin coat. The hood with its snow-white lambswool was a stark contrast to her dark hair, accenting her natural beauty. She had worn the coat daily since Christmas, delighting in the reactions from men and women alike whenever she walked by. She grinned when she saw how Emiline took in the women's faces as they turned to sneak a peek at the new coat.

Ellen was often called on to sing at public gatherings. She had a gorgeous voice that often left not a dry eye in the place whenever she lifted it to old sea ballads or Irish love songs. And before she'd even gotten her coat off and taken a seat, someone begged her to sing for the ladies.

She laughed, her voice tinkling merrily. "I'll sing if someone will accompany me on the mouth organ."

Quick as a flash, one of the women took up a mouth organ and turned to give Ellen an expectant look. Without further ado, they started in on a romantic melody, and the women in the hall applauded after the first few notes, when they figured out which song she had chosen to sing. For the first time since the men had left for the seal hunt, their minds were free of worry, and the boards rattled with the tapping of feet as the sound of Ellen's voice and her accompanist filled the room.

The evening was a pleasure to all in attendance. Ellen took a breather and let the other women take turns performing, joining in now and then when the crowd was asked to sing as a group. Between songs, the women sat and gossiped while they knitted and crocheted. Everyone wanted to know all the news from around Englee, so Emiline filled them in. Times were desperate up there, she told them. There was no food, the people were starving, and the government either didn't notice their plight or chose not to.

Tea was poured by the gallon while the ladies picked at the food they had all brought to the potluck dinner. The laughter and singing continued for some time, when suddenly Ellen stood and raised her voice to get everyone's attention. She held out her hand to Emiline and beckoned her to stand. The young woman's face went white, but she obeyed.

"We have an announcement to make, ladies," Ellen said, turning to look at all the women.

"As you know, Emiline and Frank have been going steady now for a long time, and I am sure that they love each other very much." She looked at Emiline and raised an eyebrow. "Isn't that right, Emiline?"

Emiline blushed and said, "Very much."

"And of course we love her too," Ellen said, gesturing. "She has lived with us for two years, we've come to know her and her family, and as you all know, she's related to half of Conche as well."

There was some laughter. "Get on with it, Aunt Ellen," someone shouted.

"Emiline and Frank are going to get married in August, and I have been asked to say this on their behalf!"

The ladies jumped to their feet and cheered for the happy couple. Frank was the oldest son in Edward and Ellen Dower's family, and much respected in Conche. Although he was somewhere out on the icefields, warm feelings for Frank came to the ladies' hearts. Emiline's face went beet red from all the praise bestowed on her.

The commotion settled down and the women started firing questions off at poor Emiline. "What kind of a wedding dress will you be wearing, my dear? And who will be making it?"

"I plan to wear my mother's wedding dress," Emiline said. "I was going to bring it with me today to let Frank look at it, but Mother has to do some altering to make it a little smaller. She's going to send it down by the mailman next week."

Ellen jumped. "Oh my God," she exclaimed. One of the women standing nearby noticed the worried frown on her face, but quickly dismissed it in light of Emiline and Frank's exciting news.

"Where will you be living, my dear?" pressed Mrs. Hunt. "Will you be living with Mr. and Mrs. Dower?"

Emiline gave her future mother-in-law a smile and said, "No, I don't think so. I think Frank and I would like some privacy for a little while. He says that he'll be building a home next to his father's anyway, just as soon as the land grant gets straightened out. Right, Mrs. Dower?"

"Yes, the land grant," Ellen said in a distracted voice. Then her face brightened and she threw her arms around Emiline in a loving embrace. Tonight was a night for celebration, and the room burst into song and well-wishing for the blushing bride-to-be.

* * *

WHEN THE WOMEN'S AID meeting was over, Ellen and the girls went straight home, laughing as they walked. Emiline and the others went to the kitchen while Ellen removed her coat and hung it in the hallway. Not only had Edward given her such a fine garment, but he had even gone to the trouble of erecting a small clothes closet in which Ellen could keep it.

Straightening her clothes, she joined her daughters and future daughter-in-law in the kitchen and stowed her gloves on a shelf above the stove. These gloves were also a Christmas gift from her family, home-knitted with a cute diamond design on the back. She sat at the kitchen table and once again wore a distant look on her face. At first she didn't notice the girls standing around. She had other things on her mind.

"You know, Emiline," she said finally, "I'm glad you came here to Conche, my dear. If you hadn't mentioned the mailman tonight, I never would have thought about the land grant. Edward told me at Christmas to make sure and have it ready when Mr. Dempsey comes."

She thought about going to the locked trunk and retrieving the cash box right away, but it was getting late. Besides, there were still a lot of questions she wanted to ask Emiline, now that she had her all to herself.

Kizzie, Ellen's oldest daughter, was standing nearby. Ellen said to her in a soft voice, "Make us a cup of tea, my dear. The one I had up at the hall didn't satisfy me. It was too weak or something. What about you, Emiline?"

"All right, Mrs. Dower, I think I'll have one, too."

Throughout the night the two women talked about many things: the upcoming wedding, Frank and his father, the family, their future. These were happy times for the Dowers and their friends, with better days surely to follow. They each poured themselves a second cup of tea and stayed there chatting, enjoying each other's company and not caring about the lateness of the hour. With Emiline, Ellen shared a special bond, one she felt with no one else.

Finally, when the two women talked themselves out, they turned out the light and joined the rest of Conche in sleep.

* * *

THE PEOPLE OF CONCHE always worked hard for what they got in life. Fishing had always been their main source of food and revenue, and they were daring against the winds and the weather. They tilled the soil and kept cattle every year to sustain themselves, and from all corners of Newfoundland could be heard stories of their charitable nature, a tendency to help their neighbours in times of need. It was not uncommon for the families there to share the last loaf of bread with a next-door neighbour, or even to strangers who happened to come along, for that matter. Conche folk were at their best when called upon to help their fellow man. Whether it be sickness or death, the burden was shared by all.

Before she was Ellen Dower of Conche, she was Ellen Casey of St. John's. There she had received a fair education for a woman of the day. She had attended an all girls school run by a congregation of nuns and finished the equivalent of today's high school. She was an industrious woman, full of life and not afraid of hard work. Always the outgoing type who attracted others to her and was not at all bashful, it was not long after she moved to Conche as a young woman that she had declared her love for Edward to all within earshot.

Ellen was the type of person who could put any mind at ease. She was often called upon when older women died, to go and prepare them for burial. This was what they used to call "laying them out," which involved washing and dressing the deceased, then settling them into their caskets. She would also be responsible for making a shroud and a wreath of flowers.

Emiline Strong felt secure whenever she was with her. She was awed by the woman's strength.

5

The northwest wind pushed the *Elsie* at a fast pace through ice-free waters. It didn't take long to get around Cape Fox and set out for the northeast edge of the northern Grey Islands. Edward's plan was to proceed to the back side of the island to find shelter from the wind and anchor there for the night. Then in the morning they would head out toward the heavy pack ice and to the whelping grounds.

It was early yet in the season for newborn seals. Not until the eighth or tenth of March would they be prime, that is, fat enough to be of highest value. With several days at their disposal, the crew of the *Elsie* would have lots of time to seek out the whelping area and formulate a battle plan.

The cook prepared a wonderful meal, consisting of salt beef and vegetables, and of course "doughboys." Doughboys, known today as dumplings, were a favourite among Newfoundland seamen, made from baking powder, flour, and a little salt, mixed together and boiled with the vegetables. Edward's men also had their fill of fresh seal meat smothered in rich gravy.

Everyone was eager to get at the whitecoats. That evening the men sat either around the table or on their bunk beds in the forecastle, spinning yarns, singing songs and telling jokes. They were restless, Edward could tell. The thought of all those seals out there waiting for them was making them fidgety. He had no doubt that this was a crew who would make him proud.

At ten o'clock that night, when the excitement started to lessen and more than a few sealers were trying in vain to stifle yawns, Edward got their attention and led them in the rosary. They prayed for a good day tomorrow and protection for their families back home.

* * *

THE VESSEL SWARMED with men at daybreak, all hands busy readying the ship for departure. Crank winches hoisted the dual anchors, making the metal squeal as they broke free from the rocky bottom. The canvas was then hoisted, and without delay the *Elsie* slipped from the sheltered little cove they had moored in overnight.

Edward stood at the wheel and watched to make sure everything ran smoothly on deck. He set his eastern course for the heavy pack ice, where he would begin his search for the whelping pans and what he hoped to be whitecoats by the thousands.

Maybe today we'll spot the large seal herd, he thought. *If we can strike a large enough patch of whitecoats, all we'll have to do is heave to and give them a few days to fatten up.*

High up in the front spar of the *Elsie* was a small box-shaped shelter called a barrel. There was a hatch at the bottom for a man to climb through, and there he would watch the ocean from a high vantage point. Once underway, the captain sent a man up into the barrel to report on the conditions ahead.

"No ice to the east, Skipper, as far as the eye can see. Only a couple of bergs to the southeast," the lookout reported.

"All right," said Edward, nodding to the wheelman. "I think we'll haul her off and set a different course." Checking his compass and pocket watch, he ordered, "Put her on a southeast course and let her run for a couple of hours. We're guaranteed to strike ice in that direction. Watch out for the small pieces." Although built to endure great pressure from pack ice, the *Elsie*'s hull was certainly not impervious to smaller, jagged pieces.

"No problem, Skipper. I'll watch her pretty close."

Edward cupped his hands around his mouth and called to the barrelman. "I want you to stay up there for awhile and keep an eye to the southern. The ice may have gone farther up that way toward the Horse Islands."

Casting his glance around the deck one last time, Edward nodded in satisfaction. "We're going down to have breakfast, so it's all yours," he said to the wheelman. He and several deckhands then descended to the forecastle.

Fish and brewis was the menu of the day, and Edward dug in with gusto. After he cleaned his plate, he returned to the deck. He observed that the ship was making little progress in the light westerly wind.

"Put all the canvas on her, men. We have to try and get more speed out of her if at all possible." He called to the barrelman. "Have you seen anything yet?"

"No, only a few loose pans. Way up ahead there's a few large islands of ice."

Edward acknowledged the lookout's report, then remarked to the helmsman, "We should see heavy ice around noon if the wind stays in our favour."

As if on cue, the wind picked up before noon, still from the west and in their favour, and driving the *Elsie* along at just under eight knots. When she listed to starboard, the steady hiss of rushing spray could be heard. The barrelman came down after a three-hour watch and another went up in his place. At noon half the crew went for lunch while the rest kept an eye on the wind, the vessel, and the ice.

Just after the watch change, the barrelman called down. "I think I see ice, Skipper Ned, but it's farther to the northeast."

Everyone on deck looked out the port bow and there was a murmur of excitement. Edward grinned and lifted a hand to the wheelsman. "All right," he said, "that's fine, but I think we should keep going on our present course and get around the back. The windward edge could be packed solid, especially with this amount of wind on it. Besides, if that's the main body and there's whitecoats around, they're guaranteed to be a couple of miles inside the western edge."

Those on board who had been to the ice before knew Edward's words to be true. He and his crew had

gleaned whatever they could from the old-timers back
home who were veterans to the seal hunt, and there had
been much discussion about this particular phenom-
enon. So the *Elsie* kept on her southeast course.

The lookout had an excited tremor in his voice
when he relayed to Edward, "It looks to me like it's the
main icefield, Skipper. There's ice out there as far as you
can see!"

Edward asked, "Do you see any open leads of water
through the ice?"

"Yes! To the northeast about ten degrees there's a
long lead of water. It runs in through to the eastern as
far as the eye can see."

The helmsman checked his position and turned the
wheel ten degrees to port, then nudged it until the
lookout signalled that they were on course for the open
lead.

"Should we take in some of the canvas?" Edward
called up to the barrelman.

"Yes, take in at least half...Skipper, I can see a lot of
seals on the ice and in the water! They're right ahead,
about a mile or so in."

Edward laughed and slapped the sealer standing
next to him on the back. The others were looking ahead
now and chattering excitedly. Those below deck, even
the cook, came up to see why there was such a commotion.

"Don't worry, the young ones aren't far away from
here," Edward stated to those just joining them.

* * *

THE ELSIE PIERCED the main icefield at four o'clock that afternoon. And as was earlier reported by the lookout, an open lead of water yawned before them and disappeared into the field. On the ice to either side of the lead, and even in the span of water itself, were thousands of harp seals.

After the *Elsie* edged her way through the lead a ways, the barrelman yelled down, "I think we're into the ice plenty far now, Skipper."

"No, not yet," Edward replied. "We should go on for another couple of miles to get as near to the whelping patch as possible. Just keep spotting us through the open lead."

"All right, sir."

Edward said to the wheelman, "With all those old seals around, the young ones are here somewhere by the thousands, don't you worry about that."

He eyed the old harps poking up through the ice. "It's better for us to be inside the patch, because we have to work our way back to the western edge anyway. If we run into a patch of whitecoats on our way back, we can always get them then."

The occasional young seal showed itself as they worked their way farther into the ice. Further evidence of their presence came by way of large flat pans of Arctic ice, the kind on which harps preferred to birth their pups.

All of a sudden, the barrelman cried, "There they are, boys! Thousands of them everywhere, just look at that!" To say there were a few whitecoats would be an understatement. Sealers watched with open mouths as pan after pan of ice bearing newborn seals drifted past. And beyond them, the crew could swear that whitecoats stretched to eternity.

There was laughter in his voice as the lookout cried, "We should stop here, Skipper."

"All right," Edward chuckled. To those standing around, he said, "Start looking for a good place to tie on, a place like we discussed last night."

A man pointed off the starboard bow. "I see a place just up ahead."

It took a handful of men to take back and fold the canvas while the *Elsie* coasted to an area locked on three sides by large pans of ice. There was enough space between them for the ship to nestle without risking being crushed. They dropped the anchors onto the ice, and several men carrying hatchets hopped down to cut holes wide enough for the anchor claws to grasp.

Edward's best estimate was that they were about eighty miles from Conche Harbour and sixty-five miles east-northeast of the northern Grey Islands. As the sun was setting, they were now, as they say, "in the seals," but not yet "in the fat." Each member of the crew, Edward included, had that hungry look in his eyes, but he cautioned his men.

"Listen. Those seals aren't going anywhere. They'll still be here a week from now, so don't worry about it, they're ours for the taking. Tomorrow we'll kill a few to see what shape they're in."

The crew weren't satisfied. "Let's kill a few this evening, Skipper," said one man. But their captain wouldn't hear of it. He had made up his mind that they would start killing the young seals around the eighth of March, and that was that. It was what the law of the colony required of them, not to mention the fact that the seals were most likely not mature enough to fetch the top price.

"No," he said, "tomorrow morning we'll kill about a half-dozen or so to eat. Young seal will be a treat for the roaster. We'll stay here in position for the next four days, then go at it full out, in the fat."

The men knew there was no use for further comment. They would just have to wait another four days.

* * *

AS SOON AS THE ANCHORS were put out and the *Elsie* was secure, Edward called all his men together to have a talk. He was more than pleased at his prospects. They were in the middle of the seals, as many as they could possibly want. They just had to wait until the time was right.

"I'm not going to tell you anything you don't already know. We are where we want to be in the Arctic ice, and you all know what happens out here. Right now everything may look beautiful, but an hour from now we could be facing a vicious storm. We don't know.

"So, we're going to work in watches 'til we get home. We'll have four groups on the ice under lead hands. Let's stay that way, at least 'til we see what we're up against."

He looked at his watch, then to the western horizon. "I don't like the look of that mackerel sky," he remarked.

Being encased in an endless field of ice on all sides was of little concern to the crew. The sound of white-coats bawling was sweeter than any love song, and any immediate fears the crew may have had for their own safety were forgotten. This is what they had come for, to kill as many seals as humanly possible and return to Conche as rich men.

"Listen up," Edward warned. The men were distracted by all the white gold surrounding them, so he would keep his final instructions brief. "This is very important. You all know what will happen if the ice damages the rudder or the rudder case."

One sealer spoke up. "I think we're in a pretty safe place, Skipper. Those three sheets of ice are going to give us a lot of protection."

"But," Edward said, raising a finger for emphasis, "sometimes out here the tide does funny things. There's one thing that I must stress to everyone. Don't be careless while moving around at night, especially when you're near the rail. If you happen to fall overboard, you're a gone goose unless there's someone there to pull you up. Another thing: don't anyone leave the vessel for any reason. If you have a problem, let us know.

"For the next few days the kettle will be on 'round the clock, and there's plenty of grub for you to have a lunch whenever you want. If you go for a mug-up, put some wood or coal in the stove."

He finished by saying, "If tomorrow morning is a good one, I want to send a couple of crews over the ice to do a survey in a three-mile radius to give us an idea of how many we can kill. You never know, we might be able to get a couple thousand whitecoats in this patch alone."

One of the sealers offered, "From what I saw, we should be able to load this one without having to move, Skipper." He cocked his ear. "Just listen."

The sealers stopped talking and heard for the first time the sounds of their quarry. It was like the sound of a dying man not yet resigned to his fate. It was as if an orchestra were playing all around them, emitting a tune as mournful and timeless as the waves beneath their feet. Edward and his men went to sleep early that night, while all around the *Elsie* the barking of seals and cracking of ice came like past misdeeds tormenting an ancient monster that lay frozen throughout the ages, trapped in a prison of its own making until the day comes when it must walk the earth again.

6

The crew from Conche spent the night tossing and turning to the unnerving sounds around them, but the day brought with it promise and ambition. The whitecoats were still there as expected. The captain said jokingly, "Those seals have only one place to go, and that's in the water. But," he added with a wink, "they're not going to do that until they get old enough to take their first dip. You can be sure that even then they'll crawl right back up."

Shortly after daylight, when the last man finished his breakfast, Edward summoned them all to the fore-castle for a meeting. "Did you fellows see that red sky this morning? There's going to be weather before noon, and I would say it will be snow. The temperature is about fifteen below, and the wind is northeast."

The more experienced sea dogs in his crew agreed. "The ice is a solid jam now. It looks like it's freezing together," called the man currently acting as barrelman as he came in from the cold.

Edward nodded knowingly.

"Now, men, as I said last evening, I want two groups of men to go out on the ice. One group can go to the south and the other to the northeast. Here's what I want you to do."

He interrupted himself to take a quick look at his watch. Putting it away, he continued. "We're not in on the back of Conche now or on a firewood road. Out here things are different. For one thing, the weather can change in five minutes from sunshine to cloudy and then to snow, so keep your eyes open. And don't go more than three miles, that's our limit."

They agreed and understood that they had better do what they were told, because Skipper Ned Dower was not one to cross. It was said of him many times that when he was good he was more than good, and that when he was bad (usually when someone disobeyed an order or spited him), then bad was not the word to describe him. He could be like the devil, and everyone knew it.

"Frank, I want you to take two men with you and go to the northeast area. You'll work as a team. Take a lunch and the usual equipment with you. Watch the vessel at all times, and at the first sign of weather, head back. You'll also put one man in charge of counting seals, and pay particular attention to their shape and size. Don't forget your gaff and hauling rope."

Frank Dower went to work assembling his team almost as soon as the words left the captain's mouth.

"Keep listening for the horn, Frank. If you hear it, start heading back. It makes no difference how far you're out, just head back."

Edward put Walter Joy in charge of another team bound south and gave the same instructions to them. Frank and Walter showed the best leadership qualities of all his men, so Edward knew the teams were in good hands.

After they had packed their lunches and gathered their sealing equipment, the two groups made ready to leave for their designated locations. Satisfied, Edward assigned a watch to each crew, to track them every minute until they returned to the ship. He also sent a man up to the barrel as per the usual routine. The change in wind and tide was a variable he needed to predict to the best of his ability, so the lookout would have to find marks and use them to see if the *Elsie* was drifting. He warned his scouting teams to stay put and signal if the tide opened up a stretch in the ice between them and the vessel.

* * *

THE BAWLING OF THE WHITECOATS pierced the still morning air. Edward's breath puffed in front of him as he surveyed the areas where he had sent his teams. After Walter and Frank left with their companies, he decided he would send a few men out to take a sample of the young seals. "I want you to walk in a straight line to the westward area for about half a mile," he said, "and kill some whitecoats, twenty at most. I want to know what shape they're in. You can bring back the livers and hearts for the cook, but leave the shoulders in the pelts. We can cut them out when we get them aboard."

They didn't have to go very far before killing their first one. The process was quick and humane; a severe blow to the top of the head was enough to crush the seal's skull and penetrate the brain. Edward's men were efficient, the four-inch steel spikes on their hand-gaffs making short work of the animals. Once the kills were made, the men skilfully removed the skeleton from the body, leaving the fat and skin intact. As instructed, they left the two front shoulders to be sculped on board. They only had to go out half a mile to kill their twentieth seal, and on the way back to the *Elsie* they hooked up the pelts they had left behind. The whole process took no more than an hour.

"Those seals are in as good a shape as I've ever seen them," Edward said proudly when the men dumped the pelts on the deck. "I see no reason why we shouldn't start killing right away."

The samplers said they saw a couple hundred or more in the half-mile stretch they had walked. Edward bent and examined the fine creatures. "We'll wait 'til the other parties get back, and we'll all sit down together and decide what to do. You fellows might have struck on a patch born early."

This was a fair assessment of what they had seen. "On a single pan we counted thirty-six whitecoats alone," argued one man, pointing to an area not far from the *Elsie*. "Let's get at it, Skipper. I bet we could load this schooner here in a couple of days." The others needed little urging and were giving their captain hopeful looks.

Before he could answer, the barrelman called down. "One of the crews is on the way back, Skipper."

"Good," said Edward, going to the rail. He watched Frank's group come back across the ice. They were all laughing and grinning at each other. Shortly, Walter's group came into view, and they looked to be in good spirits as well. Their mood was infectious, and by the time both groups returned to the ship, even those who had stayed aboard were alive with excitement.

"They're as ready now as they ever will be," Frank said to his father when both groups gathered on deck. He was referring to the amount of body fat on the whitecoats. "I'd say we counted about a thousand up to the northeast." Walter's group gave Edward the same estimate for their direction.

Edward held up his hand. "We'll go to the galley and have a mug-up, then we'll decide what to do."

Everyone descended to the forecastle and sat at the table. They munched on homemade bread and beans (baked in molasses with salt pork) while the captain outlined his plans.

"The seals are usually prime for taking around the eighth to the tenth. When I was in St. John's last fall, I was talking to the heads of the company that's going to take the pelts off our hands, and they told me they preferred pelts that have been killed after the eighth of the month. You know what that means."

The men said nothing, so he continued.

"They meant that we would get a better price for seals killed when they're in their prime. They won't be in their prime 'til around the eighth of March. What's the use of killing a load of whitecoats if they're no good? We might only get about half-price for them.

68

"We'll wait another four days at least before we start the kill. For now, we're safe as can be and we have lots of food and water. So let's hang tough and do the right thing." The crew of the *Elsie* accepted their captain's advice with no argument. They were impatient, but they respected Skipper Ned Dower more than anyone else alive.

The man who had been left on watch came to the forecastle and reported his findings. "Skipper, 'tis beginning to snow. It looks to me like the wind has pitched from the northeast."

Edward wasn't surprised. He'd seen all the signs that morning.

* * *

THEY ROSE JUST AFTER DAYBREAK the next day. The watchman came into the kitchen and said the snow from the previous evening had developed into a squall. He wiped freezing water from his reddened face and grinned. "This must be the whitecoat patch, Skipper," he said.

"Yes, I guess you're right," said Edward.

The cook placed a hearty breakfast on the table. The smell of fish and salt pork in the frying pans made everyone's mouth water.

"This snow is the stuff that puts the fat on the young ones, so they say," said the cook. "Just like salt fish and scruncheons sticks to a man's carcass."

The swilers laughed as they filled their plates from the heaping platters. After they had their fill, those who had pipes lit up and leaned back. Resting up before the big kill didn't seem like such a bad idea.

"I don't want anyone to leave the vessel today," said Edward. "We need all the hands we can get to start shovelling snow off the deck as soon as the storm lets up."

"Did you take a look at that sunset yesterday?" Walter asked incredulously. "I'd say we'll have a couple of days more of this, at least."

Edward nodded. "You're probably right. The north-east wind will drive us to the southwest for quite a long ways if it keeps up, maybe even as far as the Horse Islands or just off Fogo Island. Whatever the case, we just have to sit tight and wait. Those seals won't be going anywhere."

Frank looked worried. "What do you think will happen if this ice splits in two and starts to move away? We could miss out on most of them; they could be ten miles from here overnight or even in just a few hours."

"I know, Frank. I thought about that even when I made the decision to wait a few days. It's a gamble, but it would be useless to kill them just for the sake of killing them. They have to be in their prime in order to get a decent price for them. That's a chance we'll have to take."

Frank conceded that his father knew what he was doing. He would stick by his decision, no matter what. "I suppose I am over-anxious, Father," he said with a grin.

Edward laughed and slapped Frank on the back. He was proud of the boy's ambition. "You'll get your chance, Frank, and so will everyone else when the time comes." He looked around and saw that everyone was sipping the last of their tea and smoking their last few puffs of tobacco. He stood up. "This is a good day for us to do some work on that mainsail. We can work on it down in the hold. A couple of you can stay and give the cook a hand if he wants you."

The cook was grateful for the help, of course. He had told Edward earlier that he wanted water taken out of the casks and some coal for the stove brought down to the galley. To everyone's delight, he said, "I think we'll have another feed of fresh seal this evening. There's nothing like it."

Edward donned his coat and cap. "A couple of men can start shovelling snow now," he said. "I'm going to check along the sides to make sure there's nothing along the hull that could punch a hole in her."

* * *

THE STORM BLEW ON for three days with the wind northeast. It was not at all a major blizzard, just enough falling snow and wind to make work for the men aboard the *Elsie*. At first they were dismayed to see that they were drifting quite a ways from their original spot. But they could tell the sea was rolling in their favour by the way the seals surrounding them stayed in place, drifting right along with them.

"When the storm clears up, we'll start the kill," Edward announced to the men at the end of their third day of waiting. "Tomorrow is the eighth, men. They're all prime now, and at sunrise tomorrow I want every man on the ice with his packsack on his back and his gaff in his hand." He raised his voice and said, "We're going to do what we came here for. We're going to get the biggest load of seals anyone has ever seen!"

The men shouted and stamped their feet. Tomorrow was going to be the day. They could feel it.

All during the day of March 7, the men busied themselves at various tasks. Some shovelled snow from the deck while others helped the cook. A few men were assigned to attend to the large mainsail and splice some rope together.

Several times those on deck stopped and listened to the bawling of the whitecoats cut through the stormy gloom. This was their home. They weren't crying from the cold or for want of food, but because the adult seals were away feeding, and they craved company. Company they would get, but not the kind they wanted. The *Elsie* was lying in wait nearby, like a bird of prey waiting for an opportune moment.

Ten o'clock that night the wind swung around to the west and the stars came out. The watchman came to the forecastle and announced the news to everyone. The whole place went up, and Edward had to shout above the crew to make himself heard.

"We'll have an early rise tomorrow morning, men." When the place quieted, he outlined his plans for them. "There will be thirty-four of you, including Walter, who will be going on the ice as one party. We won't be having a free-for-all; what we'll do is hunt the north side first, and kill as we go. When a man kills a tow, he'll sculp them and take them back to the vessel.

"The cook and myself will hoist them on board and stow them in the hatch. While you're out there you can get your instructions from Walter. But remember, you have to keep your eyes wide open at all times, and if the weather starts to come in at all, you'll have to head straight back here."

Edward was as good as any seasoned sealing captain. He made a point of knowing every crewman's strengths and weaknesses, and utilized them with great efficiency. Most of all, he was a compassionate employer, always looking out for his workers. The men of the *Elsie* would tell anyone who asked that he was the finest captain you could ever want.

* * *

THE NORTHEAST WIND that blew the *Elsie* for many miles to the southwest sent a heavy field of ice to the shores between Conche and the Grey Islands. The ice formed a solid mass from shore to shore, and the men who went up on Cape Fox and surveyed the area with their spyglasses found that the ice extended as far as they could see. Here and there a few patches of seals moved about, but the stability of the icefield was a question they felt was better left unanswered.

When word of the massive field of ice reached John Dower, he looked up from the package of groceries he was preparing and said to Ellen, "I'd say we may not see Ned and the boys 'til around June, then. Even if they get their load on time, they won't be able to get in here at all."

Ellen shook her head. "Don't worry, John. Edward will find a way through. He always does."

John laughed. "Yes, he's after getting out of a lot harder jams, that's for sure." His face fell. "If there was only some way we could get a signal to him."

Ellen laughed. "We should be like the Indians and send up some smoke signals to them."

John grinned and went back to his work.

That night was a long one for Ellen Dower. At around the same time Edward was delivering instructions to an excited crew, she was saying her prayers and getting ready for bed. She wasn't tired, but she felt she needed a little rest. Edward and her two boys were on her mind constantly, and though she hadn't shown it, something of a panic had come over her when John mentioned the wall of ice that had accumulated along the shore.

As she lay in bed staring at the ceiling, her thoughts roamed over the last few days here in Conche. Emiline was an absolute joy to have around, and she treasured the long late-night talks they shared. How she had laughed when Emiline told her about how awkward Frank was when they first started courting! She smiled in the darkness when she tried to picture her son.

Ellen was lucky to have the young lady around as well, because if not for her she would likely have forgotten all about the land grant until well after the mailman came and went. Ellen broke out in a cold sweat when the thought hit her. These days, the mere thought of the document was all it took to rattle her nerves and send her mind reeling. She wondered in an offhand way if she was losing her mind.

"It's in the cash box with the paper money, I know it," she said, though she hadn't looked in there herself to confirm it. "Yes, that's where Edward put it." She resolved to get the land grant out of there well in advance of Uncle Paddy Dempsey's arrival.

Ellen was awake for a long time thinking about Edward. He was the only man she had ever known and would ever know. He had been so good to her and the family. She rolled onto her side when she heard the last of the girls come in for the night.

"Close the door, my dear," she called. "It looks like we could get a storm before the night is over."

Her daughter called back and assured her that all the doors were sealed tight.

Ellen started to drift toward sleep. Her last waking thoughts were of Edward and what he could be doing at that moment.

"Sleeping, of course," she mumbled, reaching out blindly to embrace her husband before nodding off into a deep slumber.

7

As the sun's rays streaked the morning sky, the men aboard the *Elsie* stood ready to jump onto the rough ice and begin the task of killing seals. Their faces were as hard as the ice this morning as the shrill cries of the whitecoats cut through the stillness of the predawn air. They had all finished their breakfast well before dawn broke through the night sky. Most hadn't slept at all.

"Now, men, you know what to do," said Edward. "But before you go, let's put a couple of ladders over the side. It's better to climb down than to jump. You could break an ankle or something."

The men lowered two ladders and secured them to the side of the *Elsie*.

"Well, it's time to go over the side," Edward said in a voice filled with excitement. He sounded like a young man again, out to his first hunt. Although he had been to the ice before, there was nothing like being in charge of your own crew in the greatest hunt in the world.

As it turned out, only two men used the ladders. The rest jumped and hit the ice running, heading for the seals. Edward laughed despite himself as the thirty-four crew members went among the seals and began their grisly work. He was still laughing as the cook came up on deck and joined him at the rail. Together they then cleared the deck to prepare it for a large load. Edward hung his tally board on the hatch, for easy access once the pelts started to pile up. It was a simple board with holes punched in it at regular intervals. For every five pelts that came aboard, a peg was put into a hole. Then, after the day's harvesting was over, the captain would count the pegs and multiply the number by five. Between recording pelts in his logbook, keeping an eye on his men, and watching how the *Elsie* settled in the water, Edward would be a busy man.

In half an hour the first tow of seals was brought to the side of the schooner. The man with the tow had five steaming pelts strung on his hauling rope. Shortly after, Edward leaped over the side and hooked a rope onto another four. He sidled up to the ship and helped the cook hoist them on board. When he turned around, he saw the rest of the men coming from the north with an average tow of five pelts.

* * *

AT 3:00 P.M. THE COOK went below and prepared supper for the crew. This evening they would be as hungry as wolves, and for this reason he cooked an enormous meal of salt beef and vegetables, with lots of doughboys to boot. At six o'clock the men came in from the seals and washed up for their supper.

And so it was that the crew of the *Elsie* had killed just over five hundred seals on the first day. "Plug one of the holes on the tallying board, cook!" was still ringing in the sealers' ears as they stowed the pelts below deck. Everyone was exhausted after the long day, but before going below they waited as the captain counted the tally board and told them what they had killed.

The smell of food was more than they could bear, and guaranteed there was little conversation in the forecastle as they came at the table from all directions, some stuffing their faces before they'd even sat down. The cook poured mug after mug of bubbling hot tea, each being yanked away as fast as he could fill it.

"You should have seen that old dog harp when he attacked me," said one of the sealers. Another told of how he had pulled ten pelts in one trip, looking to the captain and cook to verify his claim. One told of how he had fallen in the water and had to be pulled out, and then continued with his tow! And so the stories went, each tale sounding taller than the last.

Skipper Ned Dower was a proud man this evening. He had manoeuvred his own ship into the main patch on his first voyage as her owner. His fine crew had hauled more pelts the first day than he had dreamed possible. And there was no reason to doubt they could match or even exceed it tomorrow.

He spoke above the excited din.

"Men," he boomed, "I know you've had a long day. If all is well and the weather stays good, we should have an even better day tomorrow." He lit his pipe, then added, "We killed more than five hundred seals. To be exact, five hundred and thirty-eight. And to tell you the truth, that's not bad for a bunch of greenhorns."

He laughed. "Walter says it's as good as he's seen anyone do."

Walter grinned and nodded at the assembled crew.

"There's no doubt we should go back to the same area again tomorrow," Edward continued. "There are still a lot of whitecoats left around there, but after talking to Walter I think it would be wise for us to hunt the south side in the morning, just in case the ice splits and takes this patch of seals from us. He's seen it happen before. If you recall, when we entered this area we came in through a long opening, which means that if there's a tide rip this edge could get pushed east or west. We'll have to grab as many seals close by as possible.

"So," he continued, "tomorrow morning we'll all go to the south side and do the same as today. You're more experienced now, so I expect you to do even better. If all is well, within three days we should be half loaded or thereabouts."

The excited sealers looked at their captain as he concluded his speech.

"Today was only the beginning. Go to bed early and have a good night's sleep. We have to be on the ice by dawn. And let me stress this point—when you're out there tomorrow, keep your eyes open."

With this they all went to their bunks as Edward and the cook cleaned up the pots, pans, and other dishes from the evening's meal. This done, the two weary men retired for the night.

Edward and Walter slept in the captain's quarters along with two other men. The quarters were not very large, normally allowing only two bunks, but they had installed another two bunk beds atop these for extra boarders. The cook and the remaining sealers slept in the forecastle of the vessel.

Edward kept his large oak chest close to the foot of his bunk. It had been no small task for the two men who had carried it on board at Conche to stow it there. They had come down the seven-foot-high stairway backwards, holding the rail in a desperate effort not to overbalance. With the steepness of the companionway of the *Elsie* and the sheer weight of the chest, Edward had come close to losing a member of his crew then and there.

The walls of the captain's quarters were equipped with several oil lamps that gave the room a dim glow at best, barely adequate to work by without getting eye strain. A couple of candle lamps further illuminated the place, but even your closest friend would be a stranger at a distance of more than a few feet, and to read you would have to hold any reading material just inches from your eyes. Naturally, when the lamps were put out, the quarters were as black as a crypt.

* * *

ON THE NINTH OF MARCH the sun's burning halo lit up the eastern sky. It promised to be a clear day, and Edward told his crew as much.

"As far as the weather is concerned, we shouldn't have anything to worry about," he said. "Maybe a little breeze of southwest wind, but that shouldn't stop you fellows from killing a good lot of seals.

"The same rules and routine as yesterday apply here. And remember, Walter is in charge out there, so everyone listen to him and work together." He could see the excitement in their eyes as he signalled them to begin their day's work. The younger crewmen took off like a shot, yelling as they went over the side that no seal would be left on the ice.

As expected, it didn't take long for the first tow of seals to be hauled to the side of the *Elsie*, and likewise for Edward and the cook to hoist and stow them aboard. Edward shook his head in disbelief as the tally board report climbed higher and faster than yesterday. The crew kept working through the morning, each man concerned only with his individual haul and not yet aware that this had already been their biggest catch yet.

When noontime came the men lunched as they worked. As good as today's haul was, any sealer worth his salt knew that a large catch could dwindle to nothing in the space of a day. The wind and tide varied from day to day, working in their favour one day and against them the next. Right now the *Elsie* was in an ideal position relative to the herd, so they kept working through.

The seals were more plentiful than the day before and even in closer proximity to the vessel. The men also found the ice to be smoother and allowing better footing. One man reported that he killed fifty on a single pan, and there was little room for doubt. In fact, they were coming to the side of the *Elsie* faster than Edward

and the cook could lift them, and soon they were beginning to pile up on the ice. That afternoon, Edward inter-
cepted Walter when he caught sight of him and called
him aboard.

"We have over a thousand seals since this morning,
Walter," he said in astonishment. "I think we should
keep killing and hauling them to the side 'til it gets dark.
We can get them on board then, because it looks like
tomorrow morning there won't be anything done. I was
just down a few minutes ago and looked at the weather
glass. The hand is dropping fast."

Edward knew the weather quite well, and Walter
always deferred to his wisdom without question.

"I'm watching the sky very closely, and it looks to
me like there's something building up to the westward.
If that's the case, watch out." Edward emphasized his
warning with a wave of his arm.

Walter looked to the western sky and the bristling
sun. "You could be right, Skipper. And I think it's a
good idea to work at the seals 'til dark. If it's a bad day
tomorrow, the men will have a chance to rest up." He
was anxious to go. Edward could sense the impatience
in his friend.

"The boys are getting quite a ways away from the
vessel, Walter, don't you think?"

Walter handed his knife to the cook to give it a pass
on the whetstone. Then he turned back to the captain.
"We're only just coming to the seals now, Skipper. I have
to go. Can't wait any longer. I'm wasting time." With
that, he grabbed his knife and jumped over the side and
sped toward the others.

Edward blinked. He glanced at the cook, then said, "I think hiring Walter in St. John's was the best thing I ever did for our company."

"You're right, there," the cook said with a tired look.

* * *

FROM A FINANCIAL PERSPECTIVE, today was the best day Edward Dower saw in his entire life. It was after dark when the last tow of seals came to the side of the *Elsie*, and close to midnight when the last pelt was stowed away below deck. He took the tally board and went down into his cabin, trembling like a boy at Christmas. He had told the crew that he would let them know the exact amount of seals they had killed during this day and the total amount they now had on board.

Edward sat with his long legs stretched under the table, his hands still shining with the stubborn grease that came from handling so many pelts. The day's work was done, and he was now ready to count the tally. Walter came in and sat at the table with him. The two of them laughed with glee, like two young boys who had just stumbled upon their parents' hidden stash of candy.

"Have a guess, Skipper, before you count the tally."

Edward looked at Walter with a grin and said, "I already have a good idea how many we got today, so I think you should guess first."

Walter stared at him and shook his head slowly. "I don't know for sure how many pelts are aboard, but there's one thing I'm sure of." He poked the top of

Edward's desk with a finger. "Before I got on board, I took a look at the load mark on the hull, and this vessel is awfully close to half loaded. What I am saying to you now—because we said that she could carry about five thousand pelts—is that we put aboard close to fifteen hundred today!"

The skipper threw back his head and laughed. "We put aboard more than that, Walter my boy. Just you wait and see."

Without another word, he began his examination of the tally board in the little light the wall-mounted lamps allowed as Walter peeled off his sweat- and blood-soaked clothes. Just when he'd changed into a fresh suit of clothes, he almost jumped clear out of them when Edward let out a tremendous roar.

"Walter, today we put aboard *two thousand, five hundred and eleven pelts*. That brings the total to," he looked at the paper where he had written the total, "three thousand and forty-nine pelts. We are over half loaded."

Walter threw his hands into the air and cried, "I don't believe it!"

The two men sat staring at each other, then looked again at the tally board. "Yes, it's true, I tallied every one that came on board, and this is the correct amount," Edward said in an awed voice.

"Well, Skipper, if that's the tally, it must be right; it also shows on the waterline."

Edward scratched his chin. "According to that," he said, "we should be able to get about six thousand pelts aboard her."

"Yes, I would say we can, if she continues to load the same."

Edward sagged in his chair as his thoughts turned to the weather. "We're in for a bad storm of some kind, Walter, according to the weather glass. I've been watching it now for an hour before sunset. Not only that, the sun went down in a bank of clouds. I don't like the looks of that."

One of the men called down to the two that their supper was ready.

Edward nodded to Walter and they both got up without a word to join the others. Before leaving, Edward opened his sea-chest and deposited the tally board and the sheet totalling their harvest for March 9, 1872.

* * *

THE COOK HAD PREPARED a large roaster of baked seal shoulders with pastry, and on top of that a rich succulent gravy. As they entered the forecastle, Edward Dower and Walter Joy were greeted by its sweet aroma. They tried to hide the excitement in their faces as they calmly sat at the table and ignored the expectant looks from their crewmates.

Most of the men had washed their hands and faces, the blood and grease taken off. They had not yet changed their clothes, and most were soaked to the point where they had seal blood and grease dripping from their pants. This made the floor very slippery, and even the cook had to be careful moving between the stove and the table. However, excitement was high about the day's harvest, and no one seemed to mind.

As the newcomers sat around the table, all were silent. Even the cook, who was now leaning against the companionway stairs, had dropped everything to listen to what the captain had to say.

Edward Dower sat at the end of the table. His red hair lay matted over the side of his head, and his hand went up to brush it back over his forehead. He turned and spoke in a low voice. "Well, men, we've had a great day. In fact, I find it hard to believe the catch we got."

He drew in a deep breath, then said, "You have killed and hauled two thousand, five hundred and eleven seals."

For a split second there was dead silence. Then the cook took the lead and let out a triumphant roar. The others joined in, clapping and shouting at the top of their lungs.

Edward held up his hand, and quickly the noise came to a halt. He cleared his throat. "We now have on board three thousand and forty-nine pelts."

The men roared again as if they'd never stopped. Some even stamped their feet on the muck-covered floor.

The captain was grinning from ear to ear. "We're over half loaded," he said, "according to the way she's sitting in the water. If we can get another couple of days like today, we'll be ready for home."

There was much laughing and pounding each other on the shoulders among the sealers. The cook moved to the table with his steaming roaster, looking proudly on as the crew helped themselves to the delicious food. It was a meal fit for a king. The smell alone could bring the dead back to life for just a taste.

When they finished eating, Edward addressed his men. "I think we're in for a storm. From looking at the sky this evening, I would say the weather will be coming on after twelve tonight.

"Peter, I want you and Walter to take the first watch. You can start at ten o'clock, and I'll go on twelve o'clock with another man. Remember, if you see anything unusual about the vessel, let me know immediately."

The men didn't like what they were hearing. Seals were virtually throwing themselves onto the *Elsie*, and the sooner they got her loaded, the sooner they could leave for home. But Edward's reputation as a capable seaman stayed their tongues.

On the morning of March 10, the wind was blowing a gale with heavy snow. There was no sea heaving, though, because the field of ice encasing them prevented it from rolling too much. This could prove hazardous to the *Elsie* if the outlying floes were to grind against them with any kind of pressure. But the proud vessel had been well secured in a carefully selected spot between three large ice pans. Edward knew that before the ice could crush the vessel those three pans would have to crumble, and this could only happen if the sea started to heave. But he also knew that out here nothing was impossible, and it was the unforeseen that made him worry. He decided to stand on deck for most of the night and all of the following day to watch for the unexpected.

* * *

THE WIND AND SNOW kept up for three days, and the *Elsie* drifted in a southwesterly direction. It was noted that the ice around the vessel was getting very tight, and when the sea started to heave, all hands were on deck watching for anything that might damage the hull. As luck would have it, around midnight on the third day the weather started to clear up. It was just as Edward predicted. He had told the men at the supper table that the wind was going to haul around from the southwest after midnight, and, sure enough, it happened. The moon and stars came out and showed the clouds creeping to the northeast.

"We're going to have a fair day tomorrow," Edward said. "Maybe we'll even see land. Who knows? We've drifted a long ways to the southwest."

"There's one thing for sure," Walter added. "White Bay is full of ice by now after all this northeast wind. I'd say you could walk off to the Grey Islands if you had a reason."

Edward knew this could not be, but he agreed anyway.

Early in the morning, all the men were on deck shovelling snow and cleaning frozen ice and blood from the deck. It seemed like there was no way to get rid of the red substance. The risk was still too high to have the men on the ice, what with the snow that had drifted between the pans. On top of that, they had drifted too far from the patch of whitecoats for Edward to feel comfortable about sending the men out to work.

Frank was restless today. "How do you know we've drifted away from the seal herd, Father? I think we should go out on the ice and have a look."

Edward looked out over the icefield. "Do you see any old seals around us? If they were here, then the young ones would be here, too."

Frank shrugged and went back to cleaning the deck. His brother Peter was nearby, scooping seal remains overboard. He stood up and stretched his aching back. "Well, what do we do now, Father?" he asked.

"If the southwest wind blows strong enough, it might loosen the ice, Peter. That's our only hope to get back to the patch."

Edward and his sons resigned themselves to the task at hand, and they each picked up a shovel and doubled their pace. Nothing more was said as the crew of the *Elsie* continued their dirty work, biding their time before they could get back to what they really wanted to do—killing seals.

8

Edward was as impatient as the rest of his crew as he waited for the ice to open up. The southwest wind climbed, and by the morning of March 16, the day before St. Patrick's Day, the ice had loosened enough for them to raise the canvas. Long leads of water lay open to the northeast, but Edward didn't know for sure how far they had drifted. Whatever the case, he felt certain they were too far from the original patch of seals to even hope to return to it. After a few hours of sailing in that direction, though, some old harps appeared up ahead.

"I think we're getting close to the patch of seals that we left six days ago," Walter said eagerly to the captain.

"No, we've been steering a lot to the southeast. That should have put us much farther off shore than we were the first time." Edward kept his eyes on the seals off the port bow.

Walter looked at the compass bearing. "Yes, I suppose you're right. How far off do you think we are?"

"Well," said Edward, "we should be about ten miles farther off by sunset if the wind stays the same and the ice keeps abroad."

Walter looked around. "I wonder if the seals are out there?"

"I don't know," said Edward. He grinned and said, "There's only one way to find out."

Walter laughed.

After sunset, the *Elsie* arrived at what appeared to be a main patch of harp seals. As the leads of open water narrowed, the crew began taking the canvas down and reefing the sails. They secured the vessel to what Edward referred to as the standing edge, a body of ice that appeared not to have moved much during the storm.

As they were putting their anchors out and chopping holes in the ice for the claws to grab, the crewmen were entertained by the cries of whitecoats. They seemed to be coming from every direction.

"Good grief," said Edward. "It sounds like this is where all the seals in the world have come."

Walter was so excited he could hardly speak. He was confident this was where they would finish loading the *Elsie*. If all went well, they would be home before long.

On St. Patrick's Day, the rays from the early morning sun were setting the eastern sky aglow when the crew jumped over the side with their gaffs in their hands. The forlorn cries of the whitecoats echoed all around but didn't distract them from the task at hand.

"You can start right away," Walter Joy shouted at the men as they ran, "even near the side."

"There's whitecoats wherever you look," cried one of the swilers.

Edward and the cook were getting lines ready for the hoisting operation. It wouldn't be very long before the first man came with a tow. And sure enough, in less than fifteen minutes, a tow of five seal pelts was at the side. While they hoisted the first of many loads that day, Edward grinned and said that all Irishmen should be so lucky on St. Patrick's Day.

The cook immediately crossed himself.

Edward laughed and said, "We haven't got time for that now, cook."

The cook gave Edward a sheepish look. "But it's worth it, Skipper Ned."

Edward kept right on laughing. "You're right," he said as the steaming pelts flopped onto the deck. The men on the ice worked frantically during the break from the storm while Edward and the cook took care of business at their end. The dead seal count kept climbing higher and higher. Today would be a good day for the crew of the *Elsie*.

* * *

ON MARCH 17, ST. PATRICK'S DAY, Ellen Dower awoke early as usual. Sunlight poured in through the window and warmed the far wall of her bedroom. She lay in bed for some time before turning toward the room's only window, following the twisting patterns Jack Frost had left on the glass overnight. She stared mesmerized for a moment before calling out to

Ambrose, her youngest son, to get up and light the fire. As her eyes slipped lazily around the curious designs on the windowpane, her thoughts drifted far away, and the sounds of her son putting sticks into the wood stove came as distant and dreamy.

The storm of northeast wind and blowing snow that swept the Conche Peninsula for the past three days had been a terrible one. Yesterday, one of the old-timers said that the very foundation of Conche shook in the wind. Edward and the boys were out there somewhere. Were they all right? But the general feeling around the kitchen table was one of complete confidence in Skipper Ned's abilities.

Emiline said that Uncle Paddy Dempsey would be in town soon. "He told me that if I wanted to go back home with him again, or if I had anything to send back to Englee, to make sure and have it ready to go around St. Patrick's Day. He'll be by for the mail and anything else that has to go out." Emiline had winked at Ellen and said, "I think I'll stay on just a little longer, at least 'til Frank gets home."

Uncle Paddy is coming for the mail. At that moment, Ellen Dower sat bolt upright in her bed, panic grabbing at her heart. *The land grant! I haven't got it ready. How careless could I get? Our very future...my oh my, I wonder where my mind has been?* Her first instinct was to jump out of bed, but she fought for control and laid back, waiting until the house warmed a little and she could collect herself. Gradually she felt the thudding in her chest lessen, and she closed her eyes and fell into a light doze.

Something startled her. She opened her eyes and found herself looking directly at the phantom shapes on her window. "What a mystery," she mumbled, not aware she was saying it aloud. "It all looks so perfect. I wonder what it all means?"

Ellen leaped out of bed, knocking the bedclothes to the floor as she did. The early morning sun was just peeking over the trees outside her window.

"It's going to be a clear day," she said. "But bitter cold," she amended, shivering.

She reached with icy fingers for her housecoat and slipped it around her tiny frame. After buttoning it up and stepping into her slippers all in one motion, she took one quick look around and made for the door. All at once she stopped in her tracks, the thought of the land grant once more invading her mind.

"The land grant, yes, the land grant. I have to get it ready for Uncle Paddy when he gets here." She shook her head, angry at herself for having forgotten it a second time this morning.

Since Christmas Eve, Ellen had gone through the storage trunk several times for various reasons and had not seen the large envelope containing the grant. Through process of elimination, she had deduced that the only place it could be was in the cash box. The more she thought about it, the more likely it seemed. Her mind flashed to Edward and the icefields, and she was stricken with an empty, lonely feeling, wondering where he was and if he was all right. *What are Edward, Frank and Peter doing?* she wondered.

She knew that Edward would never leave something just lying around, let alone something as important as the land grant. This was their future. Not only for them, but for their families of future generations. "Maybe it was one of the girls who took it out of the trunk and put it in the cash box with the other envelopes," she reasoned.

No, I'm the only one with a key.

She straightened and looked out through the window again, her view of the landscape blurred by the frosty curlicues on the glass. Something was not right. Her eyes shifted and focused on the window itself.

Ellen gasped.

Side by side on the window, two images stared back at her. It was as if someone had taken a quill and somehow used the frost itself as the ink. On one side was etched a bouquet of roses with delicate sweeping strokes, intricately detailed and altogether startling in its beauty. But beside it was a bewildering array of lines. The patterns there made no sense, seeming to defy any reason. *A thing like this is not meant to be,* her mind screamed. Looking at the ugly thing actually pained her. Her spirits sagged, and a pit of hopelessness opened up deep down in her belly.

She took a step back and shook her head at the patterns, as though denying their existence. *Why would something like this happen side by side in nature? What does it mean? I've never seen anything like it before.*

Ellen was staring at the window for a long time before she realized the frost was beginning to fade. The room was warming up from the wood stove, and the heat was causing it to evaporate. "What—" she started to say, but she never got to finish. What came out of her was the beginning of a scream, and she had to bite down on her knuckle to keep herself from wailing hysterically. The bouquet of roses on her window had faded to meaningless droplets, but the monstrous insignia beside it had remained in its entirety, as if some dealer had left the Death card still facing up and turned the others down.

"Mother, are you up?"

Ellen's voice trembled as she spoke. "Yes, Ambrose, I'll be out in a moment, my dear. Put some more wood in the stove, please."

"I just filled it up. The house is warm enough now."

"All right. Thanks. I'll be out soon."

Taking her eyes from the window, she picked up a towel and wiped the residue from the glass, making a point not to look at it. "What will this day bring forth?" she whispered. With that, she turned and rushed out the door without looking back.

9

Ellen Dower came from a long line of staunch people who were very set in their ways. Her father, Captain Thomas Casey of St. John's, was an educated and well-respected man, and her mother came from the family of Edmund Burke. It was ingrained in Ellen that to make life a success one had to work hard and do what was right. The Casey motto was to owe no man.

She was preoccupied with the envelope as she came from her bedroom and walked into the kitchen. The feel of it, even the smell of the brown paper, filled her senses. She didn't even hear Emiline greet her.

Kizzie, the oldest Dower daughter, hesitated in the act of draping a tablecloth over the table. She noticed the colour had drained from her mother's face.

"Oh my, Mother. Are you sick?"

Ellen brushed her forehead with the back of her hand and replied, "No, but I didn't sleep very well last night."

Kizzie thought there might be something more than lack of sleep to her mother's condition. "Are you worried about Father and the boys? They're all right."

Ellen pulled a chair close to the table and sat down. "I'm not worried about your father this morning, Kizzie," she replied. "What I'm worried about is where he put the land grant."

Kizzie shrugged. She didn't really care for such things, and she couldn't for the life of her understand why her mother should either. "Forget about that old land grant, Mother. Don't you realize that this is St. Patrick's Day? We must celebrate. There's a time tonight, you know."

Ellen levelled a cold look at her daughter. "Kizzie, you don't have anything to worry about now, but if the time ever comes when you have to look at Maurice Power smirking out there in our garden, you'll sing a different tune." She shook her head. "But if that criminal comes into our front yard, it will be over my dead body. Your father and I know something about him that would make the hair stand up on your head."

She appeared to be very upset. In fact, she was shaking. Everyone at the table noticed it but said nothing. There was a lot on her mind, but she forced herself to drink a cup of tea and down a few pieces of bread despite not feeling hungry in the least. Getting up from the table, Ellen walked over to the Waterloo stove and held her hands out over it.

"Mrs. Dower," said Emiline, "do you intend to go to the shop today?"

"Yes."

"Is it all right if I come along and give you a hand?"

"Yes, you certainly can," Ellen replied.

The two women got their warm clothes on and went out to the hall.

"Just a moment, my dear," Ellen said.

Emiline looked at the older woman. "Yes? What is it, Mrs. Dower?" Ellen was taking off her woollen mitts and laying them on the table.

"I can't leave just yet. I promised myself I was going to have a look in the cash box for the land grant. I keep forgetting to check, but this time I'm going to do it."

The cash box would be in its customary spot, inside the large trunk upstairs in the loft. The coffers contained money and assets belonging to the two brothers and the firm. It was Edward's practice whenever he left for travel to transfer all the valuables from his sea-chest to the storage trunk. As he was now away on board the *Elsie*, she fully expected to see the land grant where he always left such items of importance. He had even told her that this is where she would find the document when the time came to mail it. Nevertheless, Ellen crossed herself when the girls weren't looking.

She retrieved the key to the cash box from Edward's overcoat pocket and went up the creaking stairs. Kizzie joined Emiline at the foot of the stairs and watched as Ellen ascended to the musty attic. She looked unsure of herself and seemed to be moving with some trepidation. Furthermore, the trembling they'd noticed in her hands at the kitchen table seemed to have worsened. Stopping, she turned and asked if Kizzie would mind accompanying her to help navigate the darkened loft.

"All right, Mother, I will," Kizzie said, and the two of them hastened upward.

Heat still emanated from the Giant, the wood Ambrose had loaded into it having not yet been reduced to ash. Ellen Dower and her twenty-three-year-old daughter went up and walked directly to the window under which sat the large trunk. The frost on this one had long since vanished, Ellen noticed, but didn't dare say aloud. Nearby was the table where Edward did most of his paperwork.

Even as she knelt by the trunk to insert the key into its locking mechanism, in her mind's eye Ellen was scanning the box's inside, trying to recreate the brown envelope. But try as she might, she could not remember seeing it there during the winter months. It had to be in the cash box, it just *had* to be. There was no room for carelessness in this matter, and she cursed herself for putting it off for so long. As if uttering the mild oath had summoned him somehow, Maurice Power's face intruded in Ellen's thoughts.

She put her hand to her forehead.

"Is there anything wrong, Mother?" asked Kizzie. There was an awkward silence. "Mother, are you all right?" she repeated.

"Yes, Kizzie, I'm all right. I was just thinking about the land grant, that's all."

"You look pale, Mother. I think you're going to faint."

"No," Ellen said more sharply than she had intended, and with that she stabbed the key into the trunk's lock. Kizzie didn't like the way her mother's hands trembled or the set of her face as she lifted the trunk's heavy lid. She threw a worried glance downstairs toward Emiline.

Nothing was disturbed from the night Edward had placed everything in the box. Paper money and gold coins, documents (maps, bills of sale for three schooners, contracts with different St. John's firms), all of these items cluttered the massive chest. The cash box lay beside the pile of papers and coins. She reached inside and put her hand on its lid. Her heart was in her mouth as she pried it open and saw...

Nothing.

* * *

ELLEN BROKE OUT in a cold sweat, and she swayed unsteadily on her knees. She closed her eyes, and when she opened them she found she could think clearly once again.

"Kizzie," she said, "for the life of me, I can't remember putting the envelope anywhere. I know I wrote the address on it, but aside from that I can't remember seeing it again after your father licked the glue and sealed it shut." Again she tried to conjure up the brown envelope and more importantly its surroundings, but she drew a blank.

"Did you find it yet?" Emiline called from the downstairs hallway.

Ellen sighed.

"We're going to have to go through all of this stuff ourselves. Tell Emiline to go on to the shop without me, Kizzie, and close the door behind you. Don't allow anyone in this room, because these are your father's private affairs. There are things in here that not even I have seen, let alone you."

It took the two Dower women a little over an hour to peruse each piece of paper inside the trunk. No sign of the envelope containing the land grant turned up, so they even searched the room itself, behind the stove and around the table, leaving nothing untouched. Finally, the two women slumped against the wall near the stove, exhausted. Tears stood in Ellen's hazel eyes, making her otherwise beautiful face appear haggard and drawn.

"Kizzie," she choked, "we're all finished. It's as though a curse has fallen on us, and I don't know what the end of it will be."

Kizzie looked at her mother with pity in her eyes. She knew that she must be suffering some untold anguish. Of course, everyone knew of the goings-on between Maurice Power and her parents over the land this grant concerned. Ellen had always been the most determined to prevent Maurice from getting it, and now as her mother sat like a broken person with tears streaming down her face, Kizzie felt a lump form in her throat at the thought of her mother being beaten by such a careless blunder.

She knew that her mother was worried, but as she knelt by the trunk and looked at her sitting there on the cold floor, she saw something else in her eyes that she had never seen before. Ellen Dower's eyes were cold and staring, like those of a wild animal in a cage. Kizzie watched her like that for some time, feeling a little frightened. The look was one she recognized.

It was a look of hate.

"Mother? Are you cold?"

Her mother didn't answer but kept staring straight out the window. No, Kizzie corrected, she was staring *at* the window, not through it. But why? She reached out again to comfort her, but her mother was unreceptive and just shrugged her off.

Kizzie sighed. Though she didn't like to leave her mother like this, she didn't know what else to do. She stood and went to the stairs, giving her mother one last look before descending to the hallway.

Emiline Strong and two other daughters of Ellen's were sitting at the table when Kizzie came down. The look on her face and the hurried way she walked was alarming. In fact, she looked downright frightened.

"Is there anything wrong?"

Kizzie nodded.

The three girls jumped from the table simultaneously. Under other circumstances, the scene would have been quite funny. "What is it, Kizzie?" they demanded.

"'Tis Mother. Something has come over her." Her face took on a look of bewilderment.

Without a word, the three girls bolted upstairs. Kizzie shook her head and followed.

The two younger girls slowed to a crawl as they neared their mother. They looked to each other and to Emiline for encouragement, and then crossed the few remaining feet to stand at their mother's side. She just sat there, her eyes wide and staring as if in deep concentration.

Or dead, Emiline thought, cursing herself at once for thinking it.

"Mother, are you sick?" squeaked Nora, the youngest.

Ellen stood without warning and walked to the stairs. She didn't look any of them in the face as she went by. "We're finished. We are all finished," she mumbled.

The girls looked from the window to the chest to each other. "I wonder what she's talking about," Nora said. "What in the world has come over Mother?"

Ellen Dower went downstairs to her bedroom and dropped the trunk's key back into the pocket of Edward's overcoat. The room by now was warm and the frost on the window was gone. She looked outside, but the cloudless day didn't register. The sound of everyday activities of the townspeople also fell on deaf ears.

It was then she cried out to Edward. "We're finished, Edward. Finished! The land grant has been stolen. We'll never get the land now; Maurice Power will take it from us. Edward, what will we do?"

It was a mournful wail that sounded beyond hope. Kizzie could hardly believe what she was hearing. This was the second time her mother had made that remark. And had there been a break-in that only her mother knew about? Kizzie knew this could not be, but the idea still nagged her.

* * *

SOMETHING WAS NOT RIGHT with Mrs. Dower, that much was certain. But what could they do? Emiline steeled herself and addressed the three Dower girls. "We'll have to go into her bedroom and have a talk with her."

"I'll go in first," said Kizzie. As Ellen's oldest daughter, she wielded an unspoken authority. But her nerve was put to the test when she walked in and saw that her mother was on her bed, groaning as if in pain.

"Mother, listen to me," Kizzie almost barked. She was pleased to see her mother open her eyes this time. "You get up out of that bed right away and go out to the kitchen."

Kizzie never knew she had it in her. She never dreamed that she would be talking to her mother in such a way, not out of fear so much as a deep love and respect. Ellen Dower was always the one who took the bull by the horns, and Kizzie found the idea of all this responsibility being thrust upon her a little frightening. But get up Ellen did, and she staggered to the kitchen.

Back in the days of wooden hulls and leather undergarments, it was not unheard of for parents to hide things of great importance from their children. There were some old-fashioned folks, of course, who even kept secrets to their dying days, taking the matter to their graves and bypassing their final opportunity to reveal on their deathbeds. Down through the years, however, as the perceived shackles of tradition and religion have loosened their grip, this practice has fallen out of use to some degree. There can be no doubt that there are some things a child should never know, and the story surrounding the land grant was a closely guarded secret known only to Edward, John, Ellen, and Ellen's father, Captain Thomas Casey.

Ellen was slowly regaining her composure. Her condition still remained a mystery to the girls, but they were too relieved to see her back to her old self to give it another moment's notice. They obeyed Kizzie's commands—even Emiline, who was her senior—and crowded the kitchen table. Kizzie was the last to sit down, and when she did they all looked to Ellen for answers.

Ellen Dower spoke in a trembling voice.

"Listen," she said in an ominous tone. "I'm going to tell you something that only your father and I know. He told me that whatever I do in my lifetime, I should never tell it to anyone." She stopped and looked each of the girls in the face. "You have to swear to me and God Almighty that you will never tell it to another soul."

The girls gave their solemn vow, and Ellen straightened in her seat and laced her fingers together on the table. She sat poised and ready now to reveal all that had come to pass. "It may mean life or death for us to get the land our home and our vegetable gardens sit on. If we don't get that grant into St. John's on time, it will be too late."

What Ellen Dower told them then was something they never forgot, but also something they never told another living soul. They took it to their graves.

10

Over time, stories of Maurice Power's origins and how he came to Harbour Grace have been told and retold so often that few actually know the real one. The true story of his first year in Newfoundland begins at the age of fifteen, when he came over from Waterford County, Ireland aboard a British square-rigger full of Irish ruffians.

In Ireland he had worked as a cooper and mastered the trade, and when he landed in Harbour Grace he got a job making barrels at the local cooper shop. Young Maurice soon got himself mixed up in several fights. He gave his opponents quite a beating, and even at such an early age developed a reputation as a scofflaw who could take care of himself. He earned a lot of respect from the Irishmen in town, and before long he was asked to join the underground movement in Harbour Grace known as the United Irish Fishermen.

This group had its sights set on causing trouble for fish merchants and anyone else who supported the truck system. They were determined not to be trod upon by anyone, and though their aim was not to start riots or kill people, they did the best they could to make life miserable for anyone who opposed them. Quite often they resorted to threats and violence not only to their enemies, but to their enemies' families as well. They hated politicians for the simple reason that sometimes the Irish weren't given the opportunity to vote. Of course, Maurice was only too willing to get involved. He became the youngest member of the UIF.

Things were going quite well for Maurice Power. He took part in a few jobs and performed admirably. Most importantly, he proved himself reliable by keeping his mouth shut. He was big and strong, and it never got too cold for him to go when asked. Neither rain, snow, nor the darkness of night frightened him in the least.

It is a well-known fact that during this time in the colony of Newfoundland the fish merchants ran the government. They shaped laws and controlled the budgets. In those days the newspapermen could say just about anything in their papers as long as it suited the fish merchants. The merchants literally had a free hand unopposed.

And so it was with one man who owned a newspaper called the *Public Ledger*. This paper at first carried domestic news while at the same time strongly advocating whatever the merchants said. However, the paper's publishing agenda began to go off in a different direction, even as far as suggesting the creation of a local legislature, and furthermore that members of government should not be selected by religion. The two reformers Dr. William Carson and Patrick Morris made use of the *Ledger* to publicize their reform efforts.

The owner of this controversial newspaper was a fellow by the name of Henry Winton, an Englishman who was also the son of an Anglican minister. Winton wanted change and would publish anything in his dogged pursuit to show the majority of the people that reform was best for the colony. Certain religious factions got swept up in his cause, and the tone of his print soon earned him the mistaken reputation of being anti-Catholic. He even got into a feud with the Roman Catholic bishop, and with all of this publicity, the *Public Ledger*'s circulation sprouted and he had to hire more staff.

Winton hired a young man from Harbour Grace by the name of Robert John Parsons. He had apprenticed with another newspaper and became experienced in lithography, so Winton assigned him to foreman, a decision that gave him six good years of service. One morning, things did not go well in the printing shop. Winton and Parsons got into a nasty quarrel over a piece of broken-down equipment, and the argument deteriorated into a terrible fist fight. The result of the row was young Parsons receiving from his employer a nasty beating, to which he replied with a civil suit. From that day forward, the newspapermen became bitter enemies.

With time, Robert Parsons started his own newspaper to compete with the *Ledger*, while Henry Winton's aspirations led him to run for a seat in the government of Newfoundland. He was travelling in the Carbonear area until one fateful night on Saddle Hill in

May of 1835, when his journey by horseback came to a sudden and brutal end.

After Winton published an article in his paper boldly stating that Irish Catholics should not be allowed to vote, a lot of people began to scream for his blood. Among those he angered were the United Irish Fishermen. There can be no doubt that Robert John Parsons, a native son from Harbour Grace, had close connections with the Irishmen. And now with Winton campaigning in the Conception Bay area for a seat in government, a golden opportunity presented itself for Parsons to get even with his old boss once and for all. So, he tipped off the UIF that Winton was scheduled to come through Conception Bay on his campaign trail.

Paddy O'Neill, present-day historian, reports in *The Log of Conche* that his grandfather, Captain Thomas Casey, told him the story of Maurice Power's deathbed confession. A lot of questions were answered that night, though Thomas had gotten the gist of it years before from his daughter, Ellen Dower.

Maurice Power had become a seasoned member, that is, a seasoned rebel with the United Irish Fishermen. He had proven himself worthy of membership many times over, and many of his peers made way for him whenever he came by. Though he never took part in anything that cost a man his life, he was not above performing acts that left people and property with permanent scars, both physically and financially. Paddy O'Neill's *Log of Conche* relates the following confession from Maurice Power.

"We got tipped off that Winton was coming through from Carbonear to Harbour Grace on horseback, so myself and four other men of our crowd got ready to give him a fright. I led the group. We went up on Saddle Hill and hid away. It was around midnight when we heard old Winton coming. It seemed like he was talking to himself or giving a speech or something, 'cause he was partly crazy, according to Robert Parsons.

"Anyway, we had our plans made, and this is what we did to him. We put the rope across the road. This was just to stop his horse, but instead it almost broke his neck. As he came along talking to himself or whatever he was at, his old grey horse tripped up in the rope and down she went, throwing old Winton, legs sticking on end. I heard him when he groaned.

"'Grab him, boys,' I said. We had hoods over our heads but had no trouble seeing him. It was a moonlit night.

"Once we had him down, we held him still. He carried a sheath knife about eight inches long on his belt—we were told that—so that was the first thing I went for. Two men grabbed an arm each and I grabbed hold to the hair of his head."

The *Log* reports that at this point Maurice Power sighed as he lay there on his deathbed. "I can still see the look on old Winton's face even now. He went wild when I grabbed him by the ears. I said to him, 'Listen, old man, you can say goodbye to the clouts on the side of your head.'

"The first thing I did was I got a handful of mud and rubbed it into his ears and stogged them full

111

where he wouldn't recognize our voices. Then I
twisted off his left ear, and it seemed to come off
some easy. But you talk about the screech that come
out of his big mouth! He thought we were going to
kill him.

"I then grabbed his sheath knife and waved it in
front of his eyes. Then just as quick as a wink I caught
hold of his other ear and with the knife I cut it off. I got
another handful of dirt then and rubbed it in the
bleeding part where the ear used to be. This almost
stopped the blood.

"We then lifted him up on the old grey horse and
gave her a cut with the rope, and away she went down
the hill carrying Winton with her. And of course we took
off our hoods and away we went back to town and went
to bed. We never got caught, although we got blamed for
it and I had to leave Harbour Grace after they ques-
tioned me. But no one ever had enough proof to charge
me for it."

Maurice Power went silent, and Captain Thomas
Casey thought that his time had come. But then the man
opened his eyes again, and Thomas knew he had a few
moments to spare. He asked Maurice what he did next,
after the Henry Winton affair.

"I went to St. John's and started looking for a job,
and that was when I met up with Ned and John Dower.
They brought me down here to Conche, to go to work in
their cooper shop." These were the last words the man
ever spoke.

* * *

ELLEN BEGAN.

"We were cursed the day your father and uncle John met Maurice Power in St. John's," she said. "I don't know what would have happened if they hadn't met him then, but I know we would be better off."

Her head drooped and she heaved a heavy sigh. She sat staring at the wooden table for a long time. When she looked up, her eyes had a defeated look to them. She continued, then, with considerable effort.

* * *

JAMES HERBERT DOWER was an Irishman who had come over to Conche directly from Waterford. Accompanying him on his journey had been a man named Cashman. It is said that Cashman was a man of education and breeding. He had a daughter named Katherine, who became Dower's wife and gave him two sons, John and Edward.

John Herbert and Cashman had come over as room keepers for the French fishermen who owned and operated large fishing rooms at Conche. But upon arriving on the shores of Newfoundland, the two enterprising young men saw for themselves the great potential of the fishery in the area, so they left the French fishermen to build their own rooms. This of course did not go over well with the Frenchmen, but to stave off any uprising among their crews, they sold some land at Conche to John Herbert and made an agreement with him. They would fish side by side if he looked after their rooms during the winter, and if he promised never to seek ownership of the land.

The years went by and trade between the British and French at that time was feudal at best. Growing tired of the constant battles regarding ownership of rights along the French Shore (sometimes referred to as the "Treaty Shore"), the French fishermen abandoned their rooms and left Conche. With a new treaty in place removing them from the picture, the land in that area became available for claim pending proper documentation.

The glory days of John Herbert Dower faded to no more than a dream, and John and Edward naturally inherited the lands he had toiled. Maurice Power, who had been hired by the two while in St. John's, came to Conche and a short time later fell in love with Mary Dower, one of John's daughters. This came as a shock to John and Edward, because as good and honest a worker as Maurice was, the man was an absolute torment. Further adding to the Dowers' misery was the news that the two young lovers were getting married.

A man named Martin Flynn, who hailed from Northern Ireland, owned a house near Maurice's in Silver Cove, located at the extreme bottom of Conche. He worked for the Dower brothers taking care of the fishing rooms at Southwest Crouse. Like Maurice Power, he had also fallen in love with one of John's daughters, another pretty young woman who was admired by all for her genial nature. But unlike Maurice, Martin was welcomed into the family with open arms after they married. He treasured his wife and doted on her every minute he was able, and this did not go unnoticed by Maurice. The scoundrel would often tease poor

Martin by making suggestive comments to Martin's wife.

The story goes that one day the two families were working their vegetable gardens when Maurice called Martin over to tell him that he was trying to get the land next to Edward Dower's house, and that he was going to have it regardless of the cost. Martin disagreed with him and told him that he had no business getting involved with Uncle Ned's land. Enraged, Maurice lifted his hand and struck Martin in the face. Of course Martin, who was as big and powerful as Maurice, wasn't about to tolerate this. A savage fist fight broke out then and there while their wives and children looked on.

According to *The Log of Conche*, both men landed several vicious blows. But as the fight wore on, Maurice proved to be the stronger of the two and gave to Martin Flynn better than he got. A month later the two neighbours got into another terrible fight, again instigated by Maurice after bragging about his plans to take over all of Conche. And again, Martin received the worst of it. Fed up, Martin took his family and belongings and moved to the other end of Conche Harbour, two miles away. When news of the beating Maurice Power had given Martin and the reason for it reached Edward and Ellen Dower, they realized that if they were to keep the peace they would have to settle the matter legally.

Maurice Power was a man of great determination. When he got it in his head that he wanted something, he was almost sure to get it. The French had full fishing rights along the French Shore at the time, as were given to them in the Treaty of Utrecht. But the words of the

King of England and the King of France were not good enough for Maurice. He decided to go fishing anyway. "No French admiral or captain or anyone else is going to stop me," he was overheard telling some of the townspeople in Conche.

And fish he did. He set his nets alongshore right next to those of the French fishermen and started catching salmon. For the first few days no one said anything to him, but that soon changed. The looks given him by the passing French became more and more menacing.

Then one afternoon, a bateau with four men aboard sidled up to the little wharf he had constructed. They tied their boat on and came ashore.

"Well, good day, me hearties," Maurice exclaimed in his Irish slang. There was no mistaking the sarcasm in his voice. One of the men could speak fluent English, and he held up his hand to get Maurice's attention.

"Good day, Maurice," he said. "I am the captain of the fishing ship out there." He pointed to the large vessel anchored several hundred yards away.

Maurice peered over the Frenchman's shoulder and noticed that all of the ship's crew members were at the rail watching their captain and his entourage. He smiled and held out his hand to the captain as if to shake hands. However, the captain was having none of that.

"You are fishing on our grounds, and it will stop immediately," he declared.

Maurice's smile melted as quickly as it had come. What these four men didn't realize was the man they were dealing with was afraid of nothing, not even the devil himself. But they had good reason to fear him; if they had seen the beating he'd given poor Martin Flynn, they wouldn't have come near him at all.

"No, my honourable captain, I am *not* going to stop fishing. In fact, I am going to *increase* my fishing and catch more."

The captain gave his men a puzzled look. He turned to Maurice again and told him that if he didn't stop, he would be punished.

Maurice just laughed at the man's vague threats. This made the captain angry, and at that moment he made a terrible mistake.

The Frenchman raised his hand and attempted to backhand Maurice across the face. But his hand never came near the ruffian. Maurice stepped back out of reach with considerable ease, then lunged forward and smashed his fist directly into the man's face. The captain fell as if he weighed a ton.

One of his lackeys advanced on Maurice, but Maurice dropped him with a well-placed right hook. The two fishermen left standing panicked and dashed for their boat, but Maurice had anticipated this. He grabbed the two of them and very calmly turned them around. He motioned for them to take their captain and crewmate with them.

As the captain staggered to his feet, Maurice caught him by the throat and gave him a cold warning: if they ever interfered with him again, he would sink their vessel in the harbour. The captain stammered in agreement, and with that the whole lot of them took off for their boat. And that was the last Maurice Power ever heard of the French fishermen.

* * *

ELLEN SHIVERED at the kitchen table. Even though the Waterloo's warmth had spread throughout the house like a blanket, her hands felt like ice. Emiline, Kizzie, and her two younger daughters saw that her fingers were stitched together so tightly her knuckles had gone white.

"Then," she managed in a shaky voice, "he had the nerve to come to the shop one day and tell your father that he was going to take over the land next to us." She swallowed hard.

"But your father told him he would never get it."

* * *

"LISTEN HERE, MAURICE POWER," said Edward. "You won't get anywhere near this land. I'm going to see to it that you won't be able to get a land application processed in St. John's."

Maurice wore a devilish grin. "You just wait and see, Dower. I happen to have good friends in the government who will see to it that I get the land."

Edward found it hard to believe that Maurice had a friend in the world, let alone the government, but he said nothing. Something in the tone of Maurice's voice told him that the man was serious. He turned his back to Maurice and walked to the rear of the shop. There was only one thing left to do. He was going to have to get a land grant of his own processed first.

It took only a day for Maurice to ready his small fishing boat for the trip to Harbour Grace, Conception Bay. He had connections there in government who could help him get the land he wanted in Conche. These people owed their current positions to him and the United Irish Fishermen. On top of all the other favours the UIF had done for them, the attack on Henry Winton had given them a landslide victory, as the old man had withdrawn from public altogether. They had promised to repay Maurice for his good deeds.

"Ned," Maurice said before he set sail for Harbour Grace, "you may have a lot of money and property, but you don't have the friends in government that I have." He cackled like a madman.

The next day, Edward received word from Martin Flynn that Maurice had gone to Harbour Grace and then to St. John's on some business. Martin had no idea what kind of business was urgent enough for Maurice to take off in such a hurry, but there was no doubt in Edward's mind. He hadn't thought Maurice would leave so soon, and he grew angry with himself for allowing the man a head start. He knew that the first application in to Crown Lands was the most likely to be processed, that is, where two or more applications for the same piece of land were submitted.

Edward left for St. John's a week later to acquire a title for his land. It was in July of 1871, and he had a full load of heavily salted fish that had to be taken to market anyway, so this was his chance to fix up with the land.

Although he was almost certain Maurice's application was being processed by now, he justified that because his family had been living on the land for so long, he was more entitled to the property than anyone who just came in waving a piece of paper. *Anyway*, he thought, *there are worse things that could happen than Maurice Power getting our land, especially with the way the fish merchants are running Newfoundland. They would give their soul for a vote.* He dismissed the idea of Maurice having friends in high places as a bluff. But he would still give this matter his full attention. If he didn't, Ellen would never forgive him. Of all the people in Conche, she was the one who feared Maurice Power most, and her heart had broken the day she heard of his engagement to Mary.

Edward's trip to St. John's lasted four days. The newly bought *Elsie* and her full load of salted cod were tossed to and fro the whole way. After he and Walter Joy supervised the unloading in the city, Edward went ashore to meet a group of friends who had extended him an invitation to one of the private clubs on Water Street.

Of course the topic of the day was politics and the tyranny of the fish merchants. Edward was chatting it up with his buddies when a long-time friend of his entered and caught his eye. The man smiled when he caught sight of Edward and came over at once, offering his hand in greeting.

"Well, how are you, Ned?" he said with a smile. "It's been almost a year since we last saw each other."

Edward shook hands with the man and smiled. "Well, Robert," he said, "it's a pleasure to see you. Won't you join us?"

Robert Parsons was the Liberal member for St. John's East, though Edward had known him long before he entered politics. He accepted the invitation and joined them.

"How is the newspaper industry treating you, Robert?"

His friend smiled and said in a weary voice, "Not bad, not bad at all." Edward caught the joke. Robert managed the *Patriot*, the most controversial newspaper in the colony. They laughed.

"What have you been up to lately, Ned? Besides the fishery?"

"A little bit of everything, Robert. Trying to keep enough grub on the table to feed the crowd."

"Yes, I can imagine," Robert said, smiling.

The conversation turned to the French Shore. Edward took the opportunity to express his views on the French captains and how they should not be allowed to control the fishing grounds around Conche.

"I'll tell you what, Ned," Robert interrupted. "How about coming to the office and giving me an article for the paper?" Edward was only too happy to have his opinions published, so he got his coat and the two exited the club and started up Water Street toward Robert's office.

Halfway to the newspaper office, Edward told Robert that he was in St. John's for another reason. The load of salted cod he had brought in the harbour was secondary in his thoughts, he told his long-time friend. The real reason he was here was to obtain legal documentation giving him title to the land on which he lived. But it seemed Maurice Power was always one step ahead of him.

Suddenly, Edward noticed that Robert was not walking alongside him anymore. He looked over his shoulder and noticed that he had stopped dead in his tracks. Robert's walking cane was firmly planted on the ground. Edward felt mild surprise at this, but he was alarmed by the look on his friend's face.

"Listen, Ned. Did you say Maurice Power? I mean, Harbour Grace Maurice Power?"

"Why, yes, Robert. I think that's where he came from, or somewhere around there."

Robert Parsons, the same Robert Parsons who years ago worked for Henry Winton but had a falling-out with him and did all he could to ruin the man, caught up with Edward. "My son," he said, "do you know who you're dealing with?"

Edward said nothing as they resumed their walk.

"You don't know what he did in Harbour Grace, Ned. Up on Saddle Hill he helped cut the ears off that scoundrel Henry Winton. I don't feel bad about it one way or the other, but what I'm saying is I don't think I would feel very comfortable having to quarrel with him over a piece of land at Conche."

Edward could hardly believe it! "Listen, Robert, I want to have a talk with you when we get off the street. This is a serious matter."

Robert Parsons and Edward Dower sat around a large table that crowded most of the newspaper office. Looking around to make sure they were alone, Robert began telling Edward the story of Saddle Hill and the part he and Maurice Power had played in Henry Winton's downfall. He trusted Edward with his life, so he felt certain that any secret he told him would be as well guarded as his wife and children.

When he finished, he said, "So, Maurice ended up in Conche. Ned, this is the way that I would handle it. I would fill in the land application and write a letter to go along with it, stating that you and your family have occupied the land for a certain number of years. This will automatically give you the first chance for a grant. Then give them to me and I'll take it to the Crown Lands office to be processed."

Edward felt like dancing. His friend had just made his life a whole lot easier. This information about Maurice Power's suspected criminal activity was just the leverage he needed. He hoped it didn't have to come to that, but he knew that Maurice was like a dog when he wanted something.

During his stay, Edward did as Robert asked and filed an application for a land grant. He added a covering letter and entrusted them to his friend. A lot of worry was lifted from him; he was confident Crown Lands would see his point of view. He returned to the *Elsie* and together with Walter Joy readied her for departure. They sailed back to Conche in high spirits, but when it was learned that Maurice Power had come back with a letter stating that there was no other application into Crown Lands at the time that his was received, and that for this reason Maurice's was being processed, his doubts resurfaced.

John Dower, Edward's brother and business partner, and, of course, Maurice Power's father-in-law, came to Edward with a copy of the letter. He had tears in his eyes as he read it to him.

"I don't know what to do," John said in a lost voice.

These were two brothers who had never shared a cross word in their entire lives. They had worked together, eaten together, and even lived together. Their wives and families had coexisted in idyllic bliss on land that John Herbert Dower had left in good faith to his sons. And these days there were no better or more resourceful caretakers of the land than the Dowers. But it appeared that unless they could straighten out the legality somehow, all that was about to change.

"Tell me something, John," Edward asked, giving his brother a piercing look. "Do you have any idea what I should do in this case?"

John didn't speak right away. He shook his head slowly after some consideration. "Have you talked to Maurice about what he's doing?" he asked.

"Yes I have, on two different occasions, but it was like talking to the stove. He just ignored me like he does to everyone else."

John looked troubled. "It's a job for me to get involved in this racket. You know where I stand in the matter, and that is with you. We've lived here for a lifetime and never had a problem, but now I don't know. If there was only some other way."

Edward swore under his breath. "I know of a way, John, but I don't want to use it, because it seems like a cowardly way to me. But, if I have to, I will."

John looked at Edward and asked, "What is it?"

Edward got up and paced the shop a couple of times. Finally, he turned to his brother and said, "I'm going to tell you something, John, but first I want you to swear to me that you will never tell anyone about it." John gave Edward his word that he would keep it a secret at all cost, no question.

"Do you know that you have a wanted man for a son-in-law? He has a bounty on his head from the British Government."

John was speechless. He remained silent while Edward filled him in on the rest of the story.

"Well, my Blessed Virgin," he said when Edward had finished. "How do you know it's true? Someone may have made it up, Ned."

Edward was sorry he had to tell his brother about this. He loved Mary like she was his own daughter. "No one made it up, John. The man who told me was also involved. He told them where Henry Winton was going to be, and guaranteed he knew they were going to do something to the old man. The newspapers carried the story for a long time, and then the British Government put up a reward of 1,500 pounds."

John Dower thought of his daughter and her three children. If they ever found out what kind of a man their father was, the children would have to live with the shame for the rest of their lives. Now he was involved, and he would have to do everything he could to avoid any unpleasantness in the family. He told Edward to leave it with him for a few days. He would have to speak with his son-in-law and try to talk some sense into him.

"All right," Edward said crisply, "I'll give you a week to see what you can do. You can tell him that if he doesn't change his mind, I'm going to write a letter to the Prime Minister and tell him that the man they're looking for is Maurice Power from Conche."

John took out his handkerchief and wiped the sweat from his face. "My great God, Ned! You'll start a war here in Conche. You know what kind of a tyrant he is when he gets mad, and you know what he will do. He'll take it out on poor Mary and the children."

"Listen, John, try and do something if you can, because if you don't Ellen is going to go out of her mind. This has to be settled soon if there is going to be any peace with Ellen and the family."

"I will, Ned, I promise," John said dejectedly.

John was a man known for his patience, but Maurice's stubbornness got on his last nerve. He tried and tried, but his son-in-law had his mind set. Maurice was determined to have that land, and he didn't care who he hurt along the way. And that was that. John was too scared to give him Edward's ultimatum, for fear that he would do something to Mary or the children.

In the meantime, Edward told Ellen the whole story involving Robert Parsons and Henry Winton, but he regretted it afterwards. Ellen was furious.

"Imagine spending the rest of your life looking out through the window at a wanted criminal! You know he's dangerous if they have a price on his head." Then one day she announced, "You have to do something, Edward. Either you get the land straightened up or we're going to have to get out of Conche."

* * *

ELLEN SAT WITH HER ELBOWS on the table and her face buried in her hands. Tears were streaming down her face and dropping heedless to the floor.

"What can we do?" she cried.

Emiline, Kizzie and the girls were crying as well. Ellen was the rock they could always depend on, and if she gave up hope, then they were all doomed. Never before had they heard such a story. Imagine! A criminal of the worst kind living just across the way from them. Their livelihoods, maybe even their lives, were at stake all because of old Maurice Power. And now it was St. Patrick's Day, and the mailman would be in town soon to pick up a letter Ellen didn't have.

Part II

11

The story of Ellen Dower has been told and retold over generations, hundreds and thousands of times. Written accounts exist in newspapers, books and magazines, but according to Paddy O'Neill and *The Log of Conche*, the right and true story has never been told. For years the truth about the lady Ellen Dower, the so-called villain Maurice Power, and the mysteries surrounding the *Elsie* have been sealed away until the time was right for the telling.

Emiline Strong, the most experienced and mature of the four girls sitting at Ellen Dower's table, was the first to compose herself. She was as shocked as the others, perhaps even more so, but she had the presence of mind to know that sitting around crying wasn't going to solve a thing. She stood up and called for everyone to be quiet.

"Mrs. Dower," she said, "I think I can safely say that Maurice Power did not come into your house and steal your land grant. It would be almost impossible for him to do it." Seeing that her words had reached Ellen, she continued with her analysis of the situation. "How would he get the key, for one thing? The key to the trunk, that is. Secondly, how could he get into the house without someone seeing him? There's always someone here, isn't there? And the third thing, even if he managed to get in, where would he know to look?"

Ellen took her hands down from her face and peered at Emiline. "What else could have happened to it, my dear?"

Emiline paced for a moment, then sat down. "Maybe the land grant wasn't taken out of the chest when Uncle Ned transferred his things to the trunk."

Ellen shook her head. "I wiped it clean with a damp cloth like I always do. My dear, there wasn't one thing left in Edward's chest when we packed his things for the seal hunt."

Kizzie interrupted. "Mother," she said, "are you sure he put the grant in the till in the first place?"

"Yes," Ellen said quickly. Her eyes narrowed. "I believe so."

"So you're not sure," Emiline reasoned.

Kizzie slapped the tabletop. "Mother, can you think? I mean, can you remember where you put it after Father signed it?"

Ellen was still unsure. She was overwhelmed by this whole mess, and soon the tears began to fall again.

Emiline turned to Kizzie. "Look, there's only one thing for us to do. We have to go over everything your mother did, step by step." She looked back at Ellen. "Can you remember anything you did before or after Uncle Ned signed the grant?"

At first Ellen didn't reply but kept on crying. Kizzie drew in a breath and snapped at her. "Mother, you stop crying right now and listen."

Ellen was not used to being addressed like this, especially by her children. Flustered, she blinked at Kizzie. "Who do you think you're talking to, Kizzie?" she demanded. "Someone out on the road? I will not stand for this kind of talk."

Kizzie was unmoved. "We have to try and get this mess straightened out, Mother, and the best way is to start from the beginning. Now tell us what happened after Father signed the grant. What did you do with it?"

Ellen looked sheepishly at her daughter. She realized she was only trying to help.

"Now get yourself together, Mrs. Dower, and go through what you did, very slowly," Emiline prodded.

"Mother, I'll get you a cup of tea," one of the younger girls offered. "It will make you feel better." She jumped to her feet, but her mother motioned her to sit down. Ellen was not interested in tea or anything else except finding the land grant.

Emiline took the lead in trying to pry information out of Ellen. "After Uncle Ned signed the land grant, what did he do with it?"

"On Christmas Eve they got all of those seals out of the nets and he was entering them in the book," Ellen said. "But in between writing down the figures, I remember he handed the grant to me in a large brown envelope. Edward licked it and closed it, then placed it on the table in front of him. I can guarantee you one thing. He went and put it in the cash box." A shadow of doubt fell across her face. "If he didn't, then I wonder what he did with it?"

"Mother," Kizzie asked, "do you remember when we came upstairs with the two parcels? Father gave you your lambskin coat, and he opened the overcoat you gave him."

"Yes, I remember that as if it was yesterday," Ellen replied in a faint voice.

"Well, what happened after that?"

Her mother was at a loss. "I don't know."

"Kizzie," Emiline said softly, "was there anything on the table when you came up? Who brought up the parcels?"

"I brought them up," Kizzie said defensively, "and I laid them on the table. I can still see the gleam in Father's eye even now when we came up carrying the two gifts. He just forgot about everything." She grinned as she remembered the excited look on Edward's face. "I put the two presents in front of Father, and after we tried to get Mother and Father to guess what their presents were, they opened them up." She burst out laughing. "If ever there were two people excited, it was Mother and Father!"

Kizzie hoped that recalling that fond moment would lighten the mood, but her mother in her distress showed only grief and weariness.

"What happened after the gifts were opened?" Emiline urged. She felt they were getting somewhere now. The answer was here somewhere; she only had to find it.

"Nothing else," Kizzie said, wide-eyed. "Mother and Father took their gifts and carried them downstairs. They put them under the Christmas tree."

Nora piped in, "They tried them on first, and Mother kept hers on when she went downstairs. Then we all got ready for the square dance at the school."

"You're right," Kizzie nodded, "but I never saw her put the coat under the Christmas tree. I stayed back and cleaned all the wrapping paper off the table and threw them in the stove."

Kizzie's voice trailed off then, because something in her mother's face had caught her attention. It had transformed into a look of horrified understanding.

"We're finished. We're all finished!" Ellen wailed.

What happened next happened very fast. She let out an ear-splitting shriek and threw her hands into the air. Everyone at the table could only stare in disbelief at Ellen's hysteria, and they were too slow to catch her when she overbalanced in the chair and hit the floor with a sickening thud. Her shrieks came to an abrupt halt. One of her daughters screamed and fainted. The others rushed to Ellen's side. Emiline lifted her head and cradled it in her lap while the rest crowded around them.

* * *

"MY BLESSED VIRGIN," cried Kizzie. "Mother is killed!"

Panic struck like a clap of thunder. Kizzie started blubbering, Nora was trembling violently, and the girl who had fainted was coming to, but upon seeing her mother lying prone went into a screeching fit.

Emiline slapped Kizzie across the face, hard. "Get a cold cloth," she barked.

Too stunned to argue, the oldest Dower daughter rushed to the washstand and snatched a face cloth. Dousing it in cold water, she scrambled out to her mother's side again. Emiline gave her an apologetic look as she took the cloth from her. She then placed it on Ellen's forehead, and there was a collective sigh of relief when her eyes fluttered.

Kizzie grabbed Nora. "Go and get the boys," she almost screamed.

Soon Ambrose and his brother, with their sister in tow, came running into the kitchen from the family's shop. They stopped and looked on, out of breath, while Emiline and Kizzie tried to coax their mother awake.

"What's wrong with Mother," Ambrose gasped. "For God's sake, what's wrong with Mother?"

It was then that John Dower shouldered his way past his nieces and nephews to stand before Ellen and Emiline. He told everyone to stand back as he knelt beside his sister-in-law. He took one look at Emiline, then gently tapped Ellen's face. Her eyes came open, and she looked around with a dazed expression.

"Ellen, my dear, what's wrong?" John asked.

He put his hand under her head and raised her to a sitting position. She whispered something in his ear.

"I can't hear you, Ellen," he said, frowning.

She whispered to him again, but he still couldn't make out what she was saying.

"Listen, boys," John said, turning to Ambrose and his brother, "lift your mother up onto the couch, for goodness' sake."

Without a word, the two boys helped John lift their mother to the couch. Kizzie went to the bedroom and returned with a blanket, draping it over her mother.

"Now, what's wrong, Ellen?" John said in a commanding voice. "Do you have the flu?"

"No, John," Ellen said weakly. "I haven't got the flu."

"Then what's wrong?"

"The land grant is gone. Kizzie burned it. Christmas Eve she threw it in the stove with the papers from the Christmas parcels." Ellen's eyes fluttered and closed. It appeared as if she had fainted.

John was speechless as he looked at Kizzie. *John, came Edward's voice unbidden to his mind, try and do something if you can, because if you don't Ellen is going to go out of her mind.* His worst nightmare was coming true. They weren't going to be able to settle the land dispute legally now, and he knew what that meant. There was going to be big trouble here in Conche, of that he was sure.

He jumped like a frightened rabbit. Spinning on his heels and knocking an empty tea mug to the floor in the process and shattering it, he ran out the door.

* * *

KIZZIE COULD HARDLY BELIEVE her ears. Imagine, she burning the land grant! Was her mother going out of her mind or something? Her brothers, sisters and Emiline looked at her as if to say "What did you do that for?" She felt faint, and hot tears coursed down her face.

137

"Mother," she shouted, "you know that I never burned the land grant. What in the world has come over you?"

She reached out and grabbed Ellen by the shoulders, lifting her off the couch and shaking her violently. Ambrose quickly stepped in and tried to restrain her, but to no avail. His sister was too far gone for him to wrestle, so his brother rushed in to give him a hand. It took the combined strength of the two of them to break Kizzie's grip on Ellen, and they held her back while Emiline gently laid their mother back to a resting position.

Ellen was petrified. She stared at her daughter with a fearful look that bordered on madness.

"Mother, what's wrong? Why are you acting like this?" begged Kizzie.

Ellen asked the boys to help her sit up. When she was comfortable and had calmed somewhat, she drew in a deep breath and started talking again.

"Listen," she said as her voice cracked and trembled, "I am sure that I know now where the land grant went." Her eyes rolled in their sockets and it seemed like she was about to faint again. Then she fixed her stare on her oldest daughter. "Kizzie threw it in the stove with the rest of the papers. There's no other place it could be. Now we're all finished! And my poor Edward, he'll have a nervous breakdown for sure when he finds out. It's good that he's out sealing."

The youngest daughter, Nora, put her hands on her hips and said to her oldest sister, "What have you got to say about that? Did you throw the land grant in the stove?"

138

THE GHOST OF ELLEN DOWER

Kizzie seethed. She stood firm against all the accusations thrown her way. She wasn't going to stand for it. "No!" she roared. "I didn't burn any land grant. When I took the parcel paper off the table and threw it in the stove, I made sure there was nothing else there but the paper. Ambrose, you believe me, don't you?" Ambrose was very intelligent for his age, and Kizzie knew that she could trust him above all.

Ambrose looked in her stern eyes and asked, "Are you sure? Did you look through the papers?"

"Yes!"

"Then what happened to it?" Ellen argued.

"I don't know, Mother. Maybe Father put it somewhere, or maybe he took it with him to the seal hunt. I don't know."

It was obvious that poor Kizzie's feelings were hurt. Ambrose felt ashamed at the unfair treatment she was receiving given the fact that no one, including their mother, had seen the grant on the table. His mind raced. Something wasn't right here, but he couldn't quite put his finger on it.

12

Celebration was the last thing on everyone's mind this St. Patrick's Day. Normally the day brought much fun and excitement, starting with a one o'clock Mass at the church, followed by an afternoon luncheon at three, and the day would be brought to a close with a big time and dance at the school in the evening. But there would be far more important things for the children of Ellen and Edward Dower to worry about this day. Like the uncertain future of their family, and their mother's failing health.

Emiline Strong sat at the table in a daze. She couldn't believe this was happening to Mrs. Dower, the strongest woman she'd ever met. It had seemed nothing could bother her, but now she was a total wreck. Could Maurice Power have such an effect on people? If it were true, then she wouldn't like living in Conche next door to such a monster.

It was better for her to go back to her home and family at Englee, she thought. If her father ever heard what Mrs. Dower had told her this morning, he would come to Conche and take her, body and bones, back home. And she would never be allowed to come back again, married or not. She wished Frank were here now, to help with his mother and maybe even persuade her to forget her troubles by attending the celebrations.

An idea came to her then.

"Oh my," she said, "why didn't I think of it before?"

"Think of what, Emiline?" Nora asked.

Emiline was a protestant, maybe the only one in Conche, but they all loved her there. Her family were merchants at Englee, and a lot of Conche's people did business with them. Of course, she had agreed to become Catholic once she married Frank. And it was this that reminded her of her family's religious practices back home. The first thing they would do in a situation such as this is go and get the minister to come and pray over the patient. However, if there were a service going on at the time, they would take the sick person to the church to receive the same ministrations.

And here they were, with a Mass starting in less than an hour. Why not take Mrs. Dower to the church? Maybe the priest could cast the devil, or whatever was giving her trouble, out of her. Now, Mrs. Dower didn't have the devil in her, at least Emiline hadn't seen one in her. But maybe the priest could give them some answers. At the very least, he could certainly make Mrs. Dower feel better, couldn't he?

Emiline got up and beckoned Kizzie to come to the inside room. She didn't really know if her idea would work, but she was willing to give it a try.

"Kizzie, I've been thinking," she began when the two young women were alone. "If we had a problem like this back home, the first thing Mother and Father would do is go and get the minister to come and pray with whoever was sick. If he couldn't get away, they would bring the person to the church." She felt a little foolish sharing this with Kizzie, but the oldest Dower girl held up her hand and grinned.

"Why didn't we think of this before?" Kizzie said.

Emiline continued in an excited tone. "Someone said there was going to be a Mass at one o'clock. If that's the case, why don't we get your mother ready and take her to the church?"

"You're right," Kizzie said, nodding. "Let's go out and tell the rest of the crowd. I know they'll agree."

Relief washed over Emiline. Mrs. Dower was such a faithful churchgoer, the young woman knew that she would not hesitate in going. She and Kizzie re-entered the kitchen and stood with the rest of the anxious family. A few of Ellen's friends had come and gathered there to help in any way they could. Emiline recognized them from the meeting she'd attended with the Women's Aid group, where Ellen had announced the young woman's wedding plans.

"Mother," said Kizzie, "we're going to take you to church. There'll be a Mass starting in half an hour and we think you should go."

Ellen stared blankly at her daughter. "What for, Kizzie? The priest can't say enough Masses to bring back the land grant you threw in the stove. You know that."

Kizzie scowled. Her blood boiled, but she forced herself to focus on what needed to be done.

"You're going to the Mass," she said, perhaps louder than she had intended, "so you might as well start getting ready." She looked around. "Nora, get your mother's boots on her feet."

Nora looked at Ambrose as much as to say "What do you think?" Ambrose just shrugged his shoulders. As far as he was concerned, something had to be done, and this was as good an idea as any they'd had that morning. In fact, he wished he'd thought of it himself.

"Yes," Ambrose said, "get her ready. We'll take her to the church."

Ellen saw there was no use fighting them on this. They were determined to see it through. She sighed, utterly depressed.

"If only Edward was here," she said. "What can I do?" She was talking to herself, oblivious to the people lining her kitchen. Finally, she took a look around as if noticing them for the first time. She nodded reluctantly, agreeing with their wishes. "I want to put on my new coat. I want to say a prayer for Edward, and it will help me think of him. Where do you think he and the boys are right now?"

"Father and the others are all right, Mother," Kizzie said, giving Emiline an uneasy look after noticing how quickly the fear had crept back into her mother's eyes. "Don't you worry about them. They'll soon be home." She hoped her tone sounded soothing.

"I don't think I will ever see your father again, Kizzie."

A deathly silence followed this declaration. Why would Ellen Dower make such a statement? Did she know something the others didn't? Impossible.

Ambrose cleared his throat. "All right, Mother, we're going to get you ready and take you to the church at one o'clock."

His mother gave him a grim look. "No, Ambrose. I want to walk to the church myself. I don't want to start a talk in Conche, you know."

* * *

MAURICE POWER AWOKE very early this St. Patrick's Day. He had made plans the night before that if this morning looked good he would go out to the headlands near Cape Fox and see if he could get a shot at some sea ducks. He ate a meagre breakfast by lamplight, then grabbed his lunch pack and his well-oiled 7/8" muzzleloader.

It was still long before daybreak, and his black-and-brown bird dog followed his snowshoe tracks to the shoreline where he had constructed a gaze the day before. The wall was made of sea ice and provided the perfect hiding spot for duck hunters. A cossack made of canvas and with a hood attached covered his upper body, while a plain pair of white pants completed the outfit and rendered him virtually invisible to animal and man alike. Now all he had to do was wait until an eider flew by. He crouched and watched patiently, his finger steady on the trigger of his powerful shotgun.

Despite his reputation as the resident monster, there was no harder worker in town than Maurice, and at times he was known to joke and kid around with people. At his worst he was like a savage, but there were few who took the time to see him at his best. The man was a mystery.

He was no fool. He knew when he was winning, and he knew when he was losing. Maurice didn't see a single duck all morning. When his pipe went out at noon, he rummaged through his supplies and swore. "I'm heading back home," he said disgustedly. "But I think I'll stop at Dowers' shop and pick up a pound of tobacco."

He picked up his things and nimbly scaled the cliffs with his muzzleloader slung over his back. He whistled to his dog as his snowshoes crunched through the crusty snow. It was going on one o'clock when he neared the Dower premises, and as he approached the shop he saw a figure coming toward him dressed in white. "Well," he said, "'tis awful. Imagine, someone just going out duck hunting this time of day. It must be one of Uncle Ned's boys coming out of his house." But as the figure neared, he noticed that it was a woman.

"My good grief," he chuckled, "it looks like old Ellen herself. And if I'm not mistaken, she's wearing that lambskin coat of hers."

What a one for duck hunting! That would be the one to sit on while in the gaze. He cackled at the thought.

When Ellen came within speaking distance, he said, "Good morning, Mrs. Dower." This was an unusual occurrence. In fact, it was the first time he had said good morning to anyone since he first came to Conche. She didn't speak, so he repeated himself.

"Good morning!"

Ellen kept walking and didn't even look his way. When she walked on by and it became apparent that she was going to ignore him completely, he shouted, "What's wrong with you? Why are you ignoring me? Have you got your tongue froze?"

Ellen turned and looked at him with her eyes blazing. But she wasn't about to frighten Maurice Power.

"Don't you stare at me, Ellen Dower. I've seen women before I ever laid eyes on the likes of you." She opened her mouth to speak, but he cut her off. "I thought you were a duck hunter, all dressed up in a white canvas suit on your way out to Cape Fox, but now I can see what you are."

His voice bubbled with enthusiasm. "'Tis that lambskin coat that Mary's been talking about all winter. This is the first time I've ever seen one like it."

Ellen turned to walk away.

"I may have that wool coat someday, Mrs. Dower," Maurice said ominously. He burst out laughing. "Yes, sir," he said as if to himself, "I may have that lambskin coat someday."

Ellen didn't respond to his taunts. Tears spilled down her cheeks as she pulled her coat tightly around her shoulders and staggered away. Maurice's demonic laughter followed her all the way to the church.

* * *

EMILINE AND THE DOWER CHILDREN watched intently from the kitchen window as Ellen walked up the narrow path, met up with Maurice Power, then continued on her way with an unsteady stride. For a minute they had stopped before passing each other, and there was a brief exchange of words. Then Maurice laughed. What was so funny? Surely he wasn't laughing at a sick woman.

They had been ready, even eager, to rush out and apprehend him, but Ellen just walked on by and proceeded to the church. Kizzie and Maurice's eyes met for just a second as he came toward the shop, and she let out a strangled gasp. Ambrose looked at her curiously but said nothing.

"My Blessed Virgin," said Nora. "Mother must have gotten some fright when she met that monster out there on the road." The girls mumbled in agreement, but Ambrose only shrugged.

They waited a few minutes before following Ellen to church. Emiline went with them, this being her first time going to a Catholic church. As they walked, Kizzie filled her in on the customs of her religion, everything from holy water to Holy Communion. As they neared the church, though, a young boy was waving his arms wildly and signalling them from the doorway. They broke into a run and covered the distance in no time. The boy's eyes were wide, but he didn't say anything. He only pointed to the door.

Emiline, Kizzie and the others bustled inside to meet the priest. He was shaking.

"There's something wrong with your mother," he said.

13

"She's on the floor up there near the altar," Father Gore pointed.

"Oh, my Blessed Virgin," several of the girls said in unison as they rushed to their mother. Kizzie dropped to her knees and held her.

"Mother, can you hear me?"

Ellen's eyes rolled, and she started shaking.

"I think your mother is having a convulsion," the priest said in alarm.

"Mother, for goodness' sake, can you hear me?"

"Yes, Kizzie, I can hear you," Ellen slurred. Her eyes focused for just a second and fixed on her daughter's face. "You burned the grant, Kizzie, you burned the grant. Now he's going to have the land."

She was referring to Maurice Power, of course. Kizzie couldn't believe what she was hearing. Would she have to take the blame for this, for something she didn't do? No, never in a million years. She stood up and put her hands to her face, sobbing uncontrollably as she bolted out the door.

Kizzie Dower was a tall, heavy-set girl whose sturdy frame was more suitable for a man, some said. She had fiery red hair and a temper to match. It was said that even the husky dogs were afraid of her. There was not a place she wouldn't go and nothing she would flinch from, whether on the darkest night or the brightest day. She could carry a sack of flour as effortlessly as any man in town, and it was also said that Kizzie Dower wasn't afraid of any man in or outside of Conche.

And that included Maurice Power.

Kizzie stalked off to her father's shop, the last known whereabouts of her mother's tormentor. There was a murderous set to her face, and she muttered as she went. "You are going to pay for this, Maurice Power, supposing I have to swing from the gallows."

But standing in the shop's doorway was her brother, Will. He had been away since early morning in the woods cutting firewood and had not heard anything about his mother's condition. He grinned when he saw his sister with her head down, coming at him like an enraged bull.

"Hey, Kizzie," he shouted. She looked up, seeing him for the first time, but didn't speak. "Kizzie, where are you going?"

Kizzie stopped and glared at Will. "I'm going in the shop to choke that Maurice Power, that's where I'm going."

Will noticed the intent on his sister's face and immediately set his axe and crosscut saw down. He shook his head in disbelief. "My Great God above," he said.

149

"Kizzie, have you been drinking or something? Have you gone out of your mind?"

"I'm not going to be blamed for something I didn't do, Will," she spat.

"Is this you, Kizzie?" he said. "Is it really you?" When his sister started forward, he straightened and spread his arms, blocking her way. "Now, you stop it, Kizzie. I want to know what's going on."

Kizzie glanced nervously at the shop's window, wondering if those inside could hear. "Will, Mother has taken seriously ill, and it's all because of that Maurice Power. He's in the shop," she said, her voice rising an octave as she stabbed a finger at the building. "We saw him go in there just now." When Will looked in the distance at their house, she said impatiently, "She's not in the house, Will. She's at the church."

"Listen, Kizzie, I just passed Maurice Power about a half a mile up the road. He's on his way home."

Kizzie turned furiously toward the home of Maurice Power, but Will took her arm.

"Kizzie, I want to know the details about this, so start talking."

"Get out of my way, Will! I can catch him before he gets home."

Will made Kizzie face him. "You must want to get yourself killed or something." He didn't know what was going on, but it had to be serious. "Tell me what happened."

Seeing that her brother wasn't going to let her anywhere near Maurice Power, Kizzie relaxed and took a deep breath. She then told Will the whole story: how their mother couldn't find the land grant; that she blamed Kizzie for burning it; and that now she was at the church, lying in a daze.

William Dower had always been a crafty man and would put this talent to great use in years to come. History records him as the shrewdest of businessmen in dealings with the fish merchants at St. John's.

"Now, Kizzie," he said, his mind working fast to defuse the situation, "you and I are grown people, and if we can't solve this problem like adults we should go home and cover up our heads." He had her full attention now, so he pressed on. "I know that you didn't burn the land grant, Kizzie, but Mother thinks you did. We'll have to make up a story to keep her quiet 'til Father comes back. Then he'll take care of everything. No one will know the difference as long as you keep that big mouth of yours shut."

Kizzie didn't like being talked to in such a gruff manner, but this was an emergency, so she remained silent and heard her brother through.

"Go back to the church and tell Mother that you were talking to me. Tell her that I know where the land grant is, that Father told me where it was before he left the harbour."

"She won't believe you."

"She'll believe me."

"I don't know, Will. You've been such a big liar all your life that she might not." Unable to come up with a better idea herself, though, she just shrugged. "All right. What should I tell her?"

"You go and tell her that Father told me before he left that the land grant is still in the sea-chest. He said that he forgot to take it out."

"That won't be any good, because she told us she helped Father transfer everything. She said that she even took a damp cloth and cleaned the inside and put cardboard down in the bottom."

Will held up a finger. "I haven't finished yet, Kizzie. Tell her that Father told me he put it down in the lining of the trunk and that he'll put it in the mail when he gets to St. John's. That should keep her at peace 'til he gets back."

Kizzie could hardly believe Will was able to make something up so quickly. "You're still the biggest liar in the world, Will," she accused. "But Mother is no fool. She has a fair idea what Father does, you know."

Will laughed. "She doesn't know everything, Kizzie, especially when Father's in St. John's and around the bars and hotels."

Kizzie didn't like that remark, and she told him so.

* * *

ELLEN WAS STILL LYING on the church floor with the crowd standing around her when Kizzie burst through the door. She was shocked to see Father Gore praying and sprinkling holy water over her mother.

"I have good news," she said, looking around and taking in the defeated expressions on everyone's face.

Father Gore stopped. "What is it, my child?"

My God, Kizzie thought. *I could never tell this pack of lies to a priest and get away with it.* But then again, she countered, Will was the one who made it up, and if it stood any chance of making her mother better and proving that she never did throw the grant into the fire, she was willing to chance it. She dismissed any doubts and concentrated on the task ahead of her.

"Tell Mother that we know where the land grant is."

The priest sprinkled a little more holy water over Ellen. "Our prayers are answered, Mrs. Dower. Arise. All is well."

Kizzie knelt and leaned toward her mother's ear. "Mother, I was talking to Will just now! He knows where the land grant is."

Ambrose looked doubtfully at Kizzie. He knew that Will would say anything to save his own skin, but he decided to keep quiet for now. Whether Kizzie believed it or not he couldn't say.

"Mother, do you hear me? We know where the land grant is. Father told Will where it was before he left for the icefield."

Kizzie's words went unheard for the most part. Until now, Ellen's eyes had taken on a dreamy, unfocused look. It didn't appear as if she were aware of her surroundings at all. Somehow she found the strength to sit up.

"Take me home, Ambrose. Now." Her voice was weak, but there was no mistaking the authority behind it.

* * *

THE DOWER FAMILY carted their mother to the house on a hand barrow. She was very weak and Kizzie had to hold her head up. Will met them halfway, and he didn't like what he saw.

"My," he said, "is Mother as bad as that? Can't she walk?"

Ambrose drew him to one side. "Will, I think Mother is dying or something," he said in a low voice.

Will was flabbergasted. "Did Kizzie tell her about the land grant, Ambrose?" he asked in a trembling voice.

"Yes, but I'm not sure if she got through. There was a lot of confusion going on around her at the church. I think you should tell her yourself when we get her back to the house."

How can I ever let myself tell Mother a pack of lies? Kizzie was supposed to do that. Will shrugged. *Oh well, anything that will set her mind at ease.*

The word had spread by the time they reached their home that Mrs. Dower was sick. They were greeted by a small crowd of people who volunteered to help in any way needed. Nodding at a few of the townspeople as they went, Will directed Ambrose to the master bedroom on the ground floor. Ellen had a habit of staying in one of the spare rooms upstairs whenever Edward was out to sea, but when he was home the master bedroom is where they slept.

The girls got their mother ready for bed. They removed her lambskin coat and returned it to its hanger in the hallway closet, then removed her undergarments and replaced them with a long nightdress. Each girl wore a worried frown as she worked; it was difficult to accept their mother's helplessness. Kizzie and Nora went into the kitchen and told the crowd that their mother was in a desperate state.

"If you could get her to drink a cup of tea, it might bring her strength back," offered one of the older ladies. "You shouldn't let her go to sleep now. She could go into a convulsion, or even suffer brain damage." It had happened before in Ireland, she said. Kizzie broke out in a cold sweat at the thought.

Nora wasn't about to let that happen. She marched back into the room and started shaking Ellen. "Wake up, Mother! Wake up!" she yelled.

Ellen opened her eyes with considerable effort.

"What's wrong, Nora, my dear?"

Kizzie came back into the room as Nora started to cry. "Mother, you have to snap out of it," said the older daughter.

Ellen looked up as she came in. "I'm not blaming you for burning the land grant, Kizzie, because you didn't know what you were doing. It's your father's fault. He should have put it in the till."

"Listen, Mother," said Kizzie, laying a comforting hand on Nora's shoulder, "I didn't burn the land grant. We know where it is."

Ellen's eyes came open now, fully alert. "Where is it, Kizzie, for God's sake?" she cried.

Kizzie's mind raced. "Now, this is what Will told us. He was talking to Father on board the schooner, and Father told him that the land grant was still in the lining of the chest. He said when he gets to St. John's with the seals he's going to take it to the Crown Lands office himself."

Ellen was more angry than relieved. "Why didn't someone tell me this? Why did you hide this from me?"

"We tried to tell you in the church, but you wouldn't listen. Now you know." Kizzie bubbled with laughter. She couldn't help it. Her mother was going to be all right now.

But her smile quickly faded when Ellen started crying and covered her face.

"What's wrong now, Mother?" Nora begged. "Why are you crying again? Everything is going to be all right."

Ellen looked at Nora with eyes filled with dread. "Did you hear what that old Maurice Power said to me?"

"No," Nora and Kizzie echoed.

"He said I looked like an old duck hunter and that he was going to have my lambskin coat. Why would he say that, Nora?"

Kizzie stood there clenching and unclenching her fists. She knew she should have gone after him when she had the chance, supposing she had to go right to his house to tackle him. If only Will hadn't interfered, she would have gotten the job done. She vowed to get even with Mr. Maurice Power one way or another.

Even more upsetting to Kizzie was the fact that her mother was still obviously not well. Her eyes were darting around nervously and she was shivering from some unknown chill. "Mother, you know that it's impossible for him to get your coat." She sighed.

"There's always someone here in the house, you know."

Her brother Ambrose, whom she trusted more than anyone else (especially that liar Will), came in. She gave him a quick look and a brief shake of her head. Bad news.

Ambrose feared his mother was losing her mind. What kind of foolishness was she getting on with? She should know better.

To their surprise, Ellen said, "I don't believe Will about the land grant; he made it up. Edward would never do it, he had no reason to."

And with that, she closed her eyes and fell into a deep sleep.

14

Late in the afternoon, the *Elsie* was "in the fat." This was a phrase used by sealers to indicate they were among the whitecoats and harvesting them. Edward's crew had been working like dogs all day, killing seals, taking the pelts off the carcasses, and pulling them to the side of the *Elsie* while they were still warm. Walter Joy had joined Edward and the cook on board to hoist the seals' pelts and stow them in the hold.

Edward wiped his brow. "If this keeps up, Walter, we'll be pretty near loaded by tomorrow evening."

"We'll be loaded before then, unless you want to swamp her," argued the cook.

Walter nodded. "That's what I'd say, too, by the way she's filling up."

"I must admit," Edward laughed, "that hold is filling up pretty fast, but it all depends on the distance the men have to tow the pelts tomorrow. I just glanced through the tally card, and if all keeps going the way it is, by sunset this evening we'll top four thousand pelts. This is unbelievable!"

The men on the ice were driving themselves to the limit of their endurance. They had elected to put off lunch at ten o'clock that morning and worked until noon. Then, requesting the cook serve them an early supper on deck, they threw themselves back into their work. The number of seals at their feet was too great an opportunity to miss.

Walter had relinquished command of the men on the ice to Frank Dower. His job was to see that all went smoothly, remaining in contact with the captain at all times and, of course, killing and hauling as many seals as he could himself. He was also responsible for watching the movement of the ice and the tide beneath it. Walter Joy knew his men were in good hands. Frank was unshakable, just like his father.

* * *

AMBROSE RACKED HIS BRAIN. His mother was going to have to think positively if her condition were to improve. He knew that if his father were here he would straighten this out in a hurry. But Edward wasn't here, so it was up to him to keep things under control. The four girls, that is, Emiline and his three sisters, were beyond consoling. They were convinced that their troubles were just beginning.

"I know it, I know it," Kizzie sobbed, "something is going to happen to Mother. You just wait and see."

Will didn't think that it was as serious as all that. He sat at the table in the corner of the bedroom with a cup of tea and some molasses bread.

159

Nora looked at Will. Seeing him casually eating away at his lunch set her off. "Will! You don't care one little bit, do you? You don't care whether Mother lives or dies."

Will raised his hand in irritation. He swallowed a large piece of bread and retorted, "Listen, Nora, do you know what you're saying? It's not only Mother that has something wrong with her. I think that you should have your head examined."

Nora dabbed her eyes with a handkerchief but didn't respond. Kizzie flew to her sister's defense and berated Will for not letting her get Maurice Power when she had the chance.

"Go on, Kizzie. Maurice could wring your neck with his little finger even before he got out of bed, so don't you go on with that to me." He heard more people coming into the kitchen, so he took his cup and plate in hand and headed for the door. But he decided he would have the last say. "It would be safe to say that you're the one who started all this mess in the first place, Kizzie. If the truth be known, you're the one who burned that land grant."

Kizzie dried her eyes and said in an even voice, "Listen to who's talking." She looked at Ambrose and gave him a sly look. Turning to face Will again, she said, "If you hadn't made up that pack of lies, she might have come around."

Ambrose struggled to his feet. "My God, Will, what in the world is Kizzie saying? Did you make up that story about the land grant being in the lining of Father's trunk?"

Will gave Kizzie a black look, then turned to leave.

"You know something, Will?" Ambrose said. "What you did is enough to bring a curse on Mother."

"Don't you be so silly, Ambrose. I'd tell her anything to get her out of the mess she's in."

Nothing more was said as Will slammed the door behind him and left them alone with their thoughts. Of course, Ambrose was far from surprised at Will's behaviour. He had a habit of talking his way out of any situation. In many ways, he was like their father.

* * *

THE CREW OF THE ELSIE finished up after dark. The hold was bulging with seal pelts, and the vessel hunched low in the water like a pregnant cow. Walter estimated she was almost fully loaded.

"If all goes well, we'll be done before noon tomorrow," Edward said. The news brought cheers from every sealer at the galley's table.

Walter was worried about overloading the *Elsie*. Although he trusted Edward's judgment, he'd seen it happen before to other sealing captains well known for their prowess on the seas.

"How many do we have on board, Skipper?" he asked.

Edward waved his hand and dismissed his first mate's concerns. "I haven't counted the tally yet. I'm going to wash up first and put on some clean clothes, then you and I will go over the tally board and make the count."

Once Edward had washed up and changed into some clean, dry clothes, he joined Walter in their quarters. Walter had likewise cleaned himself up and changed into fresh clothes. The grin on his face told Edward that he was very excited, as he was himself. Pulling a pair of chairs up to the table, Edward lit his pipe and sat for a few minutes, enjoying the sweet tobacco. Then he went to his sea-chest and lifted the cover, releasing a nice musky perfume. He was reminded of Ellen so strongly that he half expected to see her when he turned around.

My imagination, he almost said out loud.

He reached into the chest and retrieved the tally board and ship's log, in which he had recorded the total number of seals killed to date. Relighting his pipe, he blew a long stream of smoke across the table, grinning from ear to ear as he did.

"Well, Walter, my man, we will see very soon how many pelts we have on board."

Walter grinned. "I think we should have a guess first about the amount."

"We can't do that," Edward disagreed, "because we may be disappointed. After having such a great day, I don't want anything to spoil my good mood." They both laughed. "We had three thousand and forty-nine on board when we started this morning, so let's add to it now." With that, he laid the tally board in front of them, wetting the table's surface with blood and grease.

By the time the captain and his first mate had finished counting, they were hopping out of their seats. They learned that their total catch for today was two thousand and ten seals! This brought the total to five thousand and fifty-nine pelts.

Edward was clearly astonished. "We're almost loaded, Walter." He laughed crazily. "Even now I'm satisfied with what we have, and if the ice is loose when we wake up tomorrow, we'll start for home. If we're still jammed here we can take another forty-one to make it an even five thousand, one hundred."

"A wise decision," Walter approved.

"If we're icebound for any length of time, we can kill a few old harps and render out some of the fat to get a couple of barrels of seal oil."

This voyage had turned out better than either of the men had imagined. They had gotten the biggest catch of their lives, and in record time. The only thing left to do was wait and enjoy the trip home.

* * *

ELLEN DOWER RESISTED her children's efforts to revive her. At seven o'clock that evening she was still catatonic, so Ambrose sent Will up to the home of Granny Carroll, the local midwife. The old granny woman possessed a wealth of knowledge pertaining to home remedies and curatives. She was the area's doctor and undertaker.

"Get the medicine bag," Granny Carroll ordered. Will looked over at the old woman's supplies skeptically. She repeated herself a little louder this time, and this startled Will into motion.

This old lady was very dear to the Dowers and indeed all the families of Conche. She had born all of

Ellen's children and the rest of the younger generation in and around the area. The granny woman had a special place in her heart for the Dowers, for it was Edward and Ellen who kept her and her husband fed in their old age. Only days before, she had gone to the shop and been given a load of food by Ellen herself, and all Mrs. Dower had told her was, "Don't worry about it, Mrs. Carroll. Edward will get enough seals to pay for that little bit of food you have."

Granny Carroll was only too happy to help this woman whom she considered as close as any daughter.

"I hope there's something I can do for your mother," she said to Will as she pulled her coat over her narrow frame. At first she didn't believe Will when he came huffing and puffing through the door saying there was something wrong with Ellen. For one thing, this young fellow was a notorious prankster. Not only that, no stronger or harder-working person could be found than Ellen Dower, and this bit of news, that she was losing her mind, just didn't make sense.

As she and Will Dower raced to his house, Granny Carroll choked back tears at the thought of her dear, dear friend lying all alone, waiting for someone to come and save her.

15

Mrs. Carroll's specialty was homemade remedies. She had never received any formal medical or pharmaceutical training in her life, and everything she diagnosed was strictly on a "maybe," "perhaps," or "I think" basis. But for all that, her reputation boasted that she had never lost a patient.

She entered the home of Ellen Dower and saw that the place was in turmoil. The kitchen was filled with people crying and hugging each other. Kizzie and her sisters were red-eyed but had composed themselves somewhat and come out for a bite to eat. Hearing the granny woman come into the house, Ambrose poked his head out of the master bedroom and greeted her. He asked her to join him in the room, and she elbowed her way through the crowd at once.

"All right, Ambrose," she said when they closed the door behind her. "I'd like to be left alone with your mother for a few minutes. I'll call you after I examine her."

"Yes, ma'am," he said politely, exiting and easing the door closed behind him.

Ambrose and the others were famished, and they helped themselves to some tea and bread while they waited. The only sound in the kitchen was the occasional sniffle. Granny Carroll had been in the room with Ellen for about an hour when she came out and signalled for Ambrose to come inside.

"Yes, Mrs. Carroll, do you want me for anything?" he inquired when they were alone again. His heart sank when he saw the look in the old woman's eyes.

"Yes, my dear. I think it's time you went for Father Gore. Ask him to come here immediately; your mother's pulse is weak and she is not responding. I think she's slipped into a coma."

The room swam before Ambrose's eyes, and he had to reach for the table to steady himself. "Are you sure, Mrs. Carroll?" he asked, his voice cracking.

The granny woman looked at Ellen's boy tenderly. "You better get hold of yourself, son," she said softly. "You have a crowd out there who are ready to panic."

She was right, of course. Ambrose straightened and steeled himself.

"Yes, Mrs. Carroll. I will go."

* * *

THE CROWD WATCHED the bedroom door. Any minute now, Ambrose was going to come through it and say that it was just Ellen's nerves, that Granny Carroll had given her something to calm her, that she was going to be all right. The look on Ambrose's face when the door cracked open told them a different story.

"What is it, Ambrose?" asked Kizzie. "How is Mother?"

Ambrose didn't say a word. He went to the chair on which his coat was hung. Snatching it, he made his way to the door.

"Where are you going, Ambrose?" Emiline pleaded.

Ambrose squared his shoulders. Turning slowly, he looked Emiline in the eye and said, "Mrs. Carroll has asked me to go get Father Gore to give Mother extreme unction."

His words hit them all like a hammer. Ellen Dower was at death's door! Nora moaned and toppled out of her chair.

"Oh, my Blessed Virgin, my Blessed Virgin," said Kizzie. She threw her hands into the air. "Is it possible? Is it possible?"

The people there were speechless. All they could do was give Ambrose a questioning look. *What has happened to Mrs. Dower?* But he couldn't answer. He was filled with sorrow as he slipped his coat on, and his legs felt like lead.

His heart was breaking, and he wept as he ran to the church. He approached the building and rapped on the huge door. "I'll be there in a moment," came the priest's reply, but Ambrose didn't mind the wait. He secretly hoped the holy man would allow him a few moments alone to grieve.

In a minute or so, the stately old priest appeared in the doorway, his face a grim mask. He looked at Ambrose and asked, "How is your mother now?" But he knew before he even finished the question what the answer would be.

"Mrs. Carroll is at her bedside and wants you to come immediately," Ambrose croaked. "Father Gore, you have to give her extreme unction. Please come right away, because Granny Carroll says she's gone into a coma." He bent his head and his shoulders shook with his sobs.

Father Gore put his arm around him and said, "God will take care of you, Ambrose." The Dower boy just nodded and led the solemn priest to his home.

* * *

MRS. CARROLL HAD SEEN a lot in her lifetime. Hers was a heavy burden, being the person to whom everyone turned when they had serious ailments or health concerns. She could turn to no one herself, as there were no doctors, nurses, or even conventional medicine, for that matter. Granny Carroll was alone in her cause. And when she was forced to tell a patient's family of his or her passing, she could offer nothing in the way of counselling. This was understood. People had to grin and bear it.

Granny Carroll stepped out into the kitchen while Ambrose fetched the priest. She looked at Ellen's children with sympathy. "Your mother is very sick," she said, "and if the Lord doesn't intervene, I don't think she will last much longer. To be honest with you, it appears that she has slipped into a coma."

Those who had gathered in Ellen Dower's kitchen for moral support turned helpless eyes to Mrs. Dower's children. Kizzie and Nora were crying hysterically and clutching at each other, and some of the women stood nearby, ready to take either of them in their arms for comfort.

Being near families in their time of grief was nothing new to Mrs. Carroll. Under normal circumstances, she would perform her duties without emotion, but this was Ellen Dower they were talking about. "Father Gore will be here soon," she said with deliberate slowness, trying to control her voice. "He will hold a service for your mother when he comes."

As she predicted, Ambrose and the priest arrived shortly. This holy man was an awesome figure to the community. Even in the height of sorrow he carried himself with a resplendent confidence that bespoke divine importance. He came in and at once asked everyone to kneel. Then he began the Hail Mary, sprinkling holy water throughout the kitchen as he prayed.

The priest then joined Granny Carroll and together they entered the master bedroom, requesting Ambrose come in with them. The boy's face was drawn and haggard as he obeyed and shut the door behind him. When they were alone, Father Gore took a pair of candles out of his bag and lit them.

"Would you pillow Mrs. Dower up as high as you can, Mrs. Carroll?"

"Yes, Father."

Ambrose was struck again by the absurdity of the situation. His mother was dying, but why? What had come over her? He had many questions, but no answers.

It was then that Ellen opened her eyes and looked around. "Oh my, oh my," she mumbled, "oh dear." Her breath came out in a wheeze. She raised a feeble hand to her forehead. "What am I going to do at all? I am going to have to go out, yes, that's what I'm going to have to do." She moved her head from side to side.

Ambrose moved to his mother's side. "What is it, Mother?" he asked. "What do you want to do?"

Ellen closed her eyes again and was very still. It appeared to the three standing in the room that she had stopped breathing. Mrs. Carroll took her arm and felt for a pulse, then placed her hand on Ellen's forehead.

"I think she's gone, Father."

Suddenly, Ellen's chest swelled and she started breathing again.

"I'll perform extreme unction before it's too late," Father Gore said, thumbing through his prayer book. He took out a small crucifix and laid it on Ellen's chest. Then he took her fingers and wrapped them around one of the candles. That done, he blessed her with more holy water and read aloud several passages from the book.

This was the worst day of Ambrose's life. Not only would he never see his mother alive again, his father wasn't even here to say goodbye to her. He stood with his back to the wall, his head bowed, muttering over and over, "My Blessed Virgin."

Finally he could take no more, and he yanked open the bedroom door before his emotions got the better of him. He marched into the kitchen and was met by his brothers and sisters and half of Conche. Some were perched by the door leading to the master bedroom, listening as the priest administered last rites. Most of the people wore blank expressions, too far gone with their own grief to even summon a tear. He knew how they felt. The reality of it hit him all at once, and he was lucky there was a chair nearby, otherwise he would have collapsed.

"May God rest your soul," the priest's voice floated into the kitchen. "Amen."

Kizzie snapped. She started jumping up and down and screaming like a wild woman. Two older ladies stepped quickly to her side and tried to calm her. "Mother is dead, oh my, Mother is dead," she shrieked. Nora had fainted again and lay on the couch near the window while someone applied a wet cloth to her forehead.

Father Gore came out and addressed the crowd. They quieted immediately upon seeing him. All, that is, except Kizzie. But the ladies on either side of her did manage to get her to stop jumping and lower her voice to a hoarse whisper.

The priest cleared his throat. "We are all gathered here tonight unexpectedly. If someone had told me yesterday that tonight I would be reading the last rites of the Church for Ellen Dower and preparing her for her heavenly home, I would never have believed them. However, this is the case, whether we believe it or not, and may we all realize that life has no guarantee for any of us. Because even when we are in the midst of life we are also near death."

He walked over to Kizzie, who looked like a caged animal eager to strike. Laying a hand on her forehead, he said in a low voice, "Your mother is not dead yet, but her time is near. May God help you, my child."

At this Ellen's oldest daughter buried her face in her hands, and Father Gore turned and asked if everyone would kneel again for a moment of silence to honour poor Mrs. Dower.

The priest suggested to the children that now would be a good time to say some final words to their mother. "She might be able to say a word or two to you." He closed his fist around his crucifix. "The end for her anguished soul is near."

Those children who were present agreed that they would like to say farewell to their beloved mother, even Will, who was having a harder time of it than Ambrose. The priest left them then and told them he would return within the hour. Preparations had to be made for the impending funeral of Ellen Dower, survived by her nine loving children, and her husband, Edward.

16

The Dower children went into the master bedroom where their mother lay dying on the big family bed. The thoughts of each child were much the same. Father Gore had done his job, and it appeared that Mrs. Carroll had done hers, but what could they have done to prevent all this? Were they in some way to blame?

Kizzie was becoming unglued. She tugged at her hair, and her eyes stared fixedly at her dying mother. "Mother, oh Mother, can't you wake up?" she wailed. Her brothers were getting worried about her own mental state, but Will and Ambrose never expected what their sister did next. She hopped up onto the bed and started shaking Ellen by the shoulders. Before they could yell at her to stop, their mother opened her eyes.

Mrs. Carroll hauled Kizzie out of the way with a strength she didn't know she had. "You have disturbed your mother's soul, Kizzie," she moaned. "You have awakened her from eternal rest! It may cause her to suffer."

That got Kizzie's attention. She blinked, finally regaining her senses. "Here it goes again, I'm about to get blamed for something else that I didn't do. Mother is not dead, Mrs. Carroll. Look—she wants to say something."

All eyes were on Ellen. She had raised her hand. Nora was the first to move close to her. "Mother, what is it you're saying? Mother, can you hear me?"

"Listen to me," Ellen said in a clear voice, but then her speech became garbled and she uttered something incomprehensible. She began again. "Oh my, here I go, I am going, yes, I am leaving, oh it's cold, I'm afraid, it's dark, too, but I have to go." Her eyes widened as if in shock. "You got—"

"Hush," said Granny Carroll. She had seen this before, many times. Sometimes when dying people left things in their life unfinished, their minds experienced great unrest. This was called a sign against death. Legend has it that such turmoil in a person's soul was also the precursor to ghosts or apparitions of the deceased. She gave a quick look at Ellen's children, then removed her finger from Mrs. Dower's lips. If Mrs. Dower had unresolved issues with her children, then she would be a fool not to let her speak.

"I am going on a long journey," Ellen rambled, "yes, a long, long journey, I have to go, yes, I have to go and see the land grant, to see if it is on the schooner, yes, I have to see if Will is telling the truth, I have to go." She wrung her hands. "Edward! Oh, Edward, where are you, I can't see you, Edward, wave your hand, please, wave your hands."

* * *

ROSE DOWER WAS THE WIFE of John Dower. For years she lived in the same house as Ellen and was like a sister to her. They had raised their families together and cooked on the same stove and ate at the same table. Of course, when Rose heard that there was something wrong with Ellen, she was among the first to rush to her house.

Oh, how she and Ellen had cried when they learned that Rose's daughter Mary was going to marry Maurice Power! And now their worst fears had come to pass. Old Maurice was at the root of the problems Ellen was having, and Rose Dower couldn't help but feel responsible in some way for Ellen's condition.

The kitchen had cleared out for the most part when Father Gore left to prepare for the funeral service. Although Ellen was not yet dead, the crowd knew the time had come to allow her family their last moments with her. Rose came into Ellen's bedroom around eleven o'clock that night. Until now, she had been waiting silently in the kitchen with the others, cooking and brewing cups of tea for the crowd. Kizzie, who it seemed was once again in control of herself, had asked her to come in and sit near her mother, and John's wife didn't need to be asked twice.

The first thing Rose mentioned as she came in was how different the dying woman looked. She took Ellen's hand and noted how icy her fingers felt, because the sweat was rolling off her own forehead from the heat in the room.

While she sat there in silence holding her dear friend's hand, a thought came to her. Why not sing to her, for old times' sake? Many times she and Ellen would sing songs together at soup suppers, dances and weddings. People often said there were times it seemed their voices echoed around the little town of Conche long after the singing was over. Tears stood in her eyes as she lifted her voice in one last song for Ellen Dower.

Kizzie, Ellen's oldest daughter, thought the song a fitting tribute to her mother. There was no use jumping or screaming. This was it, the final curtain, and going out of her mind wasn't going to stop her mother from leaving this world. She lifted her own voice with Rose's even though she was no singer herself.

Nora had been worse off than Kizzie. The slightest bit of bad news had been enough to set her off on a fainting spell. But now here she was, holding it together for the sake of her mother. She wasn't about to let the last memory her mother had of her youngest daughter be witnessing her passed out on the floor. Her voice soared with the others.

The boys, Will and Ambrose, lent their voices to the melody as well. They were the last people anyone would expect to see within five miles of a song, but they stood unashamed, belting out the tune along with the others.

The door opened, and Emiline Strong walked in on silent feet. Ellen Dower was every bit a mother to her as Mrs. Strong back in Englee. She regretted that Mrs. Dower would never get to see Frank's wedding day. The song flowed from her lips with harmonic ease.

I left my home on Ireland's green banks
And sailed away forever
The hold was full of rugged men
And women thrown in together
The ship was tossed in the mighty gales
As if she would never stand
But then we saw before our eyes
The shores of Newfoundland

Emiline was the first to see it. Her voice trailed off and the others were quick to follow when Ellen's eyes came open. Her chest started to heave with great whooping breaths. "I am on my way, Emiline," she gasped. "Tell them, Emiline, that I am going to look for Edward. If I never return from the stormy weather, you tell Kizzie and Nora to keep our secret to their dying days. Never tell anyone about the bounty on the head of Maurice Power. I'll see to it there is a curse put on him forever." Her voice dropped to barely a whisper. "I am leaving now. Goodbye."

Her chest shuddered, then stopped.

Emiline laid a tentative hand on Ellen's shoulder. "Mrs. Dower. Can you hear me?"

But there was no response. Her flesh was like clay.

Rose put her arms around the girls and held them close. She was very shaken. What a burden to leave on her daughters and Emiline! And what was this secret she was talking about?

Nora said to Granny Carroll, "Is she dead?"

The old granny woman had seen many sorrowful things in her lifetime, but this by far was the worst.

Getting up from her chair, she went out into the kitchen and to the washstand. She unhooked a small mirror from its place on the wall and came back to stand beside the bed.

Everyone watched intently as the old woman crouched and held Ellen's head upright. She held the mirror about half an inch from her mouth and waited. Her eyes never left the glass as she watched and hoped for moisture to accumulate on its surface. After several minutes in this position, the old woman sighed and laid the mirror on the bed. She looked Kizzie in the eye and made the official announcement.

"Ellen Dower has passed away at midnight, March 17, 1872. May God in His mercy rest her weary soul."

* * *

IT WAS AFTER 3:00 A.M. when Rose went home. She was escorted by her son, who stayed close to his mother for fear of seeing a ghost of his aunt Ellen. But Rose wasn't thinking about Ellen's ghost.

The final words of her sister-in-law kept coming back to her. *Never tell about the bounty on the head of Maurice Power.* "What bounty?" she blurted. "What does it mean? There must be something awful happening for Ellen to make those her dying words." Her mind struggled with this bit of information. "And a curse, yes, she said something about a curse." Her son shivered at her side but said nothing.

"I always suspected that Maurice was mixed up in something before he came to Conche. I wonder if John knows anything about this? I'm going to find out about this, supposing it's the last thing I do."

Her kitchen was aglow from the kerosene lamp. John and some of the children were still up at this late hour, no doubt unable to sleep on this terrible night. When Rose and her boy entered, John rushed over to embrace his wife.

"Poor Ellen," he said. "You never know what the day is going to bring forth when you get up in the morning." He broke down and sobbed against his wife's shoulder. "I know Ned will go out of his mind when he finds out. Can you imagine what will happen when the *Elsie* pulls into the wharf and we have to break the news to him that his wife has died?"

It was too much for John. He left the kitchen and went to his bedroom, staggering like a drunken man.

17

Midnight came and went, and Edward Dower still tossed and turned in his bunk. Try as he might, he couldn't get to sleep. He should have been happy, but an odd sense of dread had come over him and kept him from his much-needed rest. Every bone in his body ached from the brutal work he and his crew had done today.

He started to drift off a few hours after midnight, when the watch change brought him to his senses again.

"You just hear that," he heard one of the men on duty ask. There were some muffled words, then Edward managed to tune in the rest of the conversation.

"Sounds like whitecoats bawling to me," said the other man.

"I guess it's harp pups. They're scrubbing along by the side of her, not very far away."

The other man let out a cough in the cool night air. "It looks like we're just inside the running edge. I think either we're going with the tide or that edge out there is running. If only it was daylight, we would be able to see better."

"We'd better call the skipper. You know what he told us. If anything unusual starts to happen, be sure and call him right away."

"How about if we call Walter and let him know?"

There was a pause, then, "But he's not the skipper. I'm going to call him up to have a look."

The man came down into the captain's room and was surprised to see Edward dressed and ready to come up on deck. He was about to say something, but the captain raised a hand for him to be quiet and not wake the others. They ascended the stairway to see the other sealer with his ear cocked toward starboard.

"What do you think that sound is, Skipper?"

Edward laughed. "You can almost prong the white-coats aboard. I've never seen anything like it before. Either we're near the running edge and that's a big herd of seals going by, or else we're on the move and they're standing still."

The moon peeked out from beneath a blanket of cloud and gave the icefield a sheer brilliance that stretched all the way to the horizon. Ahead the three men could see what could only be seals, by the thousands, looking like eerie phantoms floating around in the dark.

"Look at that," said one of the sealers. "That looks like young hoods to me."

Edward nodded. Hood seals differ from their harp cousins in that they do not live together in large herds. They are similar in size to the harp, but their colouring varies.

"We seem to be in a safe place," Edward said. "Never mind that grinding and growling going on over there. That big sheet of ice is protecting us. We'll wait 'til daylight."

With that, Edward took his leave and returned to his quarters. He was asleep almost as soon as he hit the pillow.

Edward! Hey, Edward! Where are you? I'm coming, Edward, I'm coming!

He awoke with an awful start, his head cracking painfully against the bed above his own. His body was coated in sweat. He hopped out of his bunk, hoping he hadn't awakened the others. "What?" he asked, "What," spinning himself around as if looking for an intruder.

He looked around the room and was relieved to see that he hadn't awakened Walter or the other two sealers sharing his room. His shoulders slumped as he relaxed, and he replayed the last few seconds of his dream.

"That voice...the voice that was just calling to me sounded awfully familiar, but I can't remember who it was."

He felt his stomach cramp with worry, but for the life of him he couldn't think why. What was he worrying about?

"The *Elsie* is loaded and ready to go, the crew is fine and everything is all right at home. Isn't it?"

There would be no more sleep for Edward Dower tonight.

* * *

THE FIRST COUPLE OF HOURS were filled with shock for the Dower family. Their father was gone, so there was no one to whom they could turn for comfort or direction. Ambrose was doing the best he could, but he couldn't curb the panic that had set in with the girls. Kizzie was shouldering much of the blame herself.

"Mother has gone to her eternal reward and her last thoughts were that I burned that land grant. Oh my, is it possible that I sent my mother to her grave?" No one could pacify her, not even Will, whom it was said could charm the birds out of the trees.

Father Gore had gone back to the rectory and was busy working out the details of the funeral. This was going to be a monumental task, even for him, because Ellen Dower was one of the area's most prominent citizens. There was much to do. *If only Uncle Ned was here,* he thought.

Granny Carroll was willing to help any way she could. She hadn't slept at all that night, and the old woman surprised everyone with her strength. "Can you take care of laying her out," the priest asked, "and get someone to cut a shroud for her? There should be lots of white cotton at the shop, Mrs. Carroll."

The granny woman blinked through her tears. Mrs. Dower had done exactly that for countless women in Conche who had gone to meet their Maker. "Yes, Father, I can wash her and lay her out and put her grave clothes on her myself, you don't have to worry about that. I'll get Mrs. Simmons to cut the shroud."

The priest knew exactly who to get to make a coffin.

Martin Flynn often told people how he longed for the day when he would be called upon to make one for Maurice Power. Maurice, ever one step ahead of poor

Martin, overheard him one day and gave Mary specific orders not to let him make his casket when his time came.

News of Ellen Dower's death went out with the breaking of the dawn and spread from house to house. Some people could hardly eat their breakfast, they were that sick with grief. Those children old enough to understand what was going on were kept indoors, and every shade was drawn halfway as a show of respect for the dead. Such was the custom in those days, the shades in the house of the deceased being drawn all the way.

* * *

MAURICE ALWAYS GOT OUT of bed early in the morning, so he was surprised when there came a knock on his door even before he got up. He dressed himself in a hurry and stumbled to the door. His second surprise came early in the day as well, for the two men standing at his doorstep told him that Mrs. Ellen Dower had died. He stood there in baffled silence for a minute, then thanked the two men as they took their leave. He ran into his bedroom and shook Mary awake. Her eyes widened when he told her the news. She was speechless.

"She looked all right to me yesterday when I passed her on the way to the shop," Maurice exclaimed. "That old Ellen, I bet she thought she was never going to die. If it wasn't St. Paddy's Day yesterday I would have told her so."

"What are you talking about, Maurice?" Mary demanded. "Did you say anything to Aunt Ellen yesterday?"

"No," he replied quickly.

"Then what are you talking about?"

Maurice rolled his eyes. "I joked about that lambskin coat she was wearing and she flew into me like an old hen. I told her that she looked like a duck hunter on her way to Cape Fox. She didn't like it and attacked me!"

Mary was well aware that there was no love lost between Maurice and Aunt Ellen. But what worried her now was the extent of the argument they'd had. Would it get him in trouble?

"Listen, Maurice, last night you said that you were going down to the cooper shop this morning to get some shavings for the fire. So while you're there, find out all the news for me, all right? Ask Mother."

Maurice didn't appreciate being treated like a messenger boy and his wife knew it. But Mary was on the verge of breaking into tears, and he didn't want to be around to see it.

For peace's sake, he consoled himself.

* * *

JOHN DOWER SAT AT THE TABLE with a blank look in his eyes. He hadn't gotten much sleep last night. On top of Ellen's untimely demise, he had heard from Rose what Ellen said about Maurice Power. Of course he knew all about Maurice's shady past, but now it would be harder for him to hide the truth from the family.

"Good morning, Maurice," he said without looking up as his son-in-law strolled in. "Don't ask me how I feel this morning, because I'm rotten."

"Mary sent me down to see if there was anything she could do," Maurice said in a bored voice.

John didn't want to start anything, not this early in the day, anyway. "Not much any of us can do, Maurice," he replied. "Only pray for the family."

Maurice had never said a prayer in his life, and he wasn't about to start now.

"Tell Mary we'll be up sometime this morning," John continued, "Or, better yet, you should bring all the family down here. Mary will be better here with her mother."

"I'll see," Maurice said. He plopped his cap onto his head, punched his hands into his mitts, and left.

He walked over to the cooper shop, the place where he had spent his first two years in Conche. Edward and John had hired him to make fish barrels for the firm, and he had proven his worth as an industrious worker. They never so much as doubted his abilities, and they didn't have to ask him twice to do something. The shop held fond memories for Maurice. This was where he had met Mary and fallen in love with her.

The small trail leading to the cooper shop passed the door of Edward Dower's house, about twenty feet distant. As he walked by he wondered what was going on in there this morning. He was still thinking this as he entered the cooper shop.

"I don't suppose old Ellen took to heart what I said. That never did anything to her."

His parting words to Ellen came back to him as he bent and scooped dry wood shavings into his burlap bag. *Maybe I should go to the house and tell Will that*

I'm sorry to hear about his mother. When the bag was full, he slung it over his shoulder and went outside. A sheepish look crossed his face as he struggled with the idea of apologizing for something he didn't do. But he wanted to do it, for Mary's sake.

He gathered his courage and opened the porch door. Feeling ridiculous, he stepped through and looked around. No one was to be seen, so he walked down the hallway toward the kitchen door, not bothering to take the bag of shavings off his back. As he neared the kitchen door, he began to lose his nerve.

"What am I doing here?" he growled in disgust.

He shook his head and spun on his heels. Slamming the porch door behind him, he stalked up the road toward his home.

* * *

NORA WAS ABOUT TO POUR herself a cup of tea when she heard someone coming down the hall. She waited for the door to open, but it never did. "That's funny," she said. Laying her tea next to a half-eaten slice of bread, she opened the door to the kitchen and saw nothing but snow on the floor, left from the visitor's boots, no doubt. She went to the porch door and took a look outside, thinking that maybe a small child had wandered in. But she changed her mind when she noticed large boot tracks on the bridge. Opening the door and looking up the trail, she saw about a hundred feet away a man with a large bag on his back.

"Hey, who's there?" Nora called.

The fellow stopped and turned to face Nora.

My, she thought, *Maurice Power. What's he doing here? I bet Mary's got him down here this morning to get the news about Mother.*

Without even acknowledging the girl, Maurice turned and set off down the road again.

Nora went back into the kitchen and sat at the table. Emiline came into the room then and began to fix herself a sandwich. Nora mentioned what she had just seen, and at first the young woman didn't believe her, so Nora took her out to the porch and pointed at the figure moving up the road.

Emiline squinted. "Yes, you're right, it's Maurice Power. What do you think he has in the bag, Nora?"

Nora shrugged.

"Well, don't tell Kizzie about this," Emiline cautioned. "It may upset her more than she already is."

Nora needed no further convincing. She agreed to let it pass.

18

Martin Flynn came to take Ellen Dower's measurements in the morning, and of course his arrival did nothing to improve the overall mood in the house. The sight of him and his measuring tape was all it took for Kizzie to dissolve into helpless sobs. Martin went to her and held her close. During the night he had heard from Will what happened yesterday, how this young woman was going to tackle Maurice Power and that it took all that was in Will to stop her. He shivered at the thought of poor Kizzie facing such a man. In fact, he still hurt from the poundings Maurice had given him long ago.

"Will," Martin had said after spitting his tea in surprise, "if Maurice had beaten Kizzie, that would have brought your old man into the fray. I don't think old Maurice Power would have gotten away with it as easy as when he got into the fight with me or when he beat up that French captain, either. Uncle Ned is the only man he's afraid of, you know. He said he saw what your father did one time at a tavern in St. John's, but he wouldn't tell us what it was."

189

Kizzie liked Martin. He was tall and good-looking, with big hands and a strong body. She had gotten to know him well from the many times he'd come around to talk with her father. If the truth be known, she was in love with the man, and though he was married to her cousin, Kizzie knew she wouldn't resist him for a second if he wanted her. But all she could see in him for the time being was what he had come to the house to do.

What a task, she thought, and buried her face in his shoulder.

"Martin," she said, "we're lost here. We're all alone without Father and we need someone to help us get through this." She sniffed disconsolately. "I'm sure that if Father had been here this would not have happened."

Martin kissed her all of a sudden, and Kizzie held him that way for a few minutes before pulling away. The house was full of grief, she reminded herself. This was no time for love. Martin cleared his throat uncomfortably and asked what colour cloth the family would like to see on the outside of the coffin. Kizzie told him that grey would be fine, and she gave him a longing look before she left the bedroom to let him do his work.

* * *

GRANNY CARROLL WAS MIDWIFE and doctor for all of Conche, but today she was to take on the role of undertaker. She rose with the dawn to perform her job, despite the fact that she hadn't slept more than an hour. After she got ready, the old woman went directly to

Ellen Dower's house and started her grim work. She stripped Ellen bare and washed her, a task she had done to other deceased women dozens of times before.

She stopped when she noticed that the flesh was still supple and soft.

"That's funny," she muttered to herself. "She's been dead for over six hours now, and her jaw still falls open like she's only asleep. What in the world is causing that?"

She shrugged and dismissed it as the result of the head's positioning when Mrs. Dower died. But she had to stand back when she saw a large bruise on Ellen's right leg. The blemish had gone black. What was going on here? The third shock came when she noticed what appeared to be a fresh scrape on Ellen's knee. She covered the body, leaving only the legs exposed, and called Ambrose into the room.

At first Ambrose didn't know what to make of it. He had little experience when it came to dead people, but common sense told him that this couldn't happen to a corpse. "I'd say she must have fallen down on her way to the church or something, Mrs. Carroll. She never complained about any pain in her legs, but she had her stockings on, so we couldn't see."

Mrs. Carroll had to agree. She couldn't see any other reason for it.

* * *

IT WAS ALMOST NOON when the coffin came to the house aboard a dogsled. The dogs were barking savagely when the drivers hitched them to the fence post. Martin took one end of the casket while his companion took the other, and together they hefted the massive wooden box into the kitchen. He had built it in a rush, so it was no great beauty to behold. But the grey cloth Kizzie had requested gave it a touch of class.

The coffin was to be placed on the kitchen table. This was not typically the tradition in Newfoundland households, but it would leave the parlour available for visitors and the wake that would surely take place. In tradition with their Irish heritage, Rose Dower would attend and sing wistful ballads that spoke of heartache and yearning for their homeland. She and Ellen had always done this together at the wakes of friends and loved ones, leaving not a dry eye in the place.

They carried the coffin into the bedroom where Ellen had been laid out atop several boards. Granny Carroll, unable to explain why Ellen's mouth kept falling open and helpless to stop it, had tied it shut with a thin strip of white linen, the two ends coming together in an affectionate bow on top of her head.

Ellen had always said that she wanted to be buried wearing her wedding dress when her time came. And so it was, just hours after the last breath left her body, that her family had discussed this very thing.

Kizzie didn't know whether they should honour their mother's request or not. "What do you think Father would do if he was here?" she asked her brothers and sisters.

"He would have her dressed in her wedding gown for sure," Nora said, and no one disagreed.

This is the dress that I was married in, Ellen always said, *and it will be the robe that I'll wear on board the old ship of Zion, when I am on my way to a better world.* Then she would laugh like a little girl, her voice full of merriment.

Each of Ellen's children observed in mute admiration their mother's beauty. Even in death was she radiant, the Church insignia upon her shroud the only thing detracting from her ethereal appearance. Emiline, Granny Carroll and Martin came in and praised Ellen's beautiful wedding gown. Everyone helped lift her up and laid her with care into the wooden casket.

"She looks so cold," Kizzie observed.

Nora was in agreement. "Poor Mother, we should wrap a blanket around her," she suggested.

Kizzie snapped her fingers as an idea came to her. "Listen! I know what we're going to do."

"What?"

"We'll put her lambskin coat over her."

Everyone thought this was a great idea, and Kizzie allowed herself a little smile for the first time since this whole ordeal began.

She dashed out to the hallway and threw open the door of the closet her father had made for her mother's coat. At first she couldn't believe what she was seeing. Or, rather, what she was *not* seeing. Her mother's white coat was gone! She shut her eyes and convinced herself that she had imagined it. But when she opened her eyes, she realized horribly that her eyes were not playing tricks on her. She walked with wooden legs and a dazed expression to join the others.

"It's gone," she said, slumping into a chair. "Mother's lambskin coat is gone."

* * *

EVERYONE BLINKED.

"Gone?"

"Yes, gone."

"Where could it have gone?" Ambrose asked, frowning in consternation.

Kizzie shrugged.

The minds of all of Ellen Dower's children were racing. For some time they forgot about their mother lying dead beside them as they tried to figure out where her coat had gone.

Suddenly, Nora gasped.

"I know where it went," she shouted. Everyone was all ears, that is, everyone but Emiline. She knew what Nora was going to say even before she said it.

"Where?" Kizzie demanded.

"Maurice Power stole it!"

"What are you talking about, Nora?" Ambrose said. He was getting a little tired of people blurting out nonsensical statements and not explaining themselves.

Nora quickly went over what she had seen that morning. She finished by saying, "And that's what he had in that bag—Mother's lambskin coat. Emiline saw him too."

Emiline nodded in agreement.

Kizzie jumped to her feet. "You're right," she roared. "He told Mother yesterday that he was going to have her coat someday. Sure enough, as soon as poor Mother died he came right down here and stole it!"

Ambrose was dumbfounded. First the bruises on his mother's legs, and now this. Could a man be so low as to do such a thing? "No," he argued, "I don't think even Maurice is capable of such a thing."

"I do," Kizzie countered. "If a man is bad enough to attack and threaten a woman going to church on St. Patrick's Day, then stealing her coat is nothing."

Will wasn't convinced. "Listen," he shouted above them, "I can guarantee you one thing, and that is Maurice did not steal Mother's coat. I will put my head on the block for that."

Ambrose gave him a sour look. "All right, Will, you tell us where the coat went."

Will didn't know what to say, but he was sure of himself.

"Let us forget about the coat," Granny Carroll advised. "She won't need one in Heaven. If she does, then God will give her one." And that settled the issue.

Martin Flynn was as surprised as the rest of them when he heard the coat was stolen, and by whom. He'd never seen the likes of this before. *Maurice, you've done the wrong thing this time, old man. When Ned Dower gets back he'll break your neck.*

A wicked grin crossed his face then, and he covered it up with a cough.

Why not stir this up? Maurice has gotten away with enough stuff around here already, and it's time he got paid back. Finally, here was an opportunity to get even with Maurice Power after the abuse he'd suffered from him, not to mention catching the old goat flirting with his wife.

Being careful not to smile in front of the others, he helped the old granny woman wrap the bottom of the wedding dress around Ellen's feet. Then he took his leave. There was much to be done.

* * *

WITH THE HELP OF MARTIN FLYNN, the word quickly spread around Conche that Maurice Power had come to the home of Edward Dower that morning and snatched Mrs. Dower's lambskin coat. "Well," was the general response, "this is unforgivable." Never before had anything so cruel been done, they concurred, in the history of Conche or anywhere else.

In the late afternoon, most of the husbands and fathers and even grandfathers of Conche met to come up with a solution. Nearly all of them cried out for Maurice Power's blood, but Martin had an idea.

"Let's get Father Gore and go up to Maurice's house. We'll take the coat from him and bring it back to Mrs. Dower before she's buried. Only then will she be able to rest in peace."

What a good idea, came the vote.

* * *

AMBROSE HAD GONE to the church to have a talk with the priest. He had sneaked away from his family to get a moment's peace and to seek counsel from Father

Gore. When he mentioned his mother's missing coat, the priest nearly fell off his chair.

"I can hardly take it in," said Father Gore. "It sounds incredible to me. What will happen next if no one puts a stop to it? What can be done about it, Ambrose?"

It was at that moment he looked out the window and saw the angry mob moving fast toward the parish hall. He met them at the door. One of the men stepped forward and declared, "Father, we came to tell you what Maurice Power did." The priest raised a hand in a calming gesture and gently informed the man that he was well aware of Maurice's heinous crime. He asked what, if anything, could be done about it.

The man punched the air angrily. "We should go to his house and search it. We want that coat."

Father Gore thought it over and decided that it was a good idea, as long as there would be no violence or bloodshed.

"What do you want me to do?"

"We want you to accompany us to his home," the man replied. "We figure that when he sees you with us he'll hand over the coat and that will be the end of it. Then it will be up to Uncle Ned to deal with him when he gets home."

The priest agreed to play his part.

19

Overnight, the field of ice to the southeast had moved and brought into view the biggest herd of young hoods the *Elsie*'s crew had ever seen. By dawn the crew was on deck, and more than a few had their jaws hanging open from pure shock. It was a shame, in a way, because they couldn't afford to take on many more.

"Where's the skipper?" a sealer asked. It occurred to him that he hadn't seen Edward all morning.

"He says he has the toothache," said Walter.

The sealer didn't believe a word of it. If Edward Dower knew what kind of a catch lay before them, he would have bounded up those stairs two at a time, toothache or no toothache. However, neither Walter nor the crewman gave it another thought. Like the others, they were calculating the profits to be made if they were to take a couple of the precious seals aboard.

When Edward came up on deck, he was a mess. His vision was blurry and his stomach wrestled with the notion of staying in one place. His mind raced as he edged toward the rail, and he noticed for the first time how low the *Elsie* sat in the water.

"This is our last tow," a sealer called from the ice. He had been busy, as was evidenced by the seals trailing behind him.

"How many have we got aboard now, Walter?" Edward asked, turning to his first mate.

"We have our amount on board now. We're just going to take what the men have in tow."

"That's good," Edward said absently.

"How are you feeling, Skipper?" Walter asked with concern.

"Not bad," Edward lied.

Walter could tell there was something wrong with his captain. He had been acting strangely last night and early this morning. To his surprise, Edward had even neglected to lock his sea-chest after closing it up for the night. But it was obvious Edward didn't want to talk, so he thought it best not to bother him.

Besides, it's probably just the flu or something, he thought.

The sealers returned to the ship one at a time, each lugging an impressive tow. Five thousand, two hundred and thirty was the last count.

"What a load we've got, Skipper," Walter said gleefully. For all the success he'd gotten on this voyage, though, Edward appeared not to care too much. Walter nodded. It definitely was the flu.

"There's no need for us to kill any more seals, Walter. We'll watch our move now and get out of here."

Walter grinned and yelled at the men to finish up and come in to eat. He mentioned to Edward that fresh baked bread and pork and beans awaited them below. Rubbing his hands together, he descended to the forecastle and left Edward alone with his thoughts.

* * *

WORD REACHED WILL DOWER that Father Gore and a group of men had gone to Silver Cove to search Maurice Power's house for his mother's coat. "What a bunch of fools," he spat. "They must be trying to start a war here in Conche."

He put his snowshoes on and set off for Silver Cove himself to see what was going on. Of all the people in Conche, Will Dower was the only person Maurice could call his friend. Everyone knew it, and this along with his tendency to make up stories made Will something of a black sheep. He hadn't gone far when the men came rushing by him with dark expressions on their faces. He stopped one man and asked him what in the world was happening. The man was livid. "Maurice struck Father Gore," he shouted.

It had all started when the mob arrived at Maurice's home. Six men had accompanied the priest, but Martin Flynn was not among them. He'd been called to go to John and Rose's home to make further funeral arrangements.

Three dog teams stood by, busily scratching themselves while their masters closed in on Maurice Power's house. It was Father Gore who stepped up to the door and gave it a sharp knock. Mary Power answered and looked at him in surprise.

"Hello, Father," she said in a small voice.

"Hello, my dear," the priest said politely. "We would like to talk to Maurice. Is he in?"

"No, Father, he's out in the woodshed."

Without further ado, Father Gore and the six men walked around the house and toward the woodshed, leaving a speechless Mary standing in the doorway. The priest took the lead and called out as he walked. "Hey! Maurice, are you in there?"

There was a silence. Father Gore turned to the others and shrugged. He cleared his throat and was about to call out again, when he thought that he heard someone call out in response.

"Anyone there?"

"Yes," the priest replied with a touch of nervousness. Maurice's children had begun to mill around, no doubt curious about the crowd of men in their yard.

Maurice stopped working his pit saw and wiped sweat and sawdust from his eyes. He swore under his breath at whoever it was outside that had interrupted him while he was sawing planks for his boat. The pit saw normally required two men to operate it, but Maurice could handle one himself. He flexed his muscles and stomped out to the doorway.

"Anyone there?" he repeated.

The priest came into view as Maurice brushed more sawdust off himself. When he saw Father Gore, in his backyard of all places, he was more than a little surprised. He must have come to tell Mary all about Ellen's death. Maurice Power was not a churchgoer and made it clear to anyone who asked that he had no use for the clergy, but seeing that the priest had come to tell them the news in person, he decided he would treat the man with some respect. He took off his cap and waited for him to speak.

Father Gore couldn't quite find his voice. The other men had backed away even farther when Maurice appeared in his doorway, and the priest was beginning to have doubts of his own.

"What is it, Father Gore? What brings you here," said Maurice, losing patience with the priest. "We know all about the death of Mrs. Dower."

A sudden surge of anger at the man's use of Ellen Dower's name got the priest talking. "We came here to search your house, Mr. Power," he announced.

Maurice Power removed his sodden wool mitts and tucked them under his arm. He strode over to the priest and looked him square in the eye.

"You what?"

"Yes," the priest stammered, "we came to search your house."

Maurice calmly dropped his mitts on a pile of wood nearby and looked at the priest again, folding his massive arms in front of him while Father Gore stood there trembling. "Are you saying that you are going to go into my home to search it?"

"Y-yes."

"Tell me. What will you be searching for?"

The priest took a deep breath and tried to steady himself. Never before had he been faced by such an intimidating figure, but he wasn't going to let any man shake his faith.

"What are you going to search for? I am asking you again."

"W-we are looking for the white lambskin coat that was stolen from the Dower house."

Maurice's bloodshot eyes bulged. "What makes you think that I got it, sir?" he roared. Before the poor old priest could answer, he continued. "Are you sure that you are to the right place?" He jabbed a thumb into his own chest. "I live here, Skipper. Maurice Power."

To his credit, Father Gore didn't back down this time. "You were seen coming out of the Dower home this morning with a bag. In it you had the coat belonging to Mrs. Ellen Dower. Is this right or wrong, Mr. Power?"

Maurice thought he had been a fool to go handy to that house this morning, but now he was sure of it. Who had seen him? It must have been that girl who came to the door after he left. She must have thought that his bag of wood shavings was old Ellen Dower's lambskin coat! At first he just stared at the white-faced priest. Father Gore looked like a man who knew he was about to die. Then Maurice's massive frame lurched and heaved in a great belly laugh.

Without warning, the laughing ceased and Maurice launched himself at the priest. His face came to within a few inches of Father Gore's and he snarled, "You take one step closer to my house and it will be the last one that you will ever make on the two legs that's keeping you up, Father. I'll break them right off across the knees."

Father Gore came very close to wetting himself. He knew that Maurice Power meant what he said. Glancing back at the six men as they edged closer to the action, he somehow found his strength and retorted, "By the way, Maurice, did you not tell the late Mrs. Dower yesterday that you were going to have her coat someway or another?"

Maurice stepped back when he saw one of his children out of the corner of his eye. He looked at the ground and nodded without looking up. "Yes, Father, I certainly did, and I may have it yet before I die, and so may you. But for now, you and your gang had better haul your frames out of here, or else I'll do to you what I did to someone before I came here to this town." With that, he grabbed the startled priest by the collar and with one huge hand flung him backwards onto the hard snow.

* * *

"AS SOON AS FATHER GORE hit the snow, he got to his feet and we all ran away," the angry man told Will. "Father Gore told us he was never setting foot on Maurice Power's property again."

Will thanked the man and continued to Silver Cove. He wasn't surprised by what he heard, and a little laugh escaped him on his way to see Maurice. When he reached the house he noticed that no one was outside, so he knocked on the door and stepped in. Maurice and Mary were sitting at the table, and their children were standing around the kitchen with confused looks on their faces. Mary was crying.

Maurice didn't look like he was in a very good mood either. But Will was thankful that Maurice was not too angry to acknowledge his friend and offer his condolences.

"I"m sorry about the death of your mother, Will."

Mary also gave Will her best wishes in his time of grief. Will thanked them both as he sat at the table. He gave Maurice a playful look then. "What, has Father Gore gone out of his mind, Maurice?"

"From what we have just heard and seen, Will, everyone around here has gone out of their minds. I've never seen the likes before. It'd be better if I'd stayed at Harbour Grace, or better than that I should have stayed back in Ireland or gone to China."

Will didn't know what to say. "Why would they think that you had Mother's coat?"

Maurice started laughing. He shook all over.

Mary gave her husband a light smack. "Listen, Maurice, this is no laughing matter. Do you know that you just picked up Father Gore and shook him like a rag doll? This is going to be serious, my dear. As sure as you're alive, you're going to have to go back and apologize to him."

Will jerked his thumb toward the road. "I just passed the crowd on their way down home and they told me that you struck Father Gore."

"No, I did not strike him!" Maurice snapped. "You should know that, because if I did there would be no more Father Gore."

Will nodded.

Maurice looked at his wife to make sure she was paying attention. Then he told her and Will the truth behind the bag of shavings and the girl whom he guessed tattled on him. When he finished, Will couldn't help but laugh along with him. "No, you won't go back and apologize to anyone," he said. "They will have to come back and apologize to you before this is all over. I wish the old man was here to see this."

At the mention of Edward Dower, he bowed his head and felt guilty for laughing at a time like this. He sighed and said, "I'm going down to see if I can straighten the crowd out on this one."

"No, don't go yet, Will," Maurice said. "Have supper before you go down. Mary will have it on the table soon, and I'll give you a run home after we're done. I just have to harness the dogs. Besides, they're all gone out of their minds in Conche anyway. You could get shot if they knew you were up here with me." He grinned foolishly.

Will grinned right back and agreed to stay.

* * *

IT WAS WELL AFTER DARK when Will arrived back home. The place was full of people, both men and women, many of them very close friends of Ellen Dower. The topic of discussion was Uncle Ned and the shock he was sure to receive when the *Elsie* pulled up to the dock.

"It will kill poor Uncle Ned for sure," someone said.

"I don't want to be the one who has to break the news to him," said another.

"Why didn't he give up the coat?" a woman asked.

Will knew beyond a doubt that Maurice was once again big news in the little town.

"No one belonging to him will ever be able to wear it. And imagine a big hulk of a man like Maurice striking a poor scrawny little priest like Father Gore! It was a sin against the Church, that's what it was. For this, Maurice Power is going to pay, and pay dearly."

It was a well-known fact that Will and Maurice were the best of friends, but they didn't mind talking about the latter. Will had his flaws, but he was a likeable sort of fellow. He edged closer to his sisters and brother. Ambrose was explaining to someone that a wake was going to be held.

"But not tonight," he said, "because there are too many things we have to get straightened out first." He gave Kizzie a sidelong glance. "We have too many things on our minds, haven't we?"

Kizzie couldn't help but feel slighted by Ambrose's look.

"What things have we got on our minds?" Her voice took on a threatening tone.

He waved his hand in an apologetic gesture. "For one thing, we haven't decided whether we will bury Mother before Father gets back."

Kizzie stopped him right there. "There's no decision to be made, Ambrose. Mother is staying right here, supposing Father doesn't come back 'til the summer."

Ambrose didn't answer. He knew it was the Church's decision, not Kizzie's. "We also have to decide where we're going to bury her. Father may have to take her back home to St. John's."

"Mother will be buried here at Conche," Nora insisted. "This is what she would want. I know she would." She went on to say, "Then there's the racket about the coat. How could we have a wake for Mother with this going on?" Will cleared his throat and stopped her before she could say anything more, because Rose was only a few feet away and he didn't want to start any family infighting.

* * *

THERE WAS SOME NOISE outside, and in came Granny Carroll. She had been brought to the house by komatik to offer her services to the family. Ambrose and Kizzie and the others felt deeply indebted to her, and they used every opportunity they could to tell her so. When the old woman came in, she went directly to the table and examined Ellen's body.

That's funny, she thought. The heat in the room was stifling, but Ellen's fingernails felt icy. In fact, they glistened as if coated by a thin layer of frost. *What could cause that?* She put her hand on Ellen's face and moved it from side to side as easily as if she were sleeping. The movement caused the two large pennies that had been placed on her eyelids to fall off and rattle against the wood. *I have never seen the likes of this before*, Granny Carroll mused. *She's dead, there's no doubt about that. She hasn't breathed since midnight last night.*

She pulled up a chair and sat at the table, eyeing the coffin warily. *This whole thing looks strange to me*, she thought. *Those bruises and scrapes on her legs have me puzzled, too. But I'd better not mention this to anyone—it could start a panic.*

"Do you want a cup of tea, Mrs. Carroll?" Emiline asked.

The old woman's head snapped up in surprise. She blinked at the girl for a second, then replied, "Yes, my dear, I certainly do." She looked around the room until she caught Will's eye. "Have you been out on Cape Fox today?" she asked.

Will nodded. "Yes, there's been a crowd out there off and on all day. It's all clear water out between the two Grey Islands as far as you can see, but there's a lot of ice east of the northern Grey Islands."

"How much ice is out there?"

"From what I've seen, you could get on the ice near Cape Fox and walk right out to the eastern end of the northern Grey Islands."

* * *

FATHER GORE WAS ORDAINED at a young age and had spent nearly his entire adult life as a priest. He had weathered many storms in his day, having come close to starving to death on two separate occasions and almost freezing more than once. But what happened to him this evening was by far the worst thing he'd ever experienced, or so he told himself. His neck and throat felt like they were on fire. Maurice Power had given him a heave as if he were no more than a kitten.

He sat in the rectory, shivering with a blanket covering him like a death shroud. The memory of the man's steel grip was doing all kinds of things to his nerves. "Is it any wonder that Martin Flynn wouldn't go up with them," he said aloud. His eyes narrowed. "Someone is going to hear about this, don't worry about that. I will write Bishop Fleming about this and have Maurice Power excommunicated from the Church, and I'm going to find out more about his background, too. He said he was going to do something to us like he did to someone before he came here."

As he sat in misery, his thoughts went to the untimely death of Ellen Dower. She had been a faithful parishioner. In fact, half of Father Gore's money came from the two Dower families, John's and Edward's. And without the singing of Ellen and Rose Dower making the weddings and times that much more entertaining, Conche would be just a ghost of its former self. He sighed and drifted off into a troubled sleep.

20

Edward Dower ate very little little supper in the evening. He had a fever and felt nauseous. Walter had told this to Edward's sons, Peter and Frank, and they confronted their father after the dishes were put away and before he could retire to his quarters.

"You're getting the flu, Father," Frank stated.

"Yes, perhaps I am."

"Maybe you should go to your room and turn in," Peter suggested. "Cover up warm and stay there 'til you feel better. Frank and I will take care of everything. Don't worry about a thing."

"Yes," Edward said weakly. "I think that's what I'll do."

With that he left the forecastle and went back to his cabin with Walter Joy at his side. The west wind blew strong on this starry night. Today had been a good day like the others, and Edward paused to contemplate the extraordinary week he and the crew of the *Elsie* had had. They were now en route to Conche, if the ice permitted, with a bumper load of prime young seal pelts ready for market. Edward Dower should have felt on top of the world, but he didn't. He couldn't put it in words, only that he felt deep down that something was dreadfully wrong.

The deck of the *Elsie* was slick with grease and blood as Edward and Walter ambled along in semi-darkness. The salt water and scrubbing brush were no match for the viscous blubber that came from thousands of seal pelts dragged across the deck in the past week. They descended the stairs into their quarters, taking extra care as they turned around and gripped the stairway. Splattered seal fat made the going more difficult than usual. Under ideal circumstances it was no place for anyone to be in a hurry. You just had to take your time.

Walter was the first to make the treacherous climb down. He lit the candle lamp and placed it on the table, and the room's walls glowed a dull orange. Checking the stove, he found the wood was still burning and lending warmth to the dark cabin. The floor had been built onto the timbers of the vessel, giving the room an odd shape that flattened only in the centre of the floor. When the *Elsie* was fully loaded, this area sank below sea level, and Edward was wary of this in case the hull was penetrated by ice. He knew that if this happened, anyone in the room would have mere seconds to escape before the place became a watery grave.

Walter noticed that when Edward came down into the cabin he was looking around as if expecting to see someone. This struck him as peculiar, but he let it pass.

His captain was out of sorts, and anyone in such a condition was liable to do strange things.

"Walter, you can lie down if you like and get a little sleep."

"Are you all right, Skipper? I mean, do you think you're getting a flu or something?"

"No, I'm all right," Edward said with a tired grin. "Just a bit of a headache, that's all. By tomorrow morning everything should be all right." He walked over and tapped the weather glass. "It looks like a change in the weather. The hand is moving over."

Walter peered at the barometer and nodded. "Yes, it looks like it," he agreed. "Maybe we're going to get a storm."

Edward scratched his stubbly chin. "You should take the sextant up and get a reading on our exact position. The evening star is just about in the right spot to get a good shot. You always seem to do a better job of it than I do."

"Yes, I certainly will," Walter said. He climbed up the slippery stairway and came back down in five minutes. Pointing to his chart, he said, "We're sixty miles southeast of the northern Grey Islands and seventy-two miles from Cape Fox. Our vessel is lying with her head directly in a westerly direction and ready to move at a moment's notice."

Edward was glad to hear it. He didn't know where he'd be without Walter Joy.

"Is there anything else, Skipper?"

"No, you should get a couple of hours' sleep."

"All right," Walter said and went to his bunk. He couldn't quite shake his concerns about the skipper's

well-being, but soon sleep overtook him and banished
all his worries.

* * *

EDWARD WAS NOT a sound sleeper; he heard everything that moved on or around the *Elsie*. If anyone
spoke or moved on deck he heard it, sleeping or not. His
ears were keen for his age, and the stories passed down
by people who sailed with him say that he was a man
who never slept. Often he would lie awake and listen to
the talk around him, grinning when someone told a joke
or a funny story and cocking his ear with interest when
someone divulged a secret.

He folded his hands beneath his head and let his
mind wander. *Why am I worried? I know everything is
all right at home. We never had any trouble before, so
what's wrong?* He just couldn't make any sense of it, so
he turned on his side and tried to think of something
else.

Now, there are many things in a man's life that can
drive him crazy, but the greatest thing of all is worry.
Intense anxiety has been documented in countless
medical cases as the cause of total withdrawal, phobias,
and even bizarre feelings of unreality. Men have gone
grey overnight worrying about their families, their
future, and their health. And so it was with Edward
Dower, who was so worried about his family in Conche
that he had himself completely convinced that something terrible had happened back home. "The feeling
was there," he was reported as saying after the event

that took place aboard the *Elsie*, "that almost drove me insane.

Edward had been dozing for about an hour when he thought he heard something on deck. "The boys must be changing watch," he mumbled in his half-awake, half-asleep state. He checked the time. It was nine-thirty. "It's not time for a watch change yet. It must be Frank going to bed."

The sound came again, this time much louder. He came fully awake now.

There was an unnatural silence in the room. Not even Walter's breathing could be heard. Then the companionway door opened. Edward moved only his eyes and tried to take in the darkened corner by the stairs. He had a visitor, all right, but it wasn't Frank.

It must be the cook.

Then the figure began to climb down the stairs with deliberate slowness. Something about the way it moved made Edward's heart leap into his throat.

My God! What is it?

His eyes popped open so wide they felt like they were going to burst right out of their sockets. He tried to lift his hands, but they refused to budge. The stranger (because that's what it was, a stranger) was coming down the stairs one step at a time. *The small feet*, he thought. *They are not the feet of anyone on board here.* What appeared to be soaked white rags dangled into view as the visitor took two more steps down.

In a poorly lit room such as the captain's quarters, sometimes people were deceived by what they saw. The scant light afforded by the candle lamp let only the outline of objects be known and not much in the way of detail. But, Edward's eyes were as sharp as his ears, and though he may have wished at that moment to be struck blind, there was no mistaking what he saw.

The busy streets of Halifax, the sights and sounds and smells of Christmas, Mrs. Findlay in St. John's, these things were dreams of the past for Skipper Ned Dower. But they all came rushing back now in a nightmare of white lambskin.

"My Blessed Virgin, help me," he rasped. His bladder threatened to let go.

Ellen Dower, formerly Ellen Casey of St. John's, climbed the rest of the way down the stairs and into the small cabin. Her hood was up and the coat bundled tightly around her frame, but the shape and posture of the figure left little room for doubt. It was Ellen, or something that looked very much like her. She limped to the table and stood in the light of the candle lamp. Breath steamed out of the dark cowl, as if the stranger had brought the night air inside with her. Edward was unable to see her face beneath the hood, and he wasn't sure he wanted to. Then the cowled figure removed the heavy mitts from her hands with elegant, ladylike movements.

Those hands, Edward thought. *They are not the hands of my Ellen. They are old and wrinkled and decayed. The fingernails, yes, those fingernails, they're frozen, frozen solid!* But the wedding band that glinted in the candlelight put an end to that line of questioning. It was Ellen's ornate ring, the very one he'd placed on her finger the night she'd said "I do."

The coat's hood swayed as Ellen lurched and started toward him. He felt an insane scream build in his throat, but no sound came out when he tried to release it. The figure then stumbled and almost fell, and it looked for a second like she was going to grab him—*My God, no!*—but, no, she turned at the last possible second and crouched before Edward's large oak sea-chest. The visitor's ancient hands lifted the lid with great difficulty until it rested against the wall. Then those frail hands went up, up, and grabbed either side of the hood. And pulled it back.

What Edward Dower saw then plagued him for the rest of his life.

Throwing back the woollen hood, the figure revealed for the first time Ellen Dower's beautiful face. Her skin was pallid and her lips a purple-blue. Her eyes were dead, half-open, staring eyes. Wrapped around her entire head was a thin death shroud. Etched in the fabric were the letters of the Holy Church. And what was this? A strip of cloth looped around her head from jaw to crown.

Ellen reached toward the sea-chest, but the lambskin coat limited her movement. In silence she unbuttoned it and was able to move more freely. Years ago, Edward and Ellen had agreed that on their dying days they were to be be dressed in the same clothes they had worn on their wedding day. Their wedding clothes they kept in a secured trunk, and from time to time Ellen would check on them in her fretful way to make sure they were still intact. And here it was, the memory of their pact flooding back to haunt him as had the lambskin coat.

Oh my God, Edward thought, noticing how Ellen's hair on one side fell over her eyes. *What am I seeing?*

He could feel her wintry breath on his face, freezing his tears as they fell. It occurred to him that his eyes were the only part of his body he could move. As Ellen poked around inside the chest, he noticed that the arms of the lambskin coat were soaked all the way to the elbows, and the weight of them seemed to be making her shrivelled hands tremble in protest. Her hands went to the chest's protective cardboard lining and began pulling.

Why is she tearing up the lining of the chest? he wondered. As if thinking it had given her the strength necessary to accomplish the deed, she gave the cardboard one final tug and it came free with a tearing sound.

Dear God, why is Ellen doing this?

The ghost of Ellen Dower pulled from Edward's sea-chest a large envelope. Edward nearly fainted when he saw it. Something had been wrong, all right, and he had been the cause! Again he tried in vain to scream in this crypt, because that's what it was, a crypt. He was dead, and this was hell or purgatory, and he was doomed to watch his family pay for his sins.

"The land grant," he whispered. "She's looking for the land grant. Oh my Great God, what have I done? I have killed my poor wife."

Ellen stood up, still clutching the envelope in her withered hands. She turned, almost striking Edward, and limped over to the table. Pulling the lamp toward her, she leaned in and scanned the address on the envelope. She nodded as if to say "Yes, that's the handwriting, but I wonder if the grant is still inside?" Edward wanted to tell her it was, but he couldn't.

"Come here, my dear, I'll help you," is what Edward would have said if he could when he saw his dear wife struggle to open the envelope. Her dark, silky hair was held in place by the same two silver combs she'd worn on their wedding night. Plucking one of them from her hair, she slit the sealed flap on the envelope, then placed the comb onto the table's wooden surface. The land grant slid out of the upturned envelope and into her waiting hand. Then, and only then, when the true whereabouts of the land grant were finally made known to her, did Ellen Dower smile.

She staggered back to the sea-chest and replaced the envelope inside the lining. Easing the lid down, she let out a great sigh that plumed mistily into the air. Ellen buttoned her wet lambskin coat and fastened the death shroud around her before lifting the hood back over her head. Edward got one last look at those ancient fingers with their icy fingernails before she slipped her sodden mitts back over them.

Then the figure straightened and stood stock-still for several minutes. Edward couldn't see her face, but he was sure the Ellen-figure was staring right at him. Speak or move he couldn't as she lifted the tail of her wedding dress and limped back toward the stairs. Edward could only watch in mute horror as the figure held its shredded dress in one hand and used the other to pull its way up and out to the frosty air.

Only after the ghost of his wife departed was Edward Dower able to find his voice.

Oh, how he screamed.

And screamed and screamed.

Part III

21

Walter Joy was a loyal worker who would stay with Edward and John Dower until he became too old to perform his duties. He carried enormous respect for the two men and was a lifelong friend to them both. Most days he spent with Edward, sailing in vessels headed either to the Labrador to collect salt fish or to the icefields for sealing. In his later years, he gave endless testimonials to the effect that he had seen Edward do things he could only describe as genius.

Many and untold are the Atlantic adventures of Walter Joy and his captain. Edward's strong will and his first mate's vast knowledge of the seas lifted them out of many hopeless situations. Many old-timers recall that Skipper Ned was referred to as a steel man. He was as solid as they come, never getting upset and rarely raising his voice, no matter how desperate the situation. Only once, the stories say, did Edward lose his cool.

"Oh my God, oh my God!" he wailed. "Walter, Walter, I've seen her, I've seen Ellen!" He was sitting bolt upright now, his limbs once again under his control. Sweat was rolling down his face and his body shook so violently that the perspiration jittered on his skin.

If ever there were a man who came to his feet in a hurry, it was Walter Joy. He stared at Edward's face and didn't like what he saw.

"What's happening, Skipper? For God's sake, what's happening?" Edward looked horrified, and there were tears mingling with the sweat glistening on his cheeks.

"My God, Skipper, is that you?"

Walter was scared himself. He couldn't believe it, that a man could change so much and so suddenly. He took a few steps toward the skipper, then stopped as Edward fell to his knees.

"Walter, she was here, right here," Edward cried, covering his face with his hands. "Ellen was here, dressed in her grave clothes. I saw her as plain as day, right here. I wasn't asleep, Walter."

Walter didn't know what to do. The skipper was yammering like a lunatic. "Ned," he said, ignoring ship protocol, "stay here."

With that he bolted for the stairs, not stopping to put his boots on. His thick socks slipped on the stairs at first, but with one great leap he crested the stairway and scrambled out onto the deck.

"There's something wrong with the skipper," he shouted as he burst through the companionway.

The two watchmen looked at each other and then at the first mate.

"What's wrong, Walter?"

"The skipper has something wrong with him. Go for Frank," Walter croaked, his throat dry.

In less than a minute, a small group of sealers were streaming down the stairway and cramming into the captain's quarters. Frank was pale with fright at the thought of his father suffering from some terrible illness. But he and the others were surprised to find Edward lying face down on the floor, crying in deepest sorrow.

Together the men lifted Edward onto his bed. He went limp and offered no resistance. He kept saying, "My God, my God, my Blessed Virgin, my Blessed Virgin." Then he caught his son's eye and said just above a whisper, "She was here, Frank, your mother was here."

Frank was nonplussed. He'd never seen his father come undone like this, mumbling gibberish. *Imagine,* he thought, *Father crying. Impossible.*

Frank stood very near where his mother had opened the brown envelope containing the land grant just minutes ago. He sized up his father's broken form, shaking all over and soaked with sweat. This man, who had a reputation for being invincible, now looked vulnerable, his copper-coloured hair sticking off in all directions like corkscrews.

"Father," he said in a calming voice, "you must have had a bad dream. You haven't been feeling well all day."

"My God, Frank, listen to me."

Though Edward was carrying on like a madman, something in his tone silenced the entire crew. He closed his eyes and wiped his face with his handkerchief, then began to talk slowly. "She came down the stairs and stood by the table right there."

He pointed at Frank's feet.

"Stop, Father." All eyes went to Frank as he asserted authority over his captain and father. He drew in a breath and was about to give his father a tongue-lashing, when something drew his eyes down and to his right.

"Father! What's that there?"

"What's what, Frank?" Walter interjected, trying to calm them both.

Frank reached down and drew something back from the table. He eyed his open palm and furrowed his brow in confusion.

"Where did this come from?"

Edward was not at all surprised to see what his son had in his hand. "I'm trying to tell you, but you won't listen."

Frank felt sick. He knew what the object was, but he wanted to hear his father's explanation first.

Edward choked on his words. "It's your mother's comb, Frank. She used it to open the envelope with the land grant. She must have left it on the table."

Sure enough, it was Ellen Dower's silver comb. Frank couldn't believe it! Here was proof right in front of his face. His mother *had* been here.

* * *

THROUGH HIS TEARS, Edward outlined what had happened in the last hour. He added that the awful

feeling he'd been experiencing for the last few days had
gotten steadily worse but tapered off and finally vanished when Ellen came to his room. It was out in the
open now, but there was still one thing that worried
him. He looked at Frank and then at Peter, then told
them something they already knew, that long ago he and
Ellen had planned to be buried wearing their wedding
clothes when they passed away. The wedding dress and
embroidered shroud Ellen was wearing when she visited
the cabin could mean only one thing.

"Frank, Peter, there is no doubt in my mind. Your
mother has passed away."

The boys shook their heads fervently. Not because
they didn't believe their father's words, but because they
didn't want to believe. They passed the silver comb back
and forth a few times, as if forgetting the feel of it when
it left their hands.

"There must be quite an uproar back home,"
Edward said in a distant voice.

Peter Dower held church services at Conche whenever the priest was called away. His father often praised
him for taking on such a worthwhile task. And now,
beckoning Peter to come near the bunk, Edward said to
his crew, "We're going to say the rosary now for the soul
of my dead wife." The men didn't need to be asked
twice. They knelt and followed Peter's lead when he
intoned the litany for the dead, followed by the rosary.

The writer J.W. Kinsella interviewed Edward Dower
ten years after this event and reported that the crew of
the *Elsie* "said a rosary and prayed to beg God to lib-
erate them from an unbroken sea of ice, so that they

may yet reach home in time to attend the burial of one who was revered and respected by all."

I never thought that I would have such an experience as this, Edward thought when the service came to an end. *Not in my whole life.* He wiped his eyes and said, "This is something that will follow me to my grave. I put that land grant in the lining of my chest and forgot about it. I can't understand what came over me to forget about it, and how your mother knew that I even put it there is beyond me."

Frank felt awkward when his father burst into tears then and hugged him close. "I wonder how long we'll be stuck here in this icefield?" he asked as he patted his father's shoulder, trying to break the tension. When that didn't work, he said, "Father you have to try and be strong about this. If Mother is dead, you still have to go home and go on with your life, no matter what happens." He didn't feel as strong as his words implied, but he tried to hold it together until he could be alone with his thoughts.

Frank was right, of course. Edward saw that his son was looking out for the crew's best interests, and this filled him with a profound sense of pride. He reached for Peter's hand, and they stayed like that for some time, the three Dower men grieving for mother and wife while the crew looked on in silence.

Walter Joy knew that he was going to have to take charge of the vessel and make sure things were handled properly. He had never expected to have to take over for Skipper Ned Dower, not in a million years. But, as second-in-command, his duty was clear. He looked at everything in a practical sense; though something extraordinary had obviously happened to his captain, he wasn't going to let that get in the way of what needed to be done.

The road that lay ahead was not an easy one. The Labrador Current was among the deadliest in the world, and it would take everything in Walter to navigate the treacherous undertow. Every hour, a thousand different things happened below sea level, so he would have to be alert at all times. There was no joy in Walter this morning as he assumed command of the mighty barque *Elsie* and waited for the ice to free her from its clutches.

22

E llen Dower looked like a woman who had fallen into a deep sleep as she lay in her casket on the kitchen table. She'd been dead for twenty-four hours now, and yet some colour still remained in her cheeks. Granny Carroll, after hearing that Ellen still *looked* alive, had assured the family that this was often the case when people died in their prime. "Mrs. Carroll knows," said one woman to the crowd in the parlour. "She's seen enough people die, that's for sure. Pretty near laid out all the old people who have died in Conche." Ambrose and the others didn't say anything but just sat in sombre silence.

Nora suggested they start singing a few songs. The depressed mood was starting to get to her. To her surprise, many of the others were in agreement, and Will offered to go and ask Mr. John Joyce to come and play his accordion.

"Music will help us get through this," Will said, and no one argued.

* * *

FATHER GORE SENT for Martin Flynn after he finished his lunch. When Martin arrived, the priest told him he wanted a grave dug for the deceased Ellen Dower.

"That's going to be a hard task, Father. The ground is frozen down about two feet, I'd say."

"I know, but it has to be done. The dead have to be buried, you know."

Martin nodded. "Where in the cemetery should we dig the hole? Does the family have anything in mind?"

The priest indicated where he wanted the grave made, and he instructed Martin to get as many men as necessary to get the job done in time. Meanwhile, he planned to give a special Mass for the dead and scheduled it for tomorrow afternoon.

By the time evening rolled around, a hole six feet deep had been dug in the graveyard.

* * *

ELLEN HAD BEEN DEAD going on two days, and the talk around town was of course the theft of her lambskin coat. After Maurice told Will and Mary about the girl who had seen him walking away from the Dowers' house, he had charged them not to tell anyone about the bag of shavings. "Keep your mouth shut about this," he ordered. "They won't believe you if you told them. They'll condemn you, that's what they'll do." There was no one more capable of concealing the truth than Will Dower, and this time was no exception. He grinned inwardly when he overheard some of the rumours going around.

He didn't attend the special Mass Father Gore said for his mother. Not only did he act in a contrary manner to his family, he even looked different than his brothers and sisters. But he resembled his family more than did his brother Peter, whom it was said was the spitting image of his uncle John. Instead of going to the church service, he went to his uncle John and aunt Rose's house. They hadn't gone to the Mass either, and as he entered he noticed that Rose had been crying. Her eyes were red and had a hollow look to them.

"How are you, Will, my dear?" she greeted him.

He went to her and gave her a hug.

"I wonder where all this is going to end?" she asked as she hugged him back.

Will, who cared little what people thought of him, said, "I know where all this is going to end, Aunt Rose."

Rose gave him a strange look. "Where?"

Will stood up. "In hell with the devil," he said, "Father Gore and all."

Rose's mouth fell open.

"Be careful, Will," John spoke up. "You could blaspheme, you know."

"Blaspheme, my eye."

Rose looked at the two men who looked like they were ready to argue. She thought that Will knew more than he was letting on and that John was trying to shut him up. John's refusal to elaborate on Ellen's dying words had only fuelled her curiosity that much more.

"Now, Will, you keep quiet," John threatened. "There's enough trouble going on now, so for God's sake, keep your mouth shut."

John was afraid Will was going to tell Rose about Maurice and the whole Henry Winton affair, but the young man didn't even know about it. Two days ago, when Ellen sat in her kitchen telling Emiline and the girls about Robert Parsons and that fateful night on Saddle Hill, he had been out cutting wood. No, what he wanted to tell Rose was that Maurice didn't steal the lambskin coat, that the bag Nora had seen on the man's back contained wood shavings and nothing more.

"Listen, Will, I want to know what went on between your mother and Maurice, because she wouldn't say what she said if there wasn't a reason." All Rose knew was what Ellen had revealed on her deathbed, that a bounty had been placed on Maurice's head. But for what, she couldn't say. She was getting tired of being left in the dark.

People were saying that Maurice had struck the priest, but Will knew better. At first he thought the wild rumours very funny, but now it was getting serious. It wouldn't be long before the whole town got together and lynched his friend. If he told them now that their suspicions were wrong, that Maurice had been unjustly accused of the coat's theft, then that would get him off the hook for sure. But he was torn, because he knew that's not what his friend wanted.

Rose was furious. She jumped to her feet and glared at her husband.

"Listen," she said loudly. She was known for her hot temper and the fact that she put up with no foolishness at all. "I want to know what's going on right now."

Will was in a jam. This wasn't his fight; it was up to Uncle John to deal with his wife. On the other hand, he was the only person who knew the truth behind the missing coat. Or did he? If Maurice Power didn't steal it, then who did? Maybe it was Maurice after all who stole the coat and made up the story about the bag of shavings, just to get Will to side with him. He was more confused than ever as he watched his aunt grow red with anger.

He threw up his hands and left the house without saying so much as a goodbye.

* * *

IT HAD BEEN DISCUSSED but only now decided that there would be a wake held for Ellen Dower. The family talked it over with Father Gore, and he told them it was a good idea. Traditionally, wakes were treated as celebrations of the deceased person's life, bringing much-needed closure to their loved ones and ending this transitional phase of their lives on a positive note.

Up to the late 1950s, moonshine was present in many if not all parts of Newfoundland. The small fishing villages were swimming in the stuff, and people wrote humourous songs about the old moonshine cans and the effects the potent elixir had on a fellow. The law had their work cut out for them when it came to moonshine. There were men who could not eat their meals or even step inside a church without first having a taste of the brew. And it goes without saying that the towns floated in moonshine whenever a social time was held. Those are days long gone, when Newfoundlanders danced, drank, sang songs, and cooked big scoffs at all hours of the night.

Ellen's wake called for a lot of preparation. Chairs had to be brought to the house and the parlour's furniture rearranged. The centre of the room was to be cleared for a square dance, and chairs to be provided for the best accordion players Conche had to offer. Rose Dower was asked if she would feel up to singing a few songs, but in light of recent events surrounding her sister-in-law's death, she wasn't quite sure.

"How can I sing when my best friend will be lying in her coffin only a few feet away?"

A young man set aside the chairs he was carrying. "Aunt Ellen would want you to sing to her," he said simply.

Rose let out a helpless sigh. "I've never seen anything like it. I was out to look at her again about an hour ago, and she looks like she's ready to speak! Her cheeks haven't even lost their colour. 'Tis amazing to me."

John spoke up. "We talked to Mrs. Carroll about that, Rose. Ellen has left this world forever, you can be sure." For some reason his wife was terrified by the idea that Ellen could hear her singing, so he tried to put her fears to rest. "What's in that casket is only a lump of cold clay. Mrs. Carroll said that people who die healthy stay looking like that for awhile."

A loved one's wake was an event that people would not miss if at all possible. Everyone was invited, and usually everyone showed up. Around 7:00 P.M., John sent word to Maurice Power that he should come with

Mary. They could bring the children to his house, where they would be looked after by himself.

When the invitation reached Maurice, he stamped his foot on the floor and refused to go. "I would not be caught in that house if I was in the same state as Ellen herself—dead."

Mary saw that he was adamant. "I don't mind you, Maurice, you won't go anywhere. But I'm going, you can like it or not."

"You can go, it's no difference to me." He shrugged. "I'll take you down and bring you back."

Mary gave it some thought. "Listen, Maurice, I'll tell you what we can do. Why don't you stay at Father's place? I'll go to the wake and you can stay with him."

She gave him the same sweet smile he'd fallen in love with all those years ago. He grumbled and fussed, but eventually he gave in and agreed to go.

23

No one under the age of sixteen was allowed to come to the party. The only other rule was that the dead person would not be left alone while the dance was in progress. Usually the person chosen to sit near the casket was hand-picked based on the fact that he (or she) was the drunkest. At eight o'clock everyone was ready to get the wake underway. The Dowers' parlour was filled to overflowing and many of the men were well into the moonshine. During the first hour, the guests spent some quiet time in conversation and paying respects to the deceased. Then at nine o'clock the musicians signalled that they were ready to begin. The quartet, two men on button accordions, another on the fiddle, and a woman with a harmonica, looked expectantly at the crowd.

It was a very cold March night with the stars twinkling and the wind blowing lightly from the northwest. One man remarked that it was a good night for a wake, but that it also looked like they were in for a southeaster. Before the musicians could begin their lively tunes, the same fellow asked them if Rose could sing a song first.

Rose, like Ellen, was a beautiful woman in her forties. And like her sister-in-law, she wasn't shy in front of a crowd.

"What do you want me to sing?"

Several people at once said, "Sing the one about Mother Malone."

"All right," Rose said. She gave the harmonica player a nod and the fiddler picked up his bow. Together they filled the parlour with a gentle harmony.

> *Oh take me back to the little town*
> *Where I used to live before*
> *Let me walk along the dusty roads*
> *And knock on every door*
> *Let me eat at every table*
> *And never be alone*
> *And stay in the house forever*
> *With dear old Mother Malone*
>
> *Oh Mother Malone, oh Mother Malone*
> *I can see your face so grand*
> *It's been oh so long since I left you*
> *And came to Newfoundland*
> *I can see your face now clearly*
> *Like the day we said goodbye*
> *But I know we'll meet again someday*
> *Somewhere beyond the sky*

Everyone clapped along when Rose reached the chorus, and many a tear was shed at the touching melody. When the song ended, the house roared with applause.

"Sing another one," they said.

"No, the dance must start," said the man in charge of the wake.

Rose smiled and gave a little bow, scurrying off the dance floor when couples started running to it. And so the square dance, or "lancers" locally, started. Before long, the revelling was in full swing, and it was a while before someone suggested they take a break.

The musicians sat in their chairs and tuned up, grateful for the brief respite. The crowd mingled between dances, most of the men going out back to have a drink of moonshine together. Soon came the call to start dancing again, and the men came in wearing a semi-drunk glow. This was going to be an all-night affair, so the drinks would have to be drunk in moderation. The music started up again and the dancers started swinging their partners around in mad circles. The festivities went on and on, and for a while the family and friends of the late Ellen Dower forgot about the body that lay as cold as clay in the room beyond.

* * *

MAURICE POWER SAT at the kitchen table with John and Will Dower. From John's house they could hear the music and the laughter as it shook the walls next door. Several men came over and gave them each a swallow of moonshine. They invited the three men to join in the celebration, but Will interrupted them and expressed his opinion that there should be no celebration for the death of his mother.

239

When the party-goers left, John, Will and Maurice talked about the seal hunt and and the crew of the *Elsie*.

"They've had pretty good weather for this voyage," Maurice remarked.

John leaned back in his chair. "The big thing is locating the seal herds," he said.

"It looks to me like we're in for a big breeze of southeast wind," said Will, looking out the window.

Maurice nodded. They talked on through the night as the wake raved on next door, and they enjoyed each other's company and the warmth of the fire nearby. They didn't need any silly party to have a good time.

* * *

IT WAS GETTING CLOSE to midnight when the dance started up again after another resting period. Some of the guests, especially women who had small children waiting at John's house to be taken home, said their goodbyes and left. Outside, the sky was becoming overcast and the wind was starting to pick up from the northeast. The same fellow who had mentioned the weather before said, "I would say that before daylight we could be getting a snowstorm." He shrugged and leaped back into the dance, shouting, "Let 'er swing, boys, and give Ellen a good send-off."

Sitting near the coffin in the kitchen was a young man by the name of Moses Lewis. He was just twenty-four years old and couldn't hold his liquor very well, so when he fell over in a drunken stupor it was deemed his turn to sit near the body for an hour. Resigned to his fate, Moses put the kettle on and waited, hoping that a hot cup of tea would clear his head. The door to the parlour was open a crack, and the music and stomping of feet was quickly giving him a headache. There was no sign of the singing, clapping, laughing, shouting and dancing letting up anytime soon. The lamp on the wall winked crazily from the vibration going through the house.

It was just a few minutes past midnight when, according to the Conche historian Paddy O'Neill, poor Moses Lewis thought he heard a funny noise. He had been drinking moonshine all evening and his head was in a fog. Until now, he'd been sitting with his elbow propped up on the back of his chair, peering through the narrow opening in the doorway and yearning for his shift to be over so he could return to the celebration. Sometimes he nodded off and spilled brown droplets of baccy juice onto his grey woollen sweater. Most of his shift was spent this way, passing out from drinking too much moonshine and coming to with a start when a particularly loud reveller interrupted his dreams.

Near the end of his shift, Moses awakened from a drunken sleep again, but this time not because of the rattling walls. He cast a glance over at the stove, thinking one of the wood junks had collapsed in a pile of ash and made the sound that had brought him to consciousness.

No sound there.

Almost fearfully he looked over at the casket and noticed everything there was as it should be. Ellen's head was slightly elevated so that it protruded a ways out of the coffin, making the simple wooden box look oddly surreal. No sound from there either. Hearing no further noise, he shook his head irritably and nestled back in his chair to catch a few more winks.

All the older men who attended a wake usually sat around and smoked their pipes, watching the younger men and women dance and frolic with all the energy they themselves could no longer muster. Between naps, Moses watched through the doorway and grinned when an old-timer got up and tried to take a turn on the dance floor. Sleep would soon overtake him again, and more tobacco juice would dribble from his chin onto his now filthy sweater.

Moses heard the noise again, and this time it brought him to his feet. Was there a tomcat or something in the kitchen? Had to be. "Or someone coming in," he said out loud, looking toward the kitchen door. It was still closed. Scratching his head in confusion, he turned in his chair and was about to write the whole thing off when he noticed a shadow on the wall.

Ah, they've come to relieve me and let me back in the parlour, he thought.

"It's about ti—"

It was then that Moses Lewis got the biggest fright a human being could get in his entire life. He was four feet from the kitchen table, and looking straight into the cold dead eyes of Ellen Dower. She was sitting up in her coffin, her death shroud still wrapped around her head and shoulders. For a split second his body would not move. It was as if it had become part of the chair. Then he heard a faint voice.

"Help me out, Moses."

Moses let out a scream that came from deep inside him and he flew from his chair, almost straight up. He sailed through the air and crashed through the parlour door, sending several dancers sprawling before he hit the floor. He scrambled to his feet and shrieked something incoherent. The wily old man he'd seen join in the dance grabbed him by the arm, but he shrugged the old-timer off.

"My God, she's getting out," he screamed, his bloodshot eyes threatening to pop out of his head.

The music stopped. Everything stopped. The whole crowd looked through the door into the kitchen. Sure enough, Ellen Dower was getting out of her coffin.

Then all hell broke loose.

Men and women alike clawed their way out the front door, others stood there and screamed, and more than a few fainted dead away on the spot. Absolute chaos ensued in the parlour while in the very next room Ellen Dower, who had been dead for two days now, calmly got out of her casket and tried to steady herself on the kitchen table.

The few who remained to see to the women who had fainted managed to finally rouse their loved ones, and together the last of them charged out the parlour door and into the cold night. At last, the house was completely empty.

Empty, that is, except for a very much awake Ellen Dower.

24

Maurice Power, John and Will were still sitting around John's kitchen table talking about the seal hunt when they heard a commotion outside. Will, who was not very happy the wake for his mother was being held in the first place, said, "Listen to that. They must have gone out of their minds now and decided to go on a march or something."

Maurice grinned. "'Tis all right as long as they don't go out and jump over the cliffs at Cape Fox."

John was about to comment, when, all of a sudden, the door burst open and Kizzie ran into the kitchen.

"My Blessed God, Uncle John, my God," she rambled, gasping for breath. "Mother just got out of the coffin!"

She didn't even notice her arch-enemy Maurice Power sitting at the table.

Will stood on shaky legs. "Kizzie, do you know what you're saying?"

"Yes!" she cried. "I saw her. She was stepping down on the chair when I last saw her."

The whole crowd started pouring into John's house then. In less than a minute the place was filled with wide-eyed people shouting and stammering. Women were crying and the men were shaking uncontrollably. Unbelievable! Incredible! came the cries.

"It looked like Mother, it is Mother," Kizzie said, her words almost lost in the mayhem. Someone ran by her, screaming that the world was coming to an end.

John Dower was a level-headed man. He stood up when the crowd reached a fevered pitch.

"Listen to me," he shouted above the din. "This is nonsense! This cannot be. There has to be some other explanation for this. I have an idea what's going on."

He had the people's attention now. They all stopped what they were doing and looked to him for answers. Kizzie took the lead and asked him in a frantic voice, "What's happening, Uncle John?"

John was clearly annoyed. "Listen to me. I think someone is playing a joke on us. That wasn't Ellen who got out of the coffin; it must be someone dressed up trying to frighten everybody."

Sudden understanding dawned on the townspeople. Maybe he was right. It wasn't something that hadn't happened before. Such pranks were often played on people back in Ireland.

"Who saw her first?" John demanded.

"It was Moses Lewis," someone shouted. "He was sitting near her when she sat up."

John rolled his eyes. "You must be crazy to talk after him. Where is he now?" They looked around the room, but there was no sign of the young man.

"All right," Ambrose spoke up. "Uncle John, if you think it was someone playing a joke, you go out now and see if Mother is still in the coffin."

John said nothing. He had no intentions of going in that house to have a look. Sensing his hesitation, Ambrose turned to the crowd and asked if anyone who'd been at the dance would go in and take another look. No one volunteered.

"We should go and get Father Gore," offered one of the revellers.

"A good idea," said Ambrose, and a couple of men left at once to find the priest.

All the women were milling around John Dower's kitchen in a frenzied state. The men went outside and stared at the house belonging to Edward and Ellen. The door was wide open and swinging on its hinges and all the rooms were still lit, but no movement could be detected within. Ellen, or Ellen's imposter, was nowhere to be seen.

"What should we do?" an old-timer queried.

"Should someone go in?" asked another.

"Not me, not for any money," a fisherman stated.

None of the men outside would even think about going handy to the house, not even as a group. Someone said they should go around back and peek through the kitchen window. They might get a glimpse of what was going on, to see if indeed Ellen was up and out of her coffin. A good idea, but not one soul offered to venture near the house.

* * *

IT WAS TWELVE-THIRTY when the priest and the two men who had gone for him came down the road, all out of breath. At that precise moment, they and everyone else heard a noise that sounded like it came from Ellen's house.

"Listen," one man hissed. "Did you hear that?" Those standing around him nodded emphatically. "It sounds like Ellen is calling out to someone." The man bolted into John's kitchen and informed the crowd inside, "Someone is calling from inside the house."

When he came to a stop, Father Gore wiped the sweat from his face and patted his wrinkled clothes. He looked like he'd seen better days. His eyes were white with abject terror, and the large crucifix clutched in his hand was quivering noticeably.

"We heard her calling out, Father," said one of the onlookers.

"Has anyone gone to the house?"

The man shook his head.

The priest entered John's kitchen and met a miserable-looking group of men and women. "Oh, Father Gore," one said. Before he had a chance to reply, he noticed Maurice Power sitting at the kitchen table. His heart stopped as he watched the man sitting unconcerned, as if the brute were watching a group of children playing. Father Gore turned sharply, not wanting to meet the man's gaze.

The priest cleared his throat. "What shall we do?" he asked in a voice he hoped sounded confident.

No one had an answer. That was why they had summoned him in the first place. "There isn't much I can do for now, only pray," he said. He gave the crowd a hopeful look, but they only stared back in confusion.

"Why don't you go in and see her, Father?"

The old priest felt ill at that suggestion. He swallowed hard. "I will go in if some men will go with me." He felt emboldened by his own words, but when no one offered to accompany inside the Dower house, he threw up his hands in despair.

Maurice Power had been watching the proceedings with growing amusement. *You had all the nerve in the world when you came to my house yesterday afternoon to search for a coat that I didn't have, but now you're a coward, afraid of your shadow.* Maurice laughed at the silly priest, standing there with his nightshirt dragging on the floor.

* * *

THE STORM EDWARD PREDICTED never came, only a light breeze from the northeast. Edward felt like he was going out of his mind. He couldn't eat, couldn't sleep, and he couldn't take his mind off what was lying inside his sea-chest. The crew talked about what Edward had seen the night before. During the day he and his son Frank had opened the chest, and sure enough, the brown envelope was tucked away in the lining, looking as it had on Christmas Eve.

And now here was Ellen's silver comb, a ghostly memento of her visit. Edward took it and hid it away, though at first he was loath to touch it. If he had been the first to see it, he knew in his present state that he would have hidden it away and not mentioned it, inadvertently prolonging the crew's suspicions that their captain was going crazy. But everyone had gotten a good look at the comb, and if Edward was losing his mind, then so were they. It, too, was tucked away in his sea-chest.

"I just don't know what to say or think, Frank," Edward confided. "There has to be an awful racket going on back home, and here we are, jammed solid in this icefield. Poor Kizzie, I know she must be out of her mind."

Frank didn't say anything. His sister would have to take care of herself. They had problems of their own.

The crew was restless, so early that morning they decided to kill some more seals. Hoods both old and young surrounded the *Elsie*, and the ship wasn't leaving anytime soon. Keeping the weight of their groaning vessel in mind, they took the fat off those they killed. This way ten skins weighed only as much as one with the fat left on. The pelt itself was the most valuable anyway. Edward was too depressed to do up a tally, but Walter estimated they brought aboard eight hundred of the precious pelts.

Late in the evening, Edward called everything to a halt.

"Listen, boys, you must be intending to sink her for sure." He glanced warily at the pile of skins on deck. They were pushing six thousand seal pelts now, and if not for his serious concerns for his wife and family, he would have been smiling and clapping his hands, maybe even dipping into the rum he had stowed away for special occasions.

Ten o'clock that evening, Edward decided to lie down. Frank and Walter had both gone to the forecastle to play cards with the rest of the men as they did almost every night, so he would have some blessed privacy tonight. He yanked his boots off and pulled his old grey blanket around himself. The candle lamp on the table shone more doom and gloom to him than it did light, and this was his last waking thought. He then went into a deep sleep and started dreaming.

* * *

EDWARD FOUND HIMSELF sitting down at the parlour table in his house at Conche. A mess of people were standing around outside. He tried to call to them, but they didn't see or hear him. He sat there tapping his fingers on the table until he heard someone coming in. Looking up, he saw a man open the front door and proceed to drag something in behind him.

My God! What's he dragging?

Maurice Power was dragging a coffin into the house. Edward squinted, trying to get a glimpse of the person in the casket. There was no one in it, but what he saw there made his heart thud in his chest painfully. There was Ellen's lambskin coat, all tattered, torn and dirty. Maurice made a half-turn toward the kitchen, and coming out to meet him were two of Edward's children, Kizzie and Ambrose. But— what's this? Were they bowing down to Maurice Power?

He tried to call out but couldn't. He tried to get up but the dream wouldn't let him. Then Ambrose looked straight at him.

Father, he said, and walked toward him.

* * *

"FATHER! SKIPPER! HEY SKIPPER, wake up," Ambrose said, shaking him. Edward opened his eyes and saw that it wasn't Ambrose, but Frank. He felt dizzy all of a sudden, and he wondered dreamily if his mind was finally coming unravelled.

"My God, we're all finished."

"Father, you were dreaming," Frank said.

Edward started crying. He felt like a man backed into a corner.

"Father, what's wrong?"

Through his sobs Edward told him about his dream. "If you hadn't awakened me, Ambrose might have told me what was going on."

"You have to get hold of yourself, Father," said Frank.

Relating the dream in later years, Edward Dower said, "I wasn't sleeping very long, taking into account the time the boys woke me. I might have been sleeping for about half an hour."

25

It is said that Maurice Power was afraid of nothing that crept or crawled. He was classed as the devil in Conche, and he knew it.

What a weakling, he thought, staring at the priest. *I make no wonder he left France and came over here. I'd say he was good for nothing over there anyway.*

He startled himself, because for one brief instant he thought he had said it out loud. But he saw no surprise in the faces of those nearby.

"Where's my coat?" he barked, getting up from the table.

Will pointed to a chair across the room. Several suspicious glances greeted Maurice as he stalked over to retrieve his coat, but no one challenged him. He may have been the devil in Conche, but the people had more to worry about now than old Maurice Power.

"Kizzie, what do you want me to tell your mother when I talk to her?" Maurice asked casually.

The twenty-three-year-old girl was so taken aback she couldn't speak.

"Don't bother to answer," he said in a hurry. "I'll bring her out here. Then you can ask her anything you like." Kizzie's eyes grew wide, and still she couldn't find the words.

Will stood up. "I'm going with you," he said.

"No, you're not," said Maurice. "I can do this myself, Will. Just in case something goes wrong, you stay here." He walked out the door without looking back.

* * *

LOOKING TOWARD THE HOUSE, Maurice could see that all of the rooms were lit and the doors wide open. At first he wasn't sure whether he should enter the front door or go in through the porch adjoining the kitchen. He opted for the front. But before he went in, he looked back at John's house and saw that everyone had crowded the window with expectant faces. Up the road from the house more townspeople were arriving, no doubt having heard of the visitor from beyond the grave.

Maurice took some precautions. He didn't want to be seen when he confronted Ellen Dower. If something went wrong and the people outside saw it, he knew that the people would never shut up about it, so he slammed the front door behind him when he entered the parlour. He was cut off from the others now. Taking a few steps toward the centre of the room, he was startled by a noise coming from the kitchen. It sounded like someone crying and saying, over and over, "Oh my, oh my, oh my."

He froze. "Is that you, Mrs. Dower?"

A voice replied. "Yes, it's me."

"Conche: A True Story" is an article that appeared in *Christmas Bells* in 1899, written by one J.W. Kinsella. According to Kinsella, Ellen Dower "was a most ladylike, winsome woman; tall, straight, majestic, and refined; a lady to my appearance, who once seen, never forgotten."

But the figure sitting before Maurice Power was quite the opposite. Ellen was unrecognizable, haggard and worn, her hair hanging limply over her face and touching the top of the stove. She shivered in her chair like a dog just out of frigid water, her teeth clacking like spoons. The cloth Granny Carroll had used to brace her jaw was slung over the back of the chair, and she had also removed her shroud and thrown it to the floor. The sound she made as she stared blankly at the stove struck Maurice as peculiar, kind of like a soft hiss. But something else struck him as hilarious. If young Moses Lewis hadn't taken off like a scalded cat, he could have told the people that Ellen Dower was wearing her white lambskin coat when she arose from her casket.

"What do you want, Mrs. Dower?" Maurice asked. There was no sympathy in his voice.

Ellen didn't look up. She recognized the voice. "Will you get Kizzie for me, please?" she stammered.

"All right," said Maurice. He was about to leave when he gave Ellen one last look. "You better move back from the stove a little, Mrs. Dower, before your hair catches on fire."

Ellen nodded and hopped her chair a few feet away from the stove.

Maurice strode back through the parlour and pushed open the front door. The people who had retreated to the relative safety of John's kitchen had found the courage to come as near to the house as the Dowers' front yard. Maurice grinned when he saw the silly priest among them.

"Kizzie, your mother wants you to come right away."

Ellen's oldest daughter pushed her way through the crowd and stood speechless before Maurice Power.

"Your mother wants to see you," he repeated.

Kizzie was frozen to the spot. It was said that she wasn't afraid of anything, but her courage had run out tonight. Emiline, who was standing near her, offered to go with her.

"All right, Emiline," Kizzie said, sighing. "If you go with me, I'll go."

"Well, come on," Maurice said impatiently and walked back inside. Kizzie and Emiline followed closely with their arms locked around each other.

* * *

MAURICE WENT DIRECTLY to the kitchen. Ellen was still sitting near the stove, shivering like a lost child. Casting a glance behind him, Maurice saw that the girls had stopped short of the kitchen doorway. He shook his head in disgust and went to the table. He wrapped his big meaty arms around the coffin and dragged it, cover and all, out of the kitchen and through the parlour. Stopping at the front door, Maurice drew back and heaved the wooden box into the snowbank, much to the awe of the spectators. He then went back in and slammed the door behind him. Walking up behind Emiline and Kizzie, who were huddled together in fright, he laid a reassuring hand on each girl's shoulder and they let out identical yelps.

"Listen, you two," he said. "Mrs. Dower wants you."

Summoning the courage to face whatever was in the kitchen (If Maurice Power could do it, Kizzie thought, then so could she), the two young women counted to three and took the last step to the kitchen. Kizzie's mouth dropped open and her eyes rolled up to whites. She collapsed in a heap.

"Get a cold cloth," Emiline said to Maurice.

Maurice wasn't interested in cold cloths. Instead, he went outside and scooped up a handful of snow, brought it inside and dropped it onto Kizzie's forehead. Emiline scowled at Maurice, but her anger was short-lived. Kizzie came to at once. She looked balefully at the figure that could only be her mother. Emiline helped her up, and together they approached Ellen as if she were the devil.

Emiline placed her hand on Ellen's forehead.

"I'm not dead, Emiline."

Emiline didn't think she'd ever hear her future mother-in-law speak again. But she was alive! Her face lit up in a big grin, and she hugged Ellen fiercely as though afraid she would again be taken away at any moment.

"Your mother needs you, Kizzie," Maurice said, looking at the girl who stood dumbfounded beside her mother. "You might as well stop the foolishness and get to work."

Kizzie broke down then and embraced her mother, sobbing with joy, sorrow, regret, and hope all at once.

"Oh my, Mother," was all she could manage.

"Watch out, you two. Don't fall on that stove," Maurice warned.

Kizzie and Emiline noticed for the first time that Ellen was wearing her lambskin coat.

"Mother," said Kizzie, crying and laughing at the same time, "stand up—we'll take that old coat off you."

"I can't stand up, Kizzie. I think I've got my leg broken," said Ellen. "I fell down near the Grey Islands when I went out, and I almost killed myself. Just look at my leg." She pulled her wedding dress up to her knee and exposed a nasty cut on her shin.

"Mother, what have you got done?"

The skin on her leg was torn and pulled back, and blood oozed slowly from the wound. The two young women didn't hesitate in lifting her up and stripping the sodden lambskin coat off her. Kizzie went to the master bedroom, where Ellen had lain dead two days ago, and retrieved a warm woollen blanket.

It was then that the devil in Maurice Power took over.

He snatched the lambskin coat from the floor and got a mad look in his eye. He swore as he stalked out to the front door. When he reached it, he kicked it open. The French priest was standing at the front of the crowd, and his eyes widened along with everyone else's when he spied what Maurice held in his hands.

Maurice walked up to him and started shouting. "Look at this, Father Gore! Do you recognize this coat?" Before the priest could answer, he said, "Well, it's the coat you accused me of stealing from Mrs. Dower. She says she was wearing it when she walked out to the *Elsie.* If you weren't a priest, I'd knock that holy head off your shoulders. Now, if you want it, here it is."

He tossed the wet coat at the priest with enough force to knock him backward. If there hadn't been a crowd behind him to break his fall, Father Gore would have been flattened to the snow yet again. Satisfied that his work here was done, Maurice shoved his way through the crowd and made his way to his father-in-law's house.

He called for Will when he stepped inside John's kitchen. "You better go over to your house and take over the situation. I doubt Kizzie will be able to handle it."

Will and Rose asked as one, "What's going on, Maurice?"

"She said that she went out along by the Grey Islands and fell down and almost broke her leg. Anyway, she can't stand on it."

He pointed a finger at Will. "There's only one thing I can tell you. Your mother looks a hundred years old."

When they pressed for more information, he told them to go and ask her themselves. "I'm going to turn in now," he said simply, and went into the next room.

26

About an hour later, things started to quiet down. Maurice Power had broken the tension for the crowd outside Ellen's house, so now when they peered inside it was more out of curiosity than fear. The sound of her crying drifted out to them.

With each passing minute, the pain in Ellen's legs and feet had worsened, so Kizzie called her brothers and sisters inside. Will and Ambrose sat near her alongside the stove while the girls searched the house for warm blankets and clean washcloths. None of Ellen's children spoke the whole time. They just stayed near their beloved mother, grateful to have her back. Kizzie made cup after cup of tea for her, and it was three o'clock in the morning before some warmth crept into her bones. She seemed to regain some of her energy, and Will and the others were encouraged by this.

"I'm glad you knew where Edward hid the land grant," Ellen said to Will. She took his hand in hers. "Will, I want you to forgive me for not believing you in the first place."

Will turned white. Here was his mother, back from the dead, telling him that a lie he had fabricated right off the top of his head was completely true! He struggled with it and felt reasonably certain he was dreaming all this.

Ellen's jaws were sore, she told them. "It must be from where they were shaking so much. I was afraid I was going to break my teeth. When I was coming back, I could hardly see a thing because my hair was down in my eyes all the time. I must have dropped my comb along the way." She paused to sip some more tea. "I hope I find it. That comb was given to me by your aunt Nora as a wedding gift."

The children were stunned by their mother's words. She was saying that she had gone somewhere when her body was laying here in the kitchen the whole time. Had she said something about going out along the Grey Islands? Impossible! Or was it? She was here, after all, sitting up and telling stories after having been dead for two days.

Kizzie was the only one who spoke.

"Yes, Mother," was all she could think to say.

Ellen's hands were beginning to swell. She complained that the area around her fingernails hurt in particular. Ambrose got a pan of ice water and dipped her hands in it, effectively reducing the swelling and dulling the ache. A short time later the girls helped her into the bedroom and removed her ruined wedding dress. They took the one remaining comb out of her hair and put it away, wondering where the other one had gone.

It was a mystery how Ellen could be in such a deplorable condition when she had been laid out neatly in her coffin the whole time. As far as anyone knew, there had been someone watching her at all times. Moses Lewis was the last to see her before she got up out of the casket, and he was drunk out of his mind. But that still didn't explain how their mother had gotten so dishevelled, not to mention the fact that she was standing here as alive as the rest of them. Then there was the question of the return of her lambskin coat...

They helped her into her woollen undergarments and nightdress, not minding in the least that she had to be treated delicately. She whimpered every time her foot touched the ground. Ambrose took one look at the large bruise along her shin and confirmed that the leg was indeed broken. So when she was ready to come out to the kitchen, someone stood on either side of her and eased her along.

John and Rose came in. At first it looked like all the money in the world wouldn't get them to come near Ellen, but Will came over and assured them that it was all right, his mother was going to be just fine. Rose broke down and wept, rushing over to embrace her sister-in-law. John took a few tentative steps toward her, nothing more. Tears were running freely down his face.

"Don't worry, Rose, it's me, and I'm alive," Ellen soothed, wincing when her sister-in-law bumped her broken leg. "I'm not a ghost, you know."

Rose felt a little braver then, and she stood and dried her eyes.

Ellen said, "Edward and the boys have the *Elsie* loaded to the gunwales with seals, John! They're just waiting for the ice to slacken so they can come home."

No one spoke. What Ellen was saying was pure insanity. So maybe she wasn't back to her old self after all. Before she died she had uttered some strange things, no stranger than what they were hearing now. They just stared back at her, wondering what she was going to say next.

"Kizzie, my dear, I want you to forgive me for accusing you of burning the land grant. I was wrong."

Kizzie was astounded. She had always loved her mother and still did, but the last two days were enough to break her heart, knowing that her mother had died accusing her in the wrong. But now things were set right, and this was the first rational thing she'd heard from her mother since this whole mess started. She bubbled with laughter and tears and hugged her mother fiercely.

"You're back, Mother, it's really you. I love you, Mother."

* * *

IT WAS CLOSE TO 3:30 A.M. when Will decided to go out to John's house to see if Maurice was still up. Before leaving he went into the master bedroom and told Kizzie and Nora where he was going. They were rubbing their mother's arms and legs with liniment. Soon Ellen was fast asleep in her bed. Will stared in fascination for a few moments, then bid his sisters a good night.

THE GHOST OF ELLEN DOWER

When he opened the outside door he was met by a strong gust of wind mixed with snow. "A storm coming on," he said. "I knew we were in for some snow."

He found Maurice sleeping on the couch near the stove. He was still fully clothed except for his skin boots. Will couldn't help but admire the man. If not for him, how would this evening have turned out? Not only that, the priest and the rest of the town had been up in arms thinking that Maurice had stolen his mother's coat. He shook his head in disgust at the priest, but he saved a little for himself for doubting his friend.

"Maurice won't be letting the priest get away as easy as that," he mumbled.

"No, you're right," said a voice from the couch.

Will let out a startled yelp. "I thought you were asleep, Maurice."

"Do you think I would risk going to sleep around here, Will?" Maurice asked incredulously.

Will's nerves couldn't take much more abuse tonight. "Maurice, did you ever see or hear talk of anything like this before? I mean, what happened to Mother? Am I in a daze or something?"

Maurice took out his pipe. "Listen, Will," he said between puffs, "I've seen a lot of stuff happen in my day. God knows half of it is not fit to tell, but what has gone on here in Conche in the last two days will keep me awake for a week. Not only what took place with your mother, we will leave that where it is, but the lies that were told about me. Imagine, Will, me, a man that never did anything bad in his life and getting accused of that." Maurice laughed, but Will was too shaken to join in.

Maurice blew sweet-smelling smoke across the kitchen. He got up and tossed some wood in the stove, then sat at the table. "I can tell you why that French priest wanted to cause trouble for me, Will," he said in a conspiratorial tone.

"Why, Maurice?"

"Because ever since I struck that French captain the other summer he has always looked at me with hate in his eyes, as if I was a piece of dirt under his feet."

Will wasn't sure about that, but he nodded anyway.

Maurice nudged the kettle toward the centre of the stove. "Let's have a cup of tea, Will, my boy. You never know what might happen before daylight. It seems we're living in a place now where the dead are coming to life and even the priest is shivering in his shoes, so God only knows what may crawl out of the walls and grab us before the sun comes up."

Will shuddered at the image. "Maurice," he said.

"Yes, Will, what do you want?" Maurice asked, eyeing him suspiciously.

Will didn't know if he should ask or if it were better to keep his mouth shut. The tea Maurice had brewed sat untouched in front of the Dower boy.

"Will, what do you want?" he repeated.

Will cleared his throat. "Now, Maurice, I know you're my best friend, and you know that I'm your close buddy, isn't that right?"

Maurice nodded slowly, not taking his eyes off Will's. "Whatever you've got on your mind, say it, Will. It can't be any worse than what's been said to me the last two days."

Will, a grown man, big and strong, whose size rivalled even that of Maurice Power, bowed his head and said in a shy manner, "They're saying that the reason Mother died or went into a trance, or whatever it was, is something to do with the piece of land next to us. She thinks that you want it or already own it."

Maurice stared at Will until the younger man started feeling a little uncomfortable. "Here, Will," he said finally. "Sweeten your tea while I tell you something."

Will obediently sat and shovelled three spoonfuls of sugar into his mug of strong black tea.

"What do you think, Will? Do you think that I want your land?"

"No. I told Ambrose and Kizzie this afternoon that it was a big mistake. I said that you didn't want our land and that there's plenty of it here in Conche. You only said that to old Martin Flynn to get him going. Anyway, this foolishness has to be straightened out."

Maurice tapped his pipe on the stove. He waved a finger in front of Will's face. "I don't think it would do any good for me to discuss this with you now, but when Uncle Ned gets back I'll be having a talk with him. What Rose told me last night wasn't very nice, and she was there when your mother died or whatever happened to her. So forget about it and drink your tea."

He grinned and added, "Rose baked a raisin cake this morning and put it in the pantry. Go bring it out— we'll destroy it."

* * *

ALL NIGHT LONG, Ellen Dower's family watched her attentively while she slept. She cried all night and called out to Edward in anguish. By dawn, more colour had come back into her cheeks, and the trembling in her limbs eased somewhat. When she awoke, she asked Kizzie if she would take a closer look at her feet.

Kizzie lifted the blanket off her mother's legs and brought the light closer. She worked like a surgeon, treating each foot with delicate care. Ellen drew in a sharp breath each time her daughter's fingers touched bare skin.

"Be careful, Kizzie, be very careful you don't touch my leg. My feet are as tender as boils."

What Kizzie saw when the wool socks finally came off frightened her. Her brothers and sisters sensed her alarm and crowded around her.

Ellen had the biggest blisters on her feet they had ever seen.

"My Blessed Virgin, Mother," Nora asked in surprise, "what has happened to your feet? Your two feet are all bladders and sores."

Ellen gave a shuddering sigh. "I walked over a lot of rough ice within the last two days. What I had on my feet wasn't fit to wear. They were Emiline's old skin boots. They didn't even have a pair of rubbers over them."

None of them yet believed their mother had made any trek out to the Grey Islands and beyond to the *Elsie*. But here was evidence to the contrary.

"Mother, we'll go for Mrs. Carroll and see if there's anything she can do."

All morning people came to the Dower house. They stayed only for a few minutes, long enough to put any doubts they had about Ellen Dower rising from the dead to rest. When they left, they all wore identical expressions of amazement on their faces.

People were still coming to witness Ellen's miraculous return when the old granny woman Mrs. Carroll shuttled on ahead of them aboard a dogsled. "How could this be?" began the talk, for Granny Carroll was known only to show up when someone was gravely ill. The people of Conche could only wait and pray that Ellen Dower hadn't come back from the dead only to say goodbye again.

27

Edward Dower was on deck with the rest of the crew before daylight. Overnight the wind had picked up from the southeast, and the watchmen notified the captain early in the morning that a storm was brewing. The *Elsie* was sandwiched between two bodies of ice that had come together while moving down from the Arctic. The larger of the two moved imperceptibly, appearing to be stationary, while the other was moving with the southerly Arctic current. The crew watched, powerless, as the latter flew by carrying a horde of seals.

"What can you see up ahead of her, boys?" Edward asked.

He looked up at the crow's nest. The barrelman was excited this morning, because the ice ahead had looked like it was breaking abroad for quite some time now. The last thing on Edward's mind now was dreams or supernatural visitors.

"The edge up ahead is coming open, Skipper," the lookout called. "We'll know more about it when it gets lighter, but the wind sure is picking up."

Edward called for Walter, who was up front watching the ice around the bulwarks. He came back to see what Edward wanted. Although Walter was now officially in charge due to Edward's diminished capacity, he still deferred to the captain and appreciated any advice he could give.

"What do you think of it, Skipper?"

"Start putting all the canvas on her right away, Walter."

Walter looked up at the rigging. He could hear the wind whistling through the cables, so there was no doubt that the sails would fill. But what concerned him was the thought that because the *Elsie* was heavily loaded (and overloaded, he feared), raising the canvas now might send them into a sharp piece of ice. They would be sunk, for sure.

"Maybe we should only put up part of the canvas until we get into open water."

"I know what you're getting at, Walter," Edward said, "but in order for the *Elsie* to get out of this ice, it will take every bit of canvas up there in the wind to get her free. Not only that, this wind might not keep up for long, so let's make good use of it. Get it all up for now, and we can always take some of it down later."

The captain made a strong argument, so Walter relayed the information to the men. In the space of an hour they hoisted the canvas and put it in place, and as luck would have it, it took less time for the mighty barque to escape the clutches of the ice and break into open water. Dawn was breaking when she burst through, and the whole crew let out a triumphant cheer. "We're going home," Edward shouted.

* * *

CONCHE WAS ASSAULTED by wind and snow that morning. The townspeople huddled in their homes, still in shock over the recent events surrounding Ellen Dower. They included Maurice Power in their conversations as well, and more than a few people were beginning to see him in an altogether different light.

Early in the morning Maurice harnessed his dogs and took his family home. When they reached their house in Silver Cove, he said to Mary, "I think I'll go out to Cape Fox and see if I can get a shot of ducks."

"Listen, Maurice, I don't want you to leave me this morning," Mary begged. "I'm still scared about last night. It's like Mother said, she thinks we will hear bad news before the day is out. Please, I want you to stay around."

Maurice wasn't one for taking orders or even following advice. But he felt like a changed man today. Mary hadn't gotten much sleep at her father's house, and he could tell that she was still frightened.

"All right," he surrendered. "I'll wait 'til this afternoon and go out then."

* * *

WHEN THE ELSIE GOT UNDERWAY with her canvas hoisted and her sails trimmed, Edward asked Walter, "How far do you think we are from Grey Islands Tickle?"

Walter was a man who had proven himself to be an excellent navigator over the years. He could estimate time and distance with almost pinpoint accuracy. Of course, he was the first to admit that he was no match for Skipper Ned Dower, and he would say so whenever asked.

"Last night around midnight I took a shot and estimated that we were about forty miles southeast of the northern Grey Islands, give or take."

Edward stared into the falling snow. "I'd say that you're close. What do you say we alter course a little to the western?"

Walter clasped his hands and rested his forearms on the rail. "Let her run for an hour," he said. "That'll give us a chance just in case we happen to run into heavy ice packed in on the back of the northern island. At least then we'll know what we're up against."

Edward nodded in approval. "You're right, Walter. I was thinking about that. It's better for us to be up the windward than down the leeward." He listened to the *Elsie* groan as her left gunwale dipped in the water. "If we don't strike any heavy ice, we should be close to Grey Islands Tickle by noon. The wind lop won't hurt us even though we're log-loaded. There's no heavy sea."

Walter could tell that every passing minute was taking its toll on Edward. The old sea dog still looked worried, the muscles in his ashen face appearing tight. But it wouldn't be long now before they reached home. According to the wind that now picked up from the southeast, Walter estimated they would be in Conche Harbour by evening.

* * *

MAURICE POWER LEFT his home for Cape Fox around one o'clock in the afternoon. Mary had calmed after a hot meal and some quiet time with the family. She still looked on edge like the rest of Conche, but Maurice figured that given time she would come around. He, of course, didn't need any consoling, and he took off for the headland with his spyglass slung around his neck and his team of dogs running full out.

* * *

THE ELSIE WHISKED to the northwest through snow all morning. The lookouts watched for bergs and strings of drifting ice. At eleven-thirty, Edward and Walter got together and discussed changing course.

"I think we should change our course to the west now. What do you think, Walter?"

His friend nodded.

"We should be within seven, eight miles of the Grey Islands by now," Edward explained. "Everything looks good."

"I think the snow is starting to let up," Walter said, looking around.

"I don't want it to let up yet. The wind might change to another direction if that happens," Edward replied.

A southeast gale of thirty-five knots pushed the burdened *Elsie* to the west and toward Grey Islands Tickle. Within an hour, the barrelman cried out, "Land ho, Skipper, fair ahead!" His voice carried over the spray and the creaking of the rigging.

Neither Edward nor Walter heard him. They were holding a private meeting below at Edward's insistence.

"We'll hoist one flag at half-mast."

Walter was unsure. "Listen, Skipper," he said uneasily, "just suppose Ellen is not dead."

Edward's eyes narrowed. "You're not calling me a liar, are you, Walter Joy?" His voice was like steel.

"No," Walter put in quickly, "but what I'm trying to say, Skipper, is what kind of an uproar will there be in Conche when they see us coming into the harbour with the flag at half-mast?"

Edward fell silent. When he did speak, Walter could hear the sternness in his voice.

"We will hoist the flag at half-mast for my dead wife," Edward said with a note of finality.

Walter didn't want to start an argument, not when they were this close to home. He sighed and hefted the Union Jack, taking it with him when he returned on deck. The Grey Islands loomed straight ahead now. They were almost home.

* * *

MAURICE POWER ARRIVED at Cape Fox shortly before two o'clock in the afternoon. He tied his sled to a tree in a ravine and unharnessed the dog he used for picking up shot birds. Taking his floating jigger, he walked up to the top of the hill to spy around for flying ducks, wondering as he went if there would be a company under the cliffs near the shoreline.

His spyglass showed nothing around the shoreline, just a string of heavy slob ice serving to block the eiders' access to the shoreline. This was where the shore ducks would normally feed in the late afternoon, but today there was little chance of that. To his dismay, the largest group of ducks lay far out by Crouse Gull Island; the large flocks that bobbed in the water out there taunted him.

He scanned the area through his glass and licked his lips. "If I was out there, I would only want one shot with this inch bore," he mourned. "I know there must be some awful companies of ducks out on the back of the Grey Islands. What a place to go, if only I—"

He stopped. "Wait a minute."

He thought his eyes were deceiving him.

Steadying his spyglass again, he said, "The *Elsie*. Yes, 'tis the *Elsie*, all right, with a full load." The ship wasn't yet close enough to pick out any of the people on board. "Not a thing in her way and a fair wind. She should be in the harbour in two hours."

He got another surprise then.

"Hmm," he mused. "Well hello, what's going on here?

"She's flying her flag at half-mast. Someone is dead on board the *Elsie*."

* * *

FATHER GORE KNELT in his study. He prayed all morning for Ellen Dower and her family, and of course for Edward and his crew. The thought came to him as he

274

was praying that he should hold a special Mass for them. Ellen, who was suffering untold agony in her feet and legs, could use all the support he could give. What had happened to her within the last few days was miraculous, and he was at a loss for an explanation. He was satisfied to leave it in the hands of the Man above.

He rang the bell for his assistant and asked him to go around town and notify everyone that he would be at the Dower house to say Mass for them. He would be adding his support to Granny Carroll, who had done all she could to ease the pain in Ellen's legs and feet. Father Gore was like that. He was considered a good man, always willing to drop everything when one of the people in town got into trouble.

When one o'clock came, he led a crowd of people to Ellen's house. He had sent word to the Dowers that he was coming, so Kizzie had tidied the place in advance. Father Gore entered the house with a beatific smile on his face, his purple robe and large crucifix on a chain around his neck giving him a regal appearance. He stood over a bedridden Ellen Dower and proceeded to read from the Holy Bible. After the reading, the rosary was said.

Father Gore looked at Ellen's bandaged leg. He fished around in his robe and withdrew a vial containing a clear liquid. "Mrs. Dower," he said, "I'm going to put some holy water on your feet and legs. Let us pray that they get better."

Standing near the bed was Granny Carroll. She had as strong a faith as the priest himself, but the look she gave him was laced with skepticism. Earlier, she had diagnosed that Ellen was suffering from a fractured leg, and her home remedies had given Mrs. Dower only minimal relief. Her only instructions to the family had been to keep their mother in bed and to hold her leg in an elevated position. She'd put a tight bandage over the bruised area and explained that this would prevent the leg from swelling out of shape. Of course, she volunteered to stay with the family all day.

Ellen was willing to give it a try. "Father, will you please bless my hands as well?"

"Yes, my dear," Father Gore said, and began to sprinkle the blessed water upon her wounds. When he finished, he said "Amen" and brought the service to a close.

* * *

JOHN DOWER WAS SITTING at his table nursing a cup of tea. Something caught his eye out the window. "Looks like Maurice," he said. "He must have been out on the cape looking for ducks. I hope he got some."

He watched his son-in-law hitch his dogs to the fence and make for the kitchen door. The door squealed loudly when he came in.

"Have a cup of tea, Maurice," John greeted him.

"Yes, I think I will."

The door opened again and Will stepped in, shivering from the cold.

"How's everything going, Will?" Maurice asked. "What have you been doing?"

"I just came from the Mass Father Gore had at the house for Mother."

Maurice let out a hearty laugh.

Rose spoke up from the table. "Oh, don't laugh at that, Maurice. That's too serious to laugh at."

Maurice just grinned. "This is one time that his prayers were answered."

Rose, John and Will just looked at him as he shovelled spoonfuls of sugar into his cup.

"What do you mean, Maurice?" Rose was the first to ask.

"I just came from Cape Fox. The *Elsie* is on her way in, just coming through Grey Islands Tickle. She should be in the harbour in about two hours."

Everyone threw their hands in the air and cheered. Rose blessed herself and gave thanks to the Almighty Father. There was something in Maurice's face that alerted Will, though.

"What's wrong?"

Maurice gave the three of them an uneasy look. "When I tell you this, I don't want you to panic. I have bad news for you." They fell silent at the seriousness in his voice.

"The *Elsie* is flying her flag at half-mast."

28

"Someone is dead on board the *Elsie*" came the cry that spread like wildfire throughout Conche. The uproar Walter and Edward had expected back home started about then. "It's my Jack," "It's my Frank," "It's my Jim," wailed the despairing towns-people. Men and women were running amok, darting in and out of houses and spreading the word before heading down to the waterfront with their spyglasses in hand.

The *Elsie* was halfway between Conche and the Grey Islands when the townsfolk arrived at the harbour entrance. "She's loaded to the water," someone remarked. But that was the last thing on their minds, because the Union Jack, as Maurice had said, was fluttering in the breeze at half-mast. One old fellow whose son was a crewman under Skipper Ned Dower watched the vessel with tears in his eyes. No one was happy to see the gallant vessel coming in the harbour; the sign of death seemed to blot out the horizon.

Those in Ellen's room were notified of the *Elsie* and her flag. Father Gore struggled with all that had happened within the past week. So much had happened surrounding Ellen Dower: she had died of mysterious causes and come back to life, her lambskin coat had vanished and come back in the wink of an eye, and now the *Elsie* was returning with bad news flying from her masthead. He wondered idly if this last had something to do with Mrs. Dower. But no, people died all the time. One of Edward's crew must have taken ill or drowned. He uttered a short prayer and prepared to receive the deceased.

"Someone is dead, so be prepared," he cautioned the people still in Ellen's room. Then he left to see to the people down in the harbour.

"Father is on his way in from the Grey Islands with a full load of seals," Nora said. Kizzie looked at her with a worried frown. How could she think of seals at a time like this?

To Kizzie's surprise, Ellen laughed. "Didn't I tell you that they were fully loaded?"

The girls gave each other a sidelong glance. Their mother had done nothing but groan in pain ever since she had awakened. But now when news had come that someone was dead on board the *Elsie*, she laughed! For all anyone knew, the dead person could be Edward himself. But Ellen was unconcerned. She ordered her children to bring her clothes—she was getting out of bed, fractured leg or no.

* * *

279

THE FACES THAT STARED out over the water at the approaching ship were frightened and melancholy. Death was on everyone's mind. "How could this happen?" people were asking each other. Skipper Ned Dower had never lost a man before, and despite the storms and illnesses and other misadventures he'd witnessed, he had never come home to Conche without all the bunting flying at the top of the mast and guns roaring to advertise his successful voyage. Apparently, his luck had run out.

Some of the men at the lower end of Conche saw the top of the mast slide into view.

"Here she comes, boys" said one salty old sea dog.

"She's homeward bound with our dead boys," said a bearded man. He sighed and said, "Let's get down to the wharf and tell the crowd."

The old seaman held up a hand. "Not yet, sir," he said. He'd sailed with Edward many times before. "I still think someone is telling lies. I've got to see that flag for myself."

The full breadth of the vessel crept into their field of vision. "Sure enough," said the man with the beard. "'Tis true—Uncle Ned has lost someone."

The old sea dog had his doubts, but he kept them to himself.

* * *

CONCHE HARBOUR is a well-protected place. It is sheltered from every wind that blows. There is a point at the entrance where a light has indicated to mariners for hundreds of years that the harbour is near. "Steady as she goes" has been the order given down through the centuries to well-trained sailors who approached this spot and prepared to round the point of land. Cook, Cabot, Banks and Grenfell each sailed into Conche Harbour and dropped anchor, carrying good news of exploration, discovery, knowledge and medicine, but what Edward Dower carried was something different. Was it death, disaster, tales of horror? No one knew. Soon he would be taking in his canvas and reefing the sails, and soon he would be telling the people at the harbour the news they didn't want to hear.

Kizzie helped her mother out of bed. She could hardly believe her eyes when Ellen got up and walked around the room using both feet. "Mother," she stammered, "your feet are better. I can't believe it!" She started trembling. "This is a miracle, Mother. Let me see your feet."

Ellen couldn't explain it. "Yes, it's a miracle, Kizzie," she gasped. "Ever since Father Gore put the holy water on me, I haven't felt any pain."

"Emiline! Come in and see Mother," Kizzie shouted.

But Emiline didn't answer. Kizzie stuck her head out the doorway and was about to call her again, when she noticed the young woman staring out the window. Her eyes were glued to the vessel coming in the harbour.

"My God," Emiline whispered. "It's true, the flag is flying at half-mast. I wonder if it's my Frank?"

Ellen walked out into the kitchen and joined Emiline Strong at the window. She rested a hand on the young woman's shoulder. "I'm better, Emiline," she said. "Just look at me."

Emiline couldn't look away from the Union Jack billowing in the wind. Her eyes welled up and she held Ellen tighter than she should have, considering Mrs. Dower's physical state. "The *Elsie*," she said, "is in the harbour. Something is wrong on board."

Ellen's smile never wavered. "Ha! Don't worry about that flag, Emiline. There's no one dead on board the *Elsie*. Edward has that flag flying for me—he thinks I'm the one who's dead. Don't you worry about it."

For the first time, Emiline noticed the woman standing next to her. She didn't see a sick woman. She didn't see anyone incapable of walking or sitting up. What she did see was someone full of vitality.

Ellen gave her shoulder an affectionate squeeze. "Help me get ready, Emiline. I'm going down to meet the *Elsie* and the crew."

* * *

EDWARD DIDN'T KNOW what to expect as he neared his hometown. Part of him felt foolish, that maybe he had imagined his wife coming into his quarters on the seventeenth of March and opening the land grant. But no, the more he thought about it, the more real it seemed. Then, of course, there was the silver comb she had left behind.

But as the *Elsie* approached Cape Fox, Edward's doubts resurfaced. "What will the people think when they see me coming in the harbour with the flag at half-mast?" he said ashamedly. *Fully loaded, with no bunting flying. Suppose all the goings-on within the last few days about Ellen was only a fantasy brought on by fatigue.*

"Should I take down the flag?"

His mind wrestled with the idea. "No," he concluded. Absolutely not.

Those on the wharf were deathly still, and Walter knew it was because of the Union Jack. He chided himself for thinking it, but the captain seemed like he was going out of his mind. The whole town was worried sick all because Skipper Ned had a dream.

"Skipper," he called down the stairway, "we're in around the point now, and in a few minutes we'll be into the wharf, so come on deck."

Edward looked up at his best friend and said with pleading in his voice, "Walter, I want you to do something for me. Promise me that if there's nothing wrong at home you'll have me put in a straitjacket and delivered to the insane asylum at St. John's."

Walter chose to ignore that. "Come on deck, Skipper," he repeated. "We've got our plans made. Before you take command again, there's just one thing I want you to do."

Edward blinked. "What's that?"

"Give me that bottle of rum."

Edward opened his sea-chest and took out the bottle of dark rum. Without a word, he handed it to Walter Joy.

* * *

THE ELSIE WAS ALMOST at the wharf by the time Nora got her mother into her lambskin coat.

"Are you sure you can walk down to the wharf, Mother?"

"Yes," Ellen said with a grin, "I'm sure, Nora. I'm as good now as I ever was." She motioned to Kizzie. "Go quickly to the trunk and bring me that silver comb that I wore in my hair, the one I wore back from my trip to the icefields. Do you remember where you put it?"

Kizzie flashed her a smile and ran upstairs to the trunk where she and Ellen had searched frantically for the land grant before this whole mess started. It seemed so long ago to the young woman now. Stopping only to cast a wary glance at the Giant stove sitting politely by the wall, she snatched the comb out of the trunk and ran downstairs.

"Now," Ellen instructed, "put it in my hair the way it was before you took it out."

Kizzie did as she was told. The comb didn't hold the hair the way it should have, but she knew her mother wanted it that way.

Ellen was grinning from ear to ear. "Nora, get me a towel that I can wrap around my head."

Emiline Strong looked at her future mother-in-law. Except for the loss of eight pounds, you would never say the woman had been dead for two days. She was alive and well and laughing like a giddy young girl. It was good to have her back.

"Come on," Ellen giggled when everything was in place. "Let's head for the wharf, all four of us, before the celebrating starts."

They couldn't help themselves. Ellen's laugh was infectious, and the four of them started laughing like madwomen as they set out for the waterfront.

* * *

EDWARD DIDN'T REMEMBER ever seeing a sorrier-looking bunch than the people crowded on the water-front. His crew stared in silence at their friends and family on shore. Among the faces were a few that caught Edward's eye: Father Gore, Moses Lewis, John and his family, Martin Flynn, Will and Ambrose. The girls were nowhere to be seen.

No sign of Ellen, either.

Martin Flynn stepped forward and caught the line. He threw it over the grump on the wharf, then looked up at the *Elsie*. He took another step toward the vessel and turned to cast one last look at the assembled people before staring up into Skipper Ned Dower's face.

"Tell us," he shouted through his cupped hands. "Is all well on board the *Elsie*?"

Edward frowned and looked at Walter. Walter caught the look and stepped up to the rail. Cupping his hands around his mouth, he replied, "All is well on board the *Elsie*, sir."

Silence.

"Tell us. Is all well ashore, sir?"

Martin threw up his hands and shouted at the top of his lungs, "All is well on shore, sir!"

The place went up. The cheer that erupted from the people standing behind the wharf was met by one equally loud from aboard the *Elsie*. The sound of their voices echoed and re-echoed throughout the hills of Conche Harbour, making a sound the likes of which had never been heard before, nor since.

Walter had everything ready to go. Earlier that day, while Edward and his sons were engaged in a private service for Ellen Dower, he had told the crew that there was a possibility their skipper was wrong in assuming Ellen was dead. So, he had instructed the men to make a few preparations of their own.

"FIRE."

Ten muskets boomed into the air in unison. Walter himself walked deliberately to the mast and raised the Union Jack until it soared high above the rigging. Then he raised his voice and ordered, "Hoist the bunting, men, for a successful voyage and a safe return."

With that, flags of every colour went aloft, and Edward choked back tears as he said, "We will drink to the people of our hometown, Conche, and to the untold mysteries that happened here."

* * *

ELLEN AND THE GIRLS pushed their way to the front of the crowd when they heard the cheering and the deafening roar of the guns. The bunting sailing high above danced in the air and filled them with a sense of pride. All was well on board the *Elsie*, just as Ellen had said, but the girls cheered and laughed along with the others anyway, not bothering to stop and question how she came by this bit of knowledge. Then someone in the crowd noticed that she was standing on her own two feet, and then another person, then another. Soon the crowd was alive with talk of yet another miracle.

* * *

EDWARD AND THE BOYS on deck gulped the heavy rum until each man felt a warm little fire in the pit of his belly. Then something caught Edward's attention, a noise from the shore. He walked over to the rail and looked out over the side. What flashed through his mind was the night Ellen, in her ghostly attire, had come aboard the *Elsie* looking for the land grant. Standing on shore was the same mysterious figure wearing Ellen's lambskin coat with the hood pulled up. When she pulled the hood down, he could see on her head a scarf or strip of cloth wrapped in an identical fashion as the shroud she had worn that night. Then that came off, and all he saw was Ellen, beautiful Ellen, smiling at him and looking very much alive. Shimmering in her hair was a silver comb, the twin of that stowed away in his sea-chest.

Edward climbed onto the rail and leaped down, landing squarely on the wharf. Ellen stood before him. He cried as he rushed to her and enfolded her in his arms.

Ellen Dower, the woman from Conche who had come back from the dead, the woman whom Edward thought he'd never see alive again, hugged him as if she would never let go.

"You're back, Edward, and so am I."

29

Maurice Power sat at his kitchen table and watched the *Elsie* with his spyglass through the window. He hadn't yet told his wife about the portentous Union Jack flying at half-mast. He laid the glass on the table and said while staring off into space, "Something is wrong."

"What did you say, Maurice?" asked Mary, coming into the kitchen at the sound of her husband's voice.

He felt a momentary twinge of guilt for not having told her. "Uncle Ned has a full load. But," he said, his voice dropping low, "he's flying his flag at half-mast. Must be something wrong."

Mary looked from her husband to the window. The *Elsie* was far away but still visible even here in Silver Cove. She could tell without the aid of a glass that the vessel was riding low on the water. Putting her hands to her face, she said in a worried tone, "I wonder what's wrong, Maurice?"

"I don't know, Mary, my dear, but it's bad news for sure."

The first thing to leap into her mind was the day her brothers joined Uncle Ned's crew. And what about Frank Dower, who was her cousin and Emiline Strong's fiancé? Was he all right? And what about his brother Peter?

"Come on, Maurice, let's head down to Mother and Father's right now. I'm not staying here."

Maurice knew it would be wise for her to be with her family in case the news involved one of her brothers. He'd held off telling her because he didn't want her to drag him down to that crowd. He was still fuming at Father Gore for having acted as judge, jury and executioner on him when he had nothing to do with the theft of Ellen's lambskin coat.

"All right," he said. "I'll get the dogs harnessed while you get the children ready."

Within five minutes they were on their way. When they arrived at John Dower's house, they saw all of the residents of Conche coming up the road. Leading them, to their utmost surprise, were Edward and Ellen Dower. Maurice saw Father Gore near the front of the crowd, so he left his family and darted into his father-in-law's house.

When he closed the door behind him, he shook his head in disbelief. "Ellen Dower walking," he said. "Must be a miracle of some kind."

* * *

THERE WAS VERY LITTLE Edward could say to his wife as they walked along the narrow path. He had hundreds of questions he wanted to ask, but as relieved as he was to see his beloved Ellen alive and well, they could wait. Word was starting to reach every corner of Conche, about Ellen's unearthly trek seventy miles out to the *Elsie*, the silver comb left behind, and the effect it had had on Edward and the crew. Most important—and most unbelievable, if the truth be known—to some was the load of over six thousand seal pelts the mighty barque *Elsie* now carried.

Edward had to get a grip on himself when the crowd told him about Ellen's death and her subsequent resurrection. He didn't miss that the two days she had spent laid out in her coffin coincided with the strange feeling he'd had aboard the *Elsie*, culminating on the night when Ellen's spirit visited him. He couldn't help but give Walter an "I told you so" look. But he put it out of his mind now, because the important thing was Ellen was here in the flesh, in spite of all his emotional turmoil since that night.

Before Edward and his family reached the house, he stopped and asked John if he would get Martin Flynn and a couple of other men to go to the *Elsie* and haul up his sea-chest for him. He then thanked everyone for their support and asked if he could be left alone with his family. "There are a lot of things left to talk about. We also have to make plans for a big time, maybe tomorrow night." They all grinned when they remembered the last time they had held.

But, there was no smile on poor young Moses Lewis's face this morning as he walked away with the crowd.

* * *

KIZZIE WAS ECSTATIC to see her father, and she refused to leave his side the whole time. Edward had a very special place in his heart for his oldest daughter. She always assumed the most responsibility when it came to housework. Cooking, cleaning, washing and ironing clothes, she was the most dependable of his children whenever these things needed to be done. The house was always kept warm, as Kizzie continually checked the stoves upstairs and down to make sure they were stocked. And no matter the time of day, she could be counted on to make breakfast or a lunch for guests under the Dower roof. Edward often said that if Kizzie ever left, the house would collapse. He laughingly referred to her as his second-in-command on shore.

After Edward and Ellen were treated by Kizzie to the first good home-cooked meal either of them had eaten in awhile, Edward sent for John and Rose. He thanked his daughter for the delicious meal and asked her if she would mind letting the adults have some privacy.

"There's something we have to take care of that's very important," he told her, "so I want you to go up to Father Gore's and ask him if he can be here at eight o'clock for a meeting with us. Tell him it's important."

Kizzie obeyed her father, whom she always treated with utmost respect. Edward then asked Will to go up to Silver Cove and ask Maurice Power if he would come down tonight at around nine. He wanted Mary to be there as well.

"Maurice and Mary are out to Uncle John's house," Will said. "They've been out there all evening."

"Good," Edward said, tapping his fingers on the table. "I want you to go out and ask him if he'll stay there 'til around nine o'clock. Tell him that I would like to talk to him and Mary."

Will nodded. "Yes, Father."

* * *

JOHN AND ROSE came out to Edward's at six-thirty that evening. Edward's brother didn't know what to make of the events here in Conche and out on the *Elsie* in the last few days. Now he had a feeling Edward wanted to talk to him about something he'd just as soon forget.

"Let's go upstairs to the loft room," Edward greeted them.

The heat emanating from the Giant bathed the guests when they reached the top of the stairs. The four of them sat around the table, and Edward got down to business right away. "Since this incident happened, I've been to hell and back, and only God knows I'm lucky to be here. It's a wonder that I didn't jump over the side and end it all.

"Now, tonight we're going to settle these goings-on once and for all. If not, I'm going to get out of Conche for good. I've made up my mind."

Rose was stunned. She knew there was something wrong all along, but she didn't have any idea what it could be. The looks passed between her husband and nephew Will in the past few days were enough to drive her crazy. Ellen's dying words had been nagging at the back of her mind as well.

"Ned, stop," she said. "Will someone tell me what this is all about? Just what is going on?"

Edward didn't know how much Rose knew about Maurice Power's attack on Henry Winton. However, he had little patience for gossip or speculation.

"That's what I'm talking about now, Rose," he said impatiently. "Maybe we should have talked about it before. Anyway, the time has come now to try and get it straightened out." He paused long enough to light his pipe. He bit down on the stem and turned to John, who looked back at his brother nervously.

"John, can you remember Father talking about the land we're on?"

"What do you mean, 'talking about this land'?"

"You're older than I am, John, so you should be able to remember better than me."

John Dower nodded in agreement. In fact, he prided himself on his good memory. "What are you getting at, Ned?"

Edward tossed his pipe on the table. "Can you remember Father talking about an old man by the name of Maurice de la Pour? He was a French pirate who jumped ship down at Fishot Island and went to Englee. He took over the French rooms as caretaker, then came here and went caretaker for the French. You know, the year before the fire burned everything down and they moved up to Silver Cove for rebuilding."

"Yes," John said. "I can remember Father talking about that now. That was a long time ago, Ned. You weren't very old then."

"I know, but I can remember it quite well all the same. I also heard Father say that this pirate said the French gave him this land as payment."

John nodded slowly. "Yes, I can remember that now. Is that the same incident he used to talk about, the time they fought over the land here and when he almost got killed?"

"Yes, that's the right time," Edward said. He grabbed his pipe and took a couple of puffs. "There's something very suspicious going on here, you know. Remember what he said about that old pirate? He said that he changed his name to Maurice Pour."

John started to laugh. "Yes! He's the fellow they used to say ran away with the Irishwoman from Herring Neck and was never heard talk of again."

"Father said that one day a schooner left here for St. John's," Edward continued, "and the skipper told him afterwards that he never gave passage to anyone by the name of de la Pour. He only had a Mr. Power and his wife aboard."

"You're right," John said. "I can hear him now. This pirate would say to Father, 'One day I will be back to get my land. If I don't get it I'll will wake up the dead and get it.'"

The two men and two woman sat for some time and just looked at each other.

Edward broke the silence. "I guess you're thinking the same thing I am. It could be possible. Yes, it *is* possible. Maurice could be the son of the pirate Maurice de la Pour."

Despite all she had been through in the past few days, Ellen was shocked most of all by this revelation.

She looked at Rose, who could only stare back in horrified silence. Her daughter was married to a pirate's son? How could this be? This was too much for her. But what she didn't know, and what John, Edward and Ellen carefully skirted around, was that her son-in-law was wanted by the British Government with a 1,500 pound price on his head for the mutilation of Henry Winton on Saddle Hill.

"Is it any wonder that Maurice just walked into this house when Ellen was laid out in her coffin, as if he was just going to a Sunday picnic?" Rose grinned like a crazy person. "The son of a pirate, hey," she mumbled.

Rose loved Maurice as a son-in-law, and she was sure that he loved her. She had never heard him say anything bad about her or anyone else since he came to Conche. Sure, he had his ways, and most of them were bad (if the people around here were to be believed), but she had never seen any bad in him. He worked night and day and would give you anything and do anything for you. She didn't care if he was a pirate or an outlaw, or even that he may have had a shady past at all. After last night, Maurice Power was a hero to Conche and would stay that way in her mind forever.

John was of the same mind as his wife. Maurice Power was a diligent worker. He honestly couldn't say anything bad about the man. He provided well for his daughter Mary, and he had never witnessed them getting in any kind of argument.

Ellen and Edward had begun to re-evaluate their opinion of Maurice Power as well. The old fellow may have done some terrible things in his younger days, but it appeared he had changed his ways. He was rough and crude, there could be no doubt. But when Ellen thought about it, most people in Conche were in some ways worse than he. The way she herself had spoken of Maurice Power made her feel like she was as guilty as the others. And Edward, he needed little convincing, especially when he heard that Maurice Power had given no thought to his own safety when he ventured into the house three nights ago and confronted what everyone thought was the devil.

"What are we going to do about this, Ned?" asked John.

"We're going to get it straightened out, once and for all."

"How do you intend to do that?"

Edward was never one to leave things half-done. "I've asked Father Gore to come here at eight o'clock, and Maurice and Mary to come at nine. We'll put an end to this problem tonight."

Rose and Ellen got up from the table wearing grim expressions. They were ready for whatever lay ahead of them now. Leaving the matter in their husbands' hands, they no longer feared for the future. With that, they went downstairs and made preparations for their guests. The first would be Father Gore, and the second Maurice Power. Or, more accurately, Maurice de la Pour.

30

Father Gore arrived on time for his meeting with the Dowers. He was bundled up in his winter outfit, because the temperature had dropped drastically since this morning. He was met at the door by Edward Dower himself and led upstairs to the loft room. Ellen was present and she greeted him warmly.

The priest removed his heavy coat and was invited to sit down in an easy chair. Ellen served him a cup of tea and some cookies. Father Gore mumbled his thanks around mouthfuls of Kizzie's delicious home cooking. When he finished, he said, "There's no doubt that miracles are still happening to us. After today, we should all believe in the Cross."

"Father Gore," Edward began right away, "we've invited you here tonight to help solve a problem. In fact, the problem we're trying to cope with is at the root of what happened here in Conche."

"I don't know what I can do," the priest said, "but I am willing to listen, my son."

Edward outlined the dispute they were having with Maurice Power concerning the land the man swore he

EARL PILGRIM

would take from them. Of course he omitted the details surrounding Henry Winton and the United Irish Fishermen, but he felt the information he gave to the priest was sufficient.

"We wanted to ask you about Maurice Power, if he was the son of one Maurice de la Pour. He lived here years ago and claimed he had all this land given to him by the French admirals after they burned everything. Are there any records, in the church or anywhere else, to your knowledge?"

Father Gore pondered Edward's story. "I don't know of any records regarding Maurice de la Pour, only that he left here with the wife of an Irish fisherman from Herring Neck and went away somewhere. Someone said that they saw him in Waterford, Ireland a few years afterwards. I don't know if this is true or not. As for anything else, we have secrets that we never reveal."

"I know, Father," Edward said. "Thank you for your help. I can only hope this turns out all right."

"Yes, so do I," said the priest.

* * *

MAURICE AND MARY POWER left John's house at nine sharp and proceeded next door. Mary turned when she reached the doorway and saw that Maurice had stopped a few feet short of the house. Will had told both of them earlier that Father Gore was there, and Maurice had vehemently refused to set foot in the house. He repeated this sentiment to Mary when she again asked him to reconsider. He wasn't going to be caught dead in

298

the presence of that priest. So he waited outside for a few minutes while Mary went in and summoned Edward.

"Maurice," he said, cracking the door open, "I would like to talk to you if it's possible. We have John and Rose inside, along with Father Gore. He's willing to sit and listen, so won't you come in?"

"No," Maurice said flatly. "After what that priest did to me, I wouldn't sit with him if it was going to save my life, Skipper."

Edward could see that Maurice wasn't about to change his mind. "I know things have gone terribly wrong here within the last few days," he said, "but we're going to have to forget about that and move on with our lives."

"All right, Skipper if that's all you want, I'm going back to my house."

Edward sighed. "If Father Gore leaves, will you come in?"

"Yes, by all means."

"All right," Edward said. "I'll ask him to leave."

Maurice raised a hand. "I would like for Kizzie, Ambrose, and the rest of your family to be there when I come in. There's something I want them to see."

Edward raised his eyebrows. He didn't know what to say. Finally, he got out, "I will have them there."

"Skipper, Mary and I will be at John's with Will. We'll come over when you get the family together," Maurice said, and walked away.

* * *

BUT MAURICE DIDN'T GO back to John Dower's house. There was something important he had to do.

"Maurice, what are you up to?" Mary asked her husband.

"Never mind, Mary," he answered. "Will should have the kettle boiled over at John's, so you go over and join him."

Without another word, he walked on ahead and to his dogs. There was something he had to get from his home in Silver Cove. Something that would change the lives of Ellen and Edward Dower forever.

* * *

AS IT TURNED OUT, FATHER GORE was only too happy to be exempt from the meeting with Maurice Power. He left without hesitation while Edward and Ellen rounded up the children and told them they wanted to have a family discussion. Everyone gathered in the loft room, the place where Ellen's troubles began on Christmas Eve. Some of the children were worried that their father would lose his temper and make short work of Maurice Power. But whatever happened tonight, violence or no, Maurice would not be leaving without getting this mess straightened out.

Before long, the sound of Maurice's boots stomping up the stairs came to them. Kizzie went as white as a sheet, sitting with her fists clenched solid. She felt as though she would not be responsible for anything she did.

Maurice and Mary came into the loft room with Will bringing up the rear. The much-feared man from Silver

Cove walked directly to Ellen and said, "Mrs. Dower, I am glad to see you looking so good. I still haven't gotten you out of my eyes yet from the other night." He shook her hand while she just looked at him with a confused expression. "Now, Skipper," he asked, "what do you want me here for?"

Edward looked around at each and every family member. Then he stood and shook hands with Maurice. "We want to talk about the land," he said. "Let's settle it, right now."

Maurice held up a hand for silence. "Skipper, there's something I think you should see."

Everyone looked on with bated breath as he reached into his pocket and took out an old brown envelope. The paper had seen better days. It was little more than a rag, all tattered and torn. He pried it open and slid a sheet of paper from it onto the table. Maurice held it up to the light, and everyone at the table could see that it was a letter, written in French on one side, and the other in English.

"Mrs. Dower, will you read this for me, please?"

Ellen took the document from him and held it near the candle lamp. She scanned the letter first, then cleared her throat and read aloud.

"'To whom it may concern: We, the fishing captains of the Harbours of the Rouge Peninsula, Newfoundland, namely Conche, hereby declare all the land that is in the area near the buildings that were destroyed by fire as outlined in the map and diagram on this letter, signed by us today.'"

She gave Edward a frightened look as she handed the letter back to Maurice.

"Would you like to read it too, Skipper?" he asked.

"No," Edward said in a wary voice.

All was silent as Maurice stuck his hand back in the ragged envelope. He pulled out another letter, this one on newer paper. He handed this one to Ellen and asked her to read it.

The look she levelled at Maurice as he handed her the note was filled with the old hate she'd felt when she thought she had lost the land grant.

"'To whom it may concern:'" she began, "'This letter gives Maurice Power and his Heirs the full title to the parcel of land that is outlined in his letter that was given to Maurice de la Pour, his father, by the French Government as of this day, Aug. 15, 1871, signed Crown Lands Division in the Dominion of Newfoundland.'"

There it was, in black and white. There could be no doubt. The land belonged to Maurice Power.

* * *

"I KNOW YOU'RE FEELING BAD about this, Mrs. Dower," Maurice said while the entire Dower family sat in shock. "All of you are, and so am I. But you need not worry. I will not take one inch of land away from you. Although I would if I was the devil that everyone thinks I am."

Before the family could blink, he snatched the letter from Ellen and walked over to the Giant stove. Using the lifter, he opened it with the hand not holding the papers. Looking at Kizzie, who had gone even whiter than before, he winked and dropped the documents into the stove's smoldering belly.

Ellen stood on legs that didn't feel like her own and walked over to Edward's sea-chest, now safely nestled in its home in the loft. Tears streamed down her face as she lifted the heavy lid and withdrew the brown envelope she knew would be hidden in the cardboard lining. She took one last look at the document that had caused her so much grief, then stood and walked purposefully toward the stove. Lifting the cover as had Maurice Power, she deposited the cursed document. Ellen Dower dropped the cover back in place with a loud bang, closing the door on all her cares and worries.

She just stood there with her head bowed for a full minute before turning to face Edward. He was standing above his sea-chest now, holding her missing silver comb.

"Edward," she sobbed, "will you please put that in my hair?"

"No," he replied, unable to hold back his tears. "I think Maurice should. It will be a token that our land troubles are over."

Maurice Power wore a warm, slightly bemused smile as he took the comb from Edward's outstretched hand. "Come here, Mrs. Dower," he said softly, and she obeyed. He brushed her dark hair back with a gentleness that belied all the rumours and gossip around Conche, and his huge calloused hands fitted the comb neatly in place. The family let out a loud cheer in private celebration of the kindness bestowed on them by the "devil" of Conche.

Never again was the land mentioned, and Maurice Power became Edward and Ellen Dower's closest friend.

Afterword

There are many stories in Newfoundland and Labrador of people who have died and come back to life. A lot of these stories come from people who have witnessed it first-hand. I had the opportunity to talk to many people and ask all manner of questions while researching this story, and in doing so I opened up a whole new world of events that took place years ago.

I was at a supermarket not long ago and met up with an old friend. He asked me if I was indeed writing a ghost story, and I, of course, said yes. This kind of story fascinates him, he told me, and we continued talking for some time, exchanging views on the subject. Then he asked me if I'd ever heard the story about the woman over at Green Island Cove. I told him that I hadn't, so he told me a story that sent me reeling in disbelief.

"This happened many years ago," he said. "In fact, the woman's granddaughter lived at Main Brook. You knew her."

"Oh yes," I said curiously.

"She's dead now, died an old lady."

I nodded. He had piqued my interest.

"This was when the French fishermen were there. Anyway, this old woman had a ring given to her. The ring was found by some kids who were digging for worms down near the shoreline. When they were on their way home, they went into the house where the woman lived and showed it to her. She washed it and examined it closer and noticed that it looked like gold. But the stone in it seemed to be of great value. There was also a name engraved that no one in Green Island Cove could pronounce."

As the story goes, the old woman took the ring and gave the two young boys a bit of money and a slice of molasses bread. They were very thankful and went on their way. After they left, she tried the ring on and was delighted to see that it fit her perfectly, as if someone had made it just for her.

"I think I'll wear this," she said to herself, and so she did.

The old widow's family came home and she showed them the ring. Her son took a closer look, and he could hardly believe what he was seeing.

"Mother, this ring is worth a fortune! Look at the large diamond in it."

"I don't care what it's worth," the old lady countered. "I will never part from it."

And so it came to pass that for many years she wore the ring. During that time it was stolen twice and her son sold it once, but each time the old lady managed to get it back. "When I die," she told her family, "I will be buried wearing this ring, and no one had better take it off my finger." They respected her wishes and said it would be so.

One day a couple of men came to her house and inquired about the jewelled ring she had in her possession. They were French fishermen, they said, just out for a casual stroll, more or less to get a little fresh air. However, the old woman was no fool. The fishermen of the day wore little more than rags, and the clothes on the backs of these two men spoke of a higher class.

Nevertheless, the two strangers were invited in and treated to the old woman's home cooking. They told the family they had heard that someone in this house was in possession of a ring with mysterious writing on it. The old lady held out her hand.

"Oh no, madame," said one man. "Can you take it off? We would like to see the writing on it, if you please."

The old woman lifted her chin. "I will never take it off, sir," she said, "but I've got the letters written down, if you want to see them."

The would-be fishermen were not satisfied, but they at least agreed to see the characters this old lady had transcribed.

"We can't pick out the letters, madame. What's written here makes no sense. If you would just take it off for a minute so we could see what is written there."

The old woman grew angry. "Well, no sir," she said crisply, "I will go to my grave wearing this ring."

She had dreamed it was owned by a young prince who had been killed, she told them. "He told me that if

I had it on when I went up to the gates of Heaven, I would get in for sure. So," she reiterated, "I will never take it off."

The two strangers could tell this woman would never give the ring up without a fight, so they grudgingly took their leave.

About a week later, the old lady died suddenly. Before she was interred, the family made sure the ring was firmly placed on her finger, staying true to their word. Her body was placed in a coffin and kept in the family home until the time came to bury her. The man who had made the coffin came in and nailed it tight when the day arrived, and six pall bearers carried the woman to the church where a short service was held. After that they took her to the graveyard, where "Ashes to ashes" was said and she was put to rest six feet under.

The story goes that two nights later, two mysterious men were seen lurking around the small town. Someone said in passing that they were the same two men who came to the woman a week ago and wanted the ring. So when these two strangers came around, they were told, "Too late, boys, the old lady is gone under with the ring on her finger." Gone forever, the men were told, and they left town shortly after hearing this.

That night, around two o'clock in the morning, the family of the old woman heard someone calling from outside.

"Open up. Open up."

The old lady's grieving son answered the door, and who should be standing there but his mother, dressed in her grave clothes and all covered in mud! Well, the poor fellow just fainted away and dropped to the floor. But his eyes hadn't deceived him at all. The old woman came into the house and talked to the whole family.

"I was in my grave," she said, "when all of a sudden a shovel came down through the coffin and pried it open. Someone was taking the ring off my finger. I fought with them, but they almost broke my arm, and the next thing I knew they had the ring and ran. They were the same two men who came here the other day."

"You're back, Mother, that's all that matters," cried the family.

The old woman was inconsolable. She would never get into Heaven now, she feared. But life went on as it always does, and the heartbroken old lady would live to see another ten years.

Earl Baxter Pilgrim has seen his share of adventure. In 1960 he served as an infantryman with the Princess Patricia's Canadian Light Infantry, and while training there became Canadian light-heavyweight boxing champion. After a stint in the armed forces, he went on to become an award-winning game warden and wildlife officer in the province of Newfoundland and Labrador. His efforts as a conservationist and environmentalist continue even today and have earned him worldwide acclaim.

He makes his home in Roddickton, Newfoundland with his wife Beatrice.

Earl B. Pilgrim is at the forefront of Canadian literature, his books having sold in excess of 75,000 copies. *The Ghost of Ellen Dower* is his sixth novel.

PRAISE FOR EARL B. PILGRIM

WILL ANYONE SEARCH FOR DANNY?

"This is the gripping, inspirational story of a legendary game warden written by another legendary game warden—Earl Pilgrim, one of Canada's most successful boxers, an indefatigable crusader for the restoration of moose and caribou and a Master Raconteur. It is a proper tribute to both men and the wild, harsh, lovely land they have guarded so well."
Ted Williams, Contributing Editor of Audobon Magazine and Gray's Sporting Journal

"The descriptions of the search activities in *Will Anyone Search for Danny?* are strikingly familiar even though they occurred more than 60 years ago. I recommend this book be in the library of every search and rescue professional, career or volunteer."
Chris Long, *SARSCENE*

THE PRICE PAID FOR CHARLEY

"*The Price Paid for Charley* records historical facts generally unknown about Grenfell's famous "Ice Pan Adventure." Mr. Pilgrim's research discloses a very human Grenfell and the sometimes desperate people that he served, making this a very readable and thrilling adventure."
John McGonigle, Sir Wilfred Thomason Grenfell Historical Society

BLOOD ON THE HILLS

"There is no doubting [Earl Pilgrim] is a master storyteller."
sieved.com

"*Blood on the Hills* is a great read for anyone interested in wildlife enforcement issues, particularly poaching, and how community residents can help fight it."
Bill Power, Outdoors Columnist, The Telegram

"In *Blood on the Hills* the author uses his expert storytelling abilities to preserve some of the memories he's collected during his years working as a wildlife officer."
The Newfoundland Herald

PRAISE FOR EARL B. PILGRIM

CURSE OF THE RED CROSS RING

"The greatest Newfoundland story ever told."
The Downhomer

"Pilgrim's fourth tour de force...gives the reader an idea of how isolated communities that have no police force attempt to maintain law and order, not always successfully, and sometimes with tragic results."
Atlantic Books Today

"Pilgrim weaves [a] fascinating tale...sharply visual and amazing. It's extremely readable, because what he has is a voice, knowledgeable and authentic."
The Telegram

"*Curse of the Red Cross Ring* is full of mystery, murder and twisting plots."
The Nor'wester

"A job well done."
The Northern Pen

THE CAPTAIN AND THE GIRL

"Knock-out book...his writing is simple, yet smart, and he's a natural storyteller."
Mark Dwyer, The Newfoundland Herald

"Pilgrim skilfully builds up his story to a grisly and gripping climax."
Roberta Buchanan, The Downhomer

"Earl Pilgrim has a tendency to jump into things and come out a winner, whether it be writing, protecting wildlife or sparring in the boxing ring."
Glen Whiffen, The Telegram

"A born storyteller...the same impact he has when talking face to face translates onto the page."
Craig Welsh, The Express

"A natural-born storyteller, Earl B. Pilgrim will not disappoint his fans with...*The Captain and the Girl*."
Karen Shewbridge, The Telegram

"...gripping, inspirational..."
TED WILLIAMS

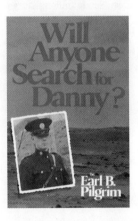

This story has been written as a memorial to the search
party from Englee, Newfoundland who went far beyond
the call of duty to search for the lost ranger, Danny
Corcoran, fighting all the elements that Nature could
unleash. *Will Anyone Search for Danny?* is the heart-
breaking true story of the townspeople who came to
love this young man and pulled together to help him
when he needed them most.

ISBN 1-894463-01-3. 270 pages. $16.95

Flanker Press Ltd.
P O Box 2522, Stn C, St. John's
Newfoundland, Canada, A1C 6K1

Toll Free: 1-866-739-4420   E-mail: info@flankerpress.com

"...*discloses a very human Grenfell...*"
GRENFELL HISTORICAL SOCIETY

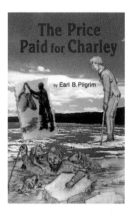

The great northern Newfoundland doctor Sir Wilfred T. Grenfell once said real joy comes not from ease or riches or from the praise of men but from doing something worthwhile. *The Price Paid for Charley* is Earl Pilgrim's tribute to the doctor from England who changed so many lives in Newfoundland and Labrador. It describes Dr. Grenfell's brave attempt to battle the elements to reach one of his patients, and the shortcut that nearly cost him his life.

ISBN 1-894463-05-6. 207 pages. $14.95

Flanker Press Ltd.
P O Box 2522, Stn C, St. John's
Newfoundland, Canada, A1C 6K1

Toll Free: 1-866-739-4420   E-mail: info@flankerpress.com

"...a master storyteller..."

Wildlife officer Earl Pilgrim is on a mission. The moose and caribou populations on the Great Northern Peninsula have been decimated, and he has promised the government of Newfoundland and Labrador to end the poaching threat. Through the character John Christian, Pilgrim takes the reader into his world of stakeouts, bare-knuckled stand-offs, and high-speed chases across the frozen barrens of the north. *Blood on the Hills* is a memoir. It is a tale of selfless determination involving great personal risk to carry out a mission that seemed impossible.

ISBN 1-894463-07-2. 143 pages. $14.95

Flanker Press Ltd.
P O Box 2522, Stn C, St. John's
Newfoundland, Canada, A1C 6K1

Toll Free: 1-866-739-4420   E-mail: info@flankerpress.com

"...Pilgrim's fourth tour de force..."
ATLANTIC BOOKS TODAY

Earl B. Pilgrim has masterfully constructed a tale of murder, betrayal, and desperation. *Curse of the Red Cross Ring* follows the trail of Sod Mugford: fisherman, lumberjack, murderer. It is based on the true happenings of 1928 and 1929, when he killed an innocent schoolteacher and fled north to the small town of L'Anse au Pigeon, Newfoundland. There he thought he would be safe from the law, but what he hadn't counted on was one man to whom the townspeople entrusted their lives in times of trouble. That man's name was Azariah Roberts.

ISBN 1-894463-11-0. 334 pages. $19.95

Flanker Press Ltd.
P O Box 2522, Stn C, St. John's
Newfoundland, Canada, A1C 6K1

Toll Free: 1-866-739-4420   E-mail: info@flankerpress.com

"...knock-out book..."

THE NEWFOUNDLAND HERALD

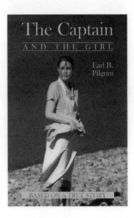

From the medical files of the great northern doctor Sir Wilfred T. Grenfell comes the story of his first year in Newfoundland and Labrador. In 1892, he came over from England to administer much-needed medical care to the colony's fishermen. In his first year he witnessed the height of famine, disease and poverty, but one case in particular would change young Dr. Grenfell forever and cause him to devote his life to improving the lives of those in Newfoundland and on the Labrador. That case involved a very sick young woman under the care of a well-intentioned but misguided sea captain.

ISBN 1-894463-18-8. 151 pages. $14.95

Flanker Press Ltd.
P O Box 2522, Stn C, St. John's
Newfoundland, Canada, A1C 6K1

Toll Free: 1-866-739-4420   E-mail: info@flankerpress.com

"...delightful collection..."
THE TELEGRAM

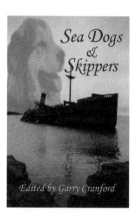

Some of Newfoundland and Labrador's finest story-tellers have collaborated to present sixteen tales of high-seas adventure. Included in this collection is "Frank and the Beothic" by Earl B. Pilgrim, the story of Frank Sheppard and the grounding of the vessel *Beothic* off the Great Northern Peninsula. Set in WWII-era Newfoundland, this tale revisits L'Anse au Pigeon and the characters Pilgrim introduced in the best-selling *Curse of the Red Cross Ring*.

ISBN 1-894463-16-1. 208 pages. $16.95

Flanker Press Ltd.
P O Box 2522, Stn C, St. John's
Newfoundland, Canada, A1C 6K1

Toll Free: 1-866-739-4420   E-mail: info@flankerpress.com

The Day Grenfell Cried

Earl B. Pilgrim

SUMMER 2003